MW01487319

Fated
Skates

ALSO BY VICTORIA SCHADE

Pick Me

A NOVEL

VICTORIA SCHADE

An Imprint of HarperCollins*Publishers*

Without limiting the exclusive rights of any author, contributor or the publisher of this publication, any unauthorized use of this publication to train generative artificial intelligence (AI) technologies is expressly prohibited. HarperCollins also exercise their rights under Article 4(3) of the Digital Single Market Directive 2019/790 and expressly reserve this publication from the text and data mining exception.

This is a work of fiction. Names, characters, places, and incidents are products of the author's imagination or are used fictitiously and are not to be construed as real. Any resemblance to actual events, locales, organizations, or persons, living or dead, is entirely coincidental.

FATED SKATES. Copyright © 2026 by Victoria Schade. All rights reserved. No part of this book may be used or reproduced in any manner whatsoever without written permission except in the case of brief quotations embodied in critical articles and reviews. For information, address HarperCollins Publishers, 195 Broadway, New York, NY 10007. In Europe, HarperCollins Publishers, Macken House, 39/40 Mayor Street Upper, Dublin 1, D01 C9W8, Ireland.

Dedicated to you, the reader

Fated Skates

Prologue

I was on my hands and knees on the ice again, with the entire world watching.

Get up, get up, get up, get up!

The way the music kept echoing around the auditorium felt like an insult. I was in agony, but the lark in the song was still joyfully soaring toward the clouds. It struck me how huge the disconnect was between my body and the performance part of my brain, because in my head I was still dutifully skating my choreography. The sweeping violin meant that I was supposed to be twisting in midair right *now* . . . then landing perfectly on one blade . . . into a step sequence . . . preparing for a triple lutz . . .

Get up.

I already had, twice.

I could hear murmurs from the crowd starting, and the vibe in the Olympic auditorium shifting. I was used to feeling embraced by the collective energy of audiences. Whatever was raining down on me now—disappointment? disbelief? anger?—was keeping me anchored to the ice.

It's over, they told me.

Get up, the voice in my head demanded.

Eventually, I did.

I blinked back the tears pooling in my eyes, ignored the flames shooting up my leg, and tried to inhabit the final, floaty moments of the song. I'd never agreed with my coach that *The Lark Ascending* sounded wistful. To me, it was a mournful piece of music, and as I stretched my hand over my head on the last note, I might as well have been waving a white flag of surrender.

There was a pause of pin-drop silence after the music faded, while the audience collectively decided how to respond to their favorite Olympic hopeful crashing out before their eyes.

It didn't matter if they gave me thunderous applause or golf claps, I couldn't hear it. I was sobbing, hiding my face in my hands as I skated off the ice.

I kept my eyes down and refused to look at the camera poised behind the source of all my pain. Carol stood in the middle of the rink door, practically blocking me from leaving the ice, because she was about to play her part. To everyone watching, she was my concerned coach, taking me into her arms and whispering encouragement in my ear.

But what she'd actually said, raising her hand to cover her mouth so no lip-readers could catch it, was, *Why the hell did you give up?*

The resulting dagger to my chest hurt almost as badly as the pain radiating from my ankle.

I pushed past her and had no choice but to move on to Tricia. I was sure this hug looked more convincing, because she'd spent her life calibrating how she appeared.

Neither embrace comforted me in any way.

I put on my guards and walked to the postperformance waiting area called the kiss and cry with the two of them following behind me. We sat down and a camera pushed in close, forcing me to find other places to look, like down at my nails and up at the ceiling beams. I tried to force myself to stop crying, because I could already see the headlines beneath the close-ups of me. Tricia handed me a tissue and motioned that I needed to wipe my face because mascara was running down my cheeks.

For the first time in my life, I didn't rush to follow her instruction.

I was devastated, and the two women whose opinions had formed the foundation of my skating career couldn't even muster half-hearted support for me.

So I decided to let the world see what being broken looked like.

I finally raised my watery eyes and stared directly into the camera.

Chapter One

Zamboni Frank was my biggest fan.

Our rink's adorable white-haired Zamboni driver thought I could do no wrong, so that meant I'd still hear him clapping even when I accidentally popped a jump or, worse, fell on my ass.

"You'll get it next time, sweetheart," he'd always yell from the entry to his cave. "Keep going!"

I didn't love when people watched me practicing, but Frank's stooped figure in the shadows was a good omen. I considered him the Phantom of the ice rink; always around, always watching, but never wanting to be the center of attention unless he was on his machine.

Like just now. My swingy takeoff on a triple axel resulted in me needing to touch my free foot to the ice when I landed. It was messy, but his applause still echoed around the rink. I gave him a little thank-you wave and he blew me a kiss.

It wasn't the best place to end my session, but I felt fried, and nothing good happened on tired skates.

"Phenomenal, Quinn," Melanie called to me as I glided to where she was waiting in the players' box, "but I wish we could hit your axel *one* more time today. That leg was loose, right? I wonder if Frank would mind if we did another . . ."

She trailed off as the Zamboni slid onto the ice and the few remaining skaters hurried off.

"Okay, I guess we're done," she said, eyes still on the beast. "That's a good place to end. You looked *really* strong today. I'm pleased."

Even after three years it was still a shock that I had a coach who praised me, freely and without hesitation. I never imagined that it was possible after a decade of Carol telling me that I was as massive as a linebacker, and "gravity's bestie," because my jumps weren't high enough, and that my blood on the ice after a hard fall was "part of the deal, now go do it again."

All when I was eleven years old.

"You okay?" Melanie asked.

I shook off the old dread and refocused on the now. "Yup."

She studied me as she handed me my hard guards and black fleece. "Tell me."

"Just in my head, as usual," I said as I slipped the guards on. I was still too warm for the fleece. "We're a little under a month and a half out. I feel like I need six."

"Nope, I'm not letting you do this." Melanie attempted her version of a glare. All the elements were present—narrowed eyes, furrowed brow—but there was something about her sweet face that prevented it from having the intended effect.

I was plenty used to glares from a coach, but in a "you suck and I'm ashamed to have my name associated with yours" kind of way, not a "quit the negative self-talk" way.

"We are *exactly* where we need to be," she continued. She held up her phone. "You'll see when you watch today's videos. You're there. All we have to do is stay consistent, and polish. And nail those axels, right?"

I answered with a snort.

"But other than that, you're on it. Trust me."

I did trust her, more than anyone. The problem was I didn't trust myself.

I'd already blown it once on the world's stage; there was always a chance I could make it a twofer if I didn't get my head game in order.

Four years later and all it took was a passing thought about my first Olympics to make my heart feel like it was trapped in a vise. I'd come a long way in the time since thanks to my new direction and team, but the blocks I had with certain jumps still popped up at the worst possible moments.

And *that* was what kept me awake at night.

"I know that look, knock it off," Melanie scolded me. "You're stuck on the axel. Everything else was phenomenal, stop obsessing. That's my job. Now park it for a minute, I have some stuff I want to go over with you."

I sat down on the bench while Melanie swiped at her phone, squinting at the screen. She defiantly refused to buy readers because she claimed it was the first sign of giving up and getting old, which left her holding her phone as far away from her face as her arm would allow anytime she needed to read something. It wasn't like she came across as just past forty, though. Her bob was jet black without even a whisper of gray, and the "wrinkles" on her face only existed in her imagination. She'd always been the tiniest skater on her team, and though she finally allowed herself to enjoy food, she was still a slip of a human. Sometimes I felt like a giant standing next to her, and I wasn't exactly known for my height.

"Okay, here it is," she said, holding her phone up triumphantly. "It's really good news. I got an email out of the blue, from a producer at that streaming show *The Score*. They're interested in doing a feature on you, which, no-brainer."

A chill ran through me. Yeah, I could command the attention of an arena filled with people and make them fall in love with me for four minutes, but sitting down one-on-one with a reporter and giving them access to my demons was *not* something I wanted to do. Especially because I could predict their angle.

Failed Olympic figure skater's second chance at gold.

The Score was a great show and seemed fair to the athletes they featured, but I'd watched enough episodes to know how they'd spin my story. It didn't take much to get me to cry when the Switzerland Games came up—especially when they rolled the footage—and that wasn't the version of myself that I wanted to present to the world. No, this time around I was going to be a completely different Quinn Albright.

I was stronger and fiercer. Bulletproof, just like my long program song said.

"I don't know . . ." I trailed off as Mel stared at me expectantly.

"Quinn, my darling, this is *priceless* coverage and a huge compliment. It's a fantastic awareness campaign for you, and it's a chance to talk about your new direction."

Anyone who followed skating and had been watching my evolution unfold at various competitions already knew that I'd left the sparkly princess persona in Switzerland. All they had to do was look at me on the ice, before my blades even moved. No more pastel Easter egg costumes and classical music. The Swan had transformed into a dragon.

"When do they want to do it?" I asked Melanie.

She squinted at her phone again. "They said they can be flexible and work with your schedule but have lots they want to film and they're hoping to get started within the next couple of weeks."

"Get started?" I repeated back to her. "You mean this isn't a one-and-done kind of thing?"

"Oops," Melanie joked. "Did I forget to mention that part? This opportunity is a big feature, possibly an entire episode if it all goes well. They basically want to embed with you for a week to start, and follow you through your daily routine. See you practicing, in the weight room, in dance class . . . a real behind-the-curtain look at what it takes to be a gold medalist."

"*Future* gold medalist," I reminded her.

I leaned forward to pound my knuckle on the wooden boards three times. Superstitious? Who, me?

"There's one other thing," Melanie said, scrunching her nose. "If the timing works out, they want to do a home visit."

My stomach curdled at the thought of going back to Connecticut. It was my home by definition but not in my heart.

"Nope. No way." I stood up and started collecting my things and packing them into my bag. "I'm out."

"Quinn, come on, it actually might help. People can see for themselves what you were up against. Your mom isn't known for her tact."

"Is a home visit a deal-breaker?" I asked.

She shrugged. "Don't know, I can ask. That aside, I really think you should do it. It's not like they're offering it to everyone on the team. It's a chance to tell your story the way *you* want to."

"You clearly don't watch reality TV. Have you ever heard of a villain edit?" I snorted as I shoved the fleece in my bag.

"Stop. Be serious for a minute and really think about how this could play out. You'll be your usual charming, gorgeous self on camera, and potential sponsors will see you as someone who's multidimensional. Not just a pretty face. I can picture it now . . . Coke, Nike, Omega, all fighting to sign you. This interview is another chance to bank your future."

My future. What did that even mean? My tunnel vision didn't expand beyond the next two months.

"It's a no-brainer, I'm forwarding you the email so you can see the specifics," Melanie added as she bent her head to tap on her phone. "I'd never force you to do it, of course, but I strongly, *strongly* suggest you agree to it. I'll be right there with you, if you want me to."

I busied myself wiping down my blades and putting on my soakers.

"I know," I finally answered. "Thank you."

"I think you'll get a kick out of who they want to interview you," Melanie added. "It's fun synergy."

My hackles went up, because I had zero in common with the three hosts of the show, other than us all being athletes. Darian Young was a former NFL quarterback, Maizey Liu was a retired Wimbledon champ, and Zach Bell was a former pro golfer.

"Who is it?"

"Bennett Martino! I love that guy. I mean, who doesn't? Four years postretirement and he's as droolworthy as ever."

The name made every muscle in my body constrict in tandem, a system-wide cramp that made me glitch for a few seconds.

"Oh, *absolutely* not," I finally answered. "It's a hard no for me."

Chapter Two

*H*ow the hell had Bennett Martino gone from being a three-time Olympic Gold speed skater, to starring in his own failed reality series called *Skate Fast, Live Loud*, to a DUI, to winning *Dancing with the Stars*, to being a spokesperson for some sort of disastrous crypto thing, to *this*? A cohosting gig on a well-respected streaming sports program. The man was human Teflon, because nothing stuck to him.

But there was no way I wanted to be a part of his latest redemption arc. Not after the way he'd treated me.

"Wait up!"

I turned to find my best friend, Zoey Chen, running to catch me as I walked out of the arena and into the parking lot. She'd been on rink two, working on her Four Continents program. I could tell she'd skated hard, because her cheeks were pink and her black hair was still damp at her temples. Without makeup she looked like a baby, a very young twenty to my absolutely ancient twenty-four.

It still smarted that I'd made the Olympics team again and she'd been a near miss, because I considered her a stronger skater.

But in typical Zoey fashion, she'd been nothing but positive about it. Sure, there was probably some envy crouching behind her cheerful smile—the uncomfortable truth of being friends with the very people you needed to beat—but like good faux sisters, we compartmentalized any weirdness and focused on cheerleading each other.

"I nailed it today," she beamed at me. "Three triples, back-to-back."

It was my turn to feel a little envy bubble up, because to me it seemed that Zoey could hit effortless triples, all day, every day.

"Congrats." I pulled her into a hug. "I hate you."

"Yeah, you can hate me all the way from Olympic Village." She laughed. "Don't start."

We walked to our cars, which were next to each other in the back corner of the parking lot, so we could avoid the minivans filled with sweaty boys getting dropped off for hockey practice.

"*The Score* wants to interview me," I said as I threw my bag in the back seat of my car.

"Wow, that's huge," Zoe said and paused with her hand on the car door. "Can I hang out in the background looking cute when they're here?"

"Nope, because I'm not doing it." I shook my head. "They hired Bennett Martino and they want to send him to interview me."

She grimaced. "Awkward."

"Tell me about it."

"Have you guys spoken since the Switzerland ghosting?"

It went so much deeper than a simple ghosting, and she knew it. I shook my head. "Not a word. And it's not like I've been keeping up with what he's doing. I had no idea that he's a correspondent now."

It was a half-truth. I'd unfollowed him, but of course I'd kept up with most of what he was doing, because it was impossible not to. He *always* found a way into the headlines. The man was even more unavoidable than usual with the Games on the horizon, because his final speed-skating run four years prior was legendary. I wanted to scream and plug my ears every time I heard the words "Magic Martino."

"I think you should do it," Zoey said as she slid into her car. "Show him how incredible you are, and what he missed out on."

"Yeah, *no*. I told Mel to see if anyone else can interview me. Total diva move but I'm not subjecting myself to him for a week straight."

"Good," she said with nod. "Lean into your diva-hood, you deserve it." She paused a beat. "See you at home?"

We both did our usual big frowns, because I hadn't lived with the Chens in years. They'd been my surrogate family when I'd moved from my home in Connecticut to the Colorado training facility as a young skater. It was with them that I'd finally learned what a family could be.

"I wish. I'm dying for some of your mom's jiaozi."

"Come for dinner," Zoey insisted. "She'd love to see you."

My stomach growled at the thought of whatever Mrs. Chen would whip up for me. I'd deprived myself of so much good food during the dark years, and while I was better at managing my eating thanks to my nutritionist, now wasn't the time to be gorging on zhajiangmian. I had a $3,000 costume I needed to fit into that was going to be shot in unforgiving close-up HD. And then there were the figure-skating Reddit threads that would pick me apart afterward, commenting on any flaw that made me look human and not like Figure Skater Barbie.

"Can't. I'm doing an extra session on the bike tonight. Rain check?"

If there was a nonskating word to describe me, "rain check" would be it. My life was a series of missed gatherings and celebrations.

But it would all be worth it.

My phone chimed with a FaceTime call. I glanced down. "Shit. It's Tricia."

"Decline it," Zoey said.

"I've been declining her for so long that she's going to send the police to do a wellness check soon, to prove a point." I heaved a sigh. "I'll talk to you later. Love you."

"Love you back." Zoey gave me a half smile as my phone continued to ring. "Good luck."

I got into my car and checked myself out in the rearview mirror. Of course my flyaways were standing at attention on the top of my head, and I looked pale, so I ran my palm over my head to smooth them down, then pinched my cheeks Scarlett O'Hara style.

I could already hear her commentary. I sat up a little straighter, shifted my expression to neutral, and hit accept.

"Hi, Mom."

Unlike most people her age, she already had the phone perfectly positioned to avoid an unflattering angle, and the lighting around her was soft. She was in full glam makeup, with a blowout and sparkly earrings. It looked like she had a filter on too. My beautiful, always perfect mother.

"Aww, *there* you are! I've been trying to reach you, I was getting so worried. Did you see that I called?"

"I did, sorry, things are intense. I haven't had much free time. Obviously."

"Well, I guess so, because you look like an absolute *ragamuffin*, you poor little thing! Are you even sleeping? You've got massive bags, sweetheart. Do you need me to send more of the hairspray I like so your wispies aren't so obvious? Whatever you're using isn't up to the job—you look like you got electrocuted."

She laughed, and I felt the old familiar tightening in my throat, like my airway was being reduced by half.

I didn't take the bait. "Nope, I have plenty, thanks. So what's up?"

"Do I see poppy seeds in your teeth?" she play-scolded, leaning closer to the screen. "Did you eat a muffin, you naughty girl?"

Instead of using my phone to check with her watching, I held it close to my body and leaned to look in my rearview mirror, even though I knew my teeth were spotless. The last thing I'd eaten was yogurt, hours before.

"Your screen must be dirty, there's nothing in my teeth, Mom," I said evenly.

I saw a flash of frustration on her face, because she still wasn't used to my deescalation techniques. The old me would've yelled at her to stop scrutinizing me. The new me didn't care what she thought about the way I looked. I knew for a fact that she hated when I wore dark colors, which was why my practice wardrobe was almost exclusively black and gray now.

"Well, *anyway*, I wanted to talk to you because someone from *The Score* emailed me about doing an interview with you. Guess they didn't hear about the change in your support team." She sniffed and focused on something just off-screen.

My break with my former coach and my wanna-be coach mom had definitely made the news, so I wasn't sure why anyone would've reached out to her for access to me.

"Yeah, Mel told me about the interview. They must've figured out that she's my point person now."

My mom's expression went stony again, because she hated that I used Melanie's nickname. She considered it disrespectful. Plus, I think she was jealous of how close we'd become and what we'd accomplished in just three years.

"I hope you're not thinking about going on that show, sweetheart," she continued. She blinked at me, waiting for me to agree with her.

I never knew what angle she was working, so I was both surprised and not that she didn't want me to do it.

"Oh? And why is that?"

I fidgeted with the pull cord on my parka, below the screen where she couldn't see it. Yeah, I had the tools to deal with her now, but the squirrelly feelings skittered back every now and then.

"It's a distraction," she replied, ever the authority on how I was supposed to live my life. "You need to focus. We *know* what happens when you're not focused."

Shots fired.

"No, why don't you tell me," I said, smiling pleasantly with my non-poppy-seeded teeth on full display.

It was the baitiest response ever, and not what my therapist would've suggested, but I couldn't resist a little pushback.

"Quinn, *stop*. Okay? Why do you always do that? Making me the bad guy. Don't you dare blame me for what happened—"

"Mom, I'm not blaming you," I cut her off, because it was the same tired script and I wasn't in the mood to hear it. "Okay? We're just having a conversation."

The idea took shape as we stared at each other in silence. I didn't want her thinking that the reason I wasn't going to do the show was because *she* thought it was a bad idea. I couldn't let her believe she had any influence on my decision-making now.

"And yeah, I'm doing the interview."

It felt good watching her expression shift from placid to silent fury. It was rare that I made her speechless.

I *wasn't* going to agree to the interview, even if they found someone other than Ben to do it, but she didn't have to know that yet. I could say that there was a scheduling conflict and that's why it didn't happen. Anything but let her take the credit for me skipping it.

The corners of my mom's mouth turned down. "Fine." She shifted her focus away from me and started swiping at her screen, squinting as she poked at it. "Okay, it's done. You got your way. Happy?"

I heard a faint ringing in my ears, a distant siren. An emergency alert in my head. "*What's* done?"

"Well, I just emailed them back to tell them you'll do it, like you wanted. Right now. You won, Quinn. Happy?"

I watched the color drain from my face on-screen, real time.

No. That absolutely did *not* just happen.

I finally found my voice again, and not in a good way.

"What do you mean?" I shouted. "You're not even a part of my team now! Did you really send the email?"

My voice was shrill enough that someone unloading equipment from their car a few spaces over turned to see what was going on.

"I thought I was helping," my mom answered in the wounded tone that I was way too familiar with. "I was making things *easier* on you. What, did I do something wrong *again*?"

I clenched my teeth together to keep from really freaking out, because that was what she wanted. Her goal was always to neg me nonstop until I was completely unbalanced, which would then allow her to tell me all the ways I was messy.

And yeah, I was knocked off my axis by my mom yet again. It

was less common these days, but she still clung to the last bits of connective tissue between us using stunts like this one.

Deep breaths.

I convinced myself that it was fine. I could recover from her email. I'd have Mel follow up with the production team tomorrow and say there was a miscommunication. No big deal, mistakes happen. I might wind up looking unprofessional, but whatever, I'd blame my intense training schedule and they'd have to understand.

"No, it's fine," I finally answered, once I'd found my inner peace again. "I appreciate your help, but as we've discussed, it's no longer necessary. In the future, my team can handle requests like the one you received. Do you need me to forward Mel's contact info to you, so if something like this happens again you can send it her way?"

My mom made a strangled noise and rolled her eyes. "I obviously have Melanie's contact info, why would you think I didn't?"

I bit my tongue to keep from spewing a half dozen wise-ass answers.

"Okay, great. I appreciate your understanding." I was now fully inhabiting apathetic customer service mode with the woman who gave birth to me.

We stared at each other silently, and I braced myself for the next hit. I could tell it was coming by the way she was narrowing her eyes at the screen, searching, calibrating.

"I don't know why I let your father talk me out of getting that ear-pinning surgery for you." She shook her head sadly, like not subjecting her adolescent daughter to plastic surgery was a tragedy. "When I see you from this angle your ears just aren't proportional. Sweetie, I'm sorry we didn't do it when you were younger. But it's never too late . . ."

My looks were low-hanging fruit, because they were a major part of my brand that I'd had no part in cultivating. I looked how I looked, it just so happened that my features lined up in an aesthetically pleasing way. Every time someone compared me to a Disney princess, which was more frequently than I preferred, my mom was quick to mention that she'd once served as Miss Delaware, so she alone knew what it felt like to wear a crown.

If she could manage to stay out of my way for the next month and a half, *I'd* know what it felt like to wear a gold medal.

Chapter Three

*I*t didn't matter that I was exhausted and achy after practice. Thanks to the countdown clock in my head, wrung out was my level set these days. Despite it, I still felt like I needed to log a few miles on the stationary bike in my converted guest room, listening to my long program song for the billionth time.

I used to get sick of my performance music, back when my opinion on it wasn't part of the decision-making process. I liked classical music enough, but it didn't get into my marrow the way my current songs did. It took some convincing to get my choreographer, Sarah, to agree to my song choices because, yeah, the message behind both of them was as obvious as a cartoon two-by-four to the head.

"Bulletproof"? It was right there in the title. The synth pop song was cheerfully defiant, a middle-finger-to-my-haters bop that kept me smiling the entire time I was on the ice. My short program piece to the song "Movement" was just as blatant in a totally different way.

Debuting my new direction at Worlds made a few commentators compare my stylistic changes to Disney teens who went full rumspringa once their restrictive contracts ended. It tracked, though. My evolution began after I quit skating and retired for a year post-Switzerland to live a real life. I'd figured out within a few months that I'd never feel okay about my skating career until I had a shot at making things happen on my own terms.

Cut to commentators calling my new programs "sultry" and "daring."

News flash, the Swan could also be sexy.

I hated that I could trace the first inklings of my new direction to the one person who was getting harder and harder to avoid. There was no way I could let Ben into my life to help tell my story, even though he played a tiny part in waking me up to it.

If I was really honest with myself, I'd admit that he was the spark on the kindling that incinerated everything I'd hated about my old life.

I closed my eyes as the vocals in the song went softer. *This* was the moment, the lead-up to what I hoped would be my flawless triple axel, where I gathered my power to leap up and twist three and a half times in the air before landing perfectly on the outside edge of my opposite blade. I visualized nailing the move, tensing my stomach and pulling my arms to my chest as if I were actually executing it on the ice.

I loved how the song went completely silent for the second I was weightless and spinning, followed by the rush of landing *exactly* as the music exploded again. It was the ultimate feel-good moment, when I was in the homestretch of the program. I knew that going for a triple axel on performance-weary legs was an absolutely stupid idea, but how fucking phenomenal would it be when I landed it?

And then there was the 10 percent jump bonus I'd earn for even attempting it.

The song ended and I moved my arms into my final pose, eye-balling myself in the mirror across from the bike. Yes, I wanted to look as graceful as my fans remembered, but I also wanted to showcase my new strength. I loved the little extra definition on my delts and the hint of biceps.

I'd grown up hearing the mantra "be strong and light," when it seemed like only the second half truly mattered. Now I was leaning into the strong part, which was why I felt like the triple A was possible. I might not be as tiny as I once was, but I was stronger than ever, in so many ways.

At least that's what I told myself when the impostor syndrome took the wheel.

I got off my bike, sprayed it down, and mopped up the sweat. I was lucky to have the mini gym waiting for me whenever I needed to push myself a little harder. As dicey as my relationship was with my parents, I had them to thank for helping with my room and board. Without them, living on my own wouldn't be possible, since my chosen career didn't exactly pay well at this stage, if ever. My apartment wasn't huge, but they'd made sure it was in a new building, and I had a decent-size bathroom along with a balcony facing the mountains in the distance.

I think I'd sat on that balcony once since I'd moved in a few years prior.

After a shower and quick dinner of salmon, wild rice, and way too much broccoli, I strapped on my trusty plug-in air-compression massage pants and settled on the couch to scrutinize today's practice videos. Mel called just as I pushed play, like she could feel me about to tear myself to bits.

"I haven't even started watching yet," I answered.

"I can't believe you changed your mind," she replied. "Proud of you."

I warmed a little at the p-word. It didn't matter how far I went in my skating career, deep down I was still a puppy yearning to hear someone tell me "Good girl."

"Huh? About what?"

"Kim Overton from *The Score* just emailed and said you green-lighted it. I wasn't expecting such a fast change of heart. What happened?"

Fury sparked in my chest at my mom's latest overreach.

"*Damn* it," I fumed. "She literally just emailed them like three hours ago. And it's late, why are they still working at nine o'clock at night?"

"Who emailed who? I'm confused," Melanie said.

"Hurricane Tricia. Someone from the production staff accidentally sent *her* a message about me being on the show, and she mentioned it when she called me today. I lied and said I was going to do it, and she immediately took it upon herself to email them back to confirm it. Anything to keep her hooks in me."

"Huh. Well, here's to happy accidents. Thanks, Tricia."

A beat, as I prepared to deliver the punchline.

"Mel, but I'm *not* doing it."

"Excuse me?"

It was impossible to put my thoughts in order, so I just opened my mouth and let the gibberish flow. "I'm just not comfortable with any of it. It's too much, and the timing is terrible. I hate all of it. Interviewing my parents, being observed, dealing with *Ben*."

I said his name like it tasted bad.

"What's wrong with Ben?"

"Long story."

I heard a sigh. "Your flip-flopping has me really confused, but I'm going to take this little slipup as a sign from the cosmos that it's happening."

"Uh, *no*, I've been pretty consistent that I wasn't agreeing to it," I replied.

A silent stalemate stretched on.

"Well, we're painted in a corner now," Mel finally admitted. "I'm sorry, Quinn, but we can't pull out. When it comes to TV it's either at a snail's pace or a sprint, and these guys are already working on scheduling their crew. It would look *incredibly* unprofessional to confirm and then immediately cancel. We need to keep your run-up to the Games squeaky clean. If you come across as flighty, or incapable of making up your mind, people are going to uh . . . draw conclusions."

She didn't have to spell it out for me. My mental health was up for public consumption as well.

"No one would find out that I canceled it," I protested.

"Quinn, there's no such thing as privacy these days and you know it. If they sense a story in all this back-and-forth they'll find a way to leak it. Especially with your mom in the mix. I'm sorry, but you have to walk the line for the next few weeks."

The implication was loud and clear. There was no need for her to come out and say that the media would be watching me for any hints of faltering. My flameout last time was dramatic, and there was plenty of debate about my mental health after the frantic tears in the kiss and cry in Switzerland.

We both silently breathed into the phone, each unsure how to move forward. Until this point we'd always been perfectly in step, and I'd gotten spoiled by our yearslong united front. This was the first time we were at odds about something major.

I hated finally admitting to myself that she was right. I couldn't risk an ounce of negative press. I needed to go into the Games like a phoenix, rising from the ashes of my dumpster fire performance four years ago.

"Can I get some control of the edit?" I asked. "And maybe get their questions in advance?"

"I can ask, but you know how these things flow. The sit-down portions will have set questions, but I can totally see Ben riffing when you two are doing the day-in-the-life stuff."

"Did you ask if anyone else can do it?" I crossed my fingers.

My stomach twisted at the thought of giving him access to my world. I'd allowed it once and wound up getting scorched.

"I asked, but they want him because it makes sense with the whole Olympic angle. He's going to be in Italy for the entire Games."

Wonderful.

I flopped back against my couch, still trying to find an out. "Can anyone else on the team do it instead of me? Erica would be amazing."

"They want *you*," Melanie said softly.

In the old days I would've been given zero choice from the moment the offer came in. I recognized that now I could pull rank, put my foot down and refuse, but Mel's quiet resistance was working on me. No threats or intimidation, just reminders about what was at stake and what I stood to gain by doing it.

Or lose by refusing.

I closed my eyes. Could I deal with Ben for a week?

Would I make it if I let charismatic, funny, charming, maddening Bennett Martino back into my life after what he did?

I took a gut check. It didn't matter how much time had passed, I still wanted nothing to do with him. But if I was honest with myself, I couldn't ignore the tiny spark of hope buried deep inside me, an ember just waiting for the right gust of air to make it catch and burn.

After *everything*. I hated that for me.

"Thoughts?" Melanie asked.

I stubbornly refused to answer her right away. She already knew what I was going to say.

"Fine."

She knew better than to gloat. "Okay, *thank* you. I'll give you whatever support you need. You're not going to regret this."

"Too late," I said under my breath.

Chapter Four

I'm so sorry to bother you, but my daughter is a skater and she absolutely loves you. She's too scared to come over and ask you herself. Would you mind . . ." The woman trailed off and held up her phone then pointed behind me.

I was a local celebrity around Woodspring, so getting recognized at the Eagle Diner wasn't a surprise. Plus, I'd actually put some effort into the way I looked considering the reason why I was sitting in the diner instead of training during the rest of the world's breakfast time. Most folks were more familiar with shined-up performance Quinn, which meant that my makeup-free practice persona could often go undetected.

I glanced over my shoulder and spotted a little girl with dark-blond space buns peeking over the top of a booth a few feet from where I was sitting. She ducked the second I caught her eye.

I smiled at the stranger. "Of course! What's her name?"

"Addie. She's shy."

I turned completely around and the little girl dipped out of view again. "Hey, Addie, can you come over here for a sec? I need your help with a really big decision."

It was like saying her name erased her fears. She practically sprinted over and climbed into the booth next to me.

"Hi," she said. "I'm Addie and I'm six."

She was an adorable scrap of a girl, with big blue eyes that seemed to take in everything.

"Wow, you're *six*?" I asked. "That's how old I was when I started skating!"

"We just began private lessons," her mom said proudly. "They say she's showing real promise."

My chest tightened a little at the reveal—thrilled that a young skater had found her calling, and terrified about what the machine could do to the magical little creature sitting beside me. Did her mother take away her stack of pancakes before she could finish? Was she already missing birthday parties because of weekend practice?

"If you're such a good skater already it means you know how important it is to have the best gear out on the ice, right?" I asked.

Addie nodded solemnly.

"I need to get some new leg warmers for practice because my favorite pair is falling apart. I can't decide between these two colors, so can you help me make up my mind?" I grabbed my phone and navigated to the photos. "There's this pink tie-dye pair I like."

Which was a lie, but I knew my usual basic black wouldn't fly based on her glittery rainbow hair ties.

"Or this pair with the sparkly snowflakes on top." The gray knit pair I showed her was closer to what I normally wore.

"Pink," she replied, as predicted.

"Pink it is! Thanks for your help, I couldn't have made such a big decision without you."

I made a mental note to suck it up and buy them, so I could

wear them on the show during on-ice segments. I knew how excited she'd be to spot me on TV in the leggings she picked.

"Honey, we need to leave Miss Quinn alone now," the woman coaxed. "I'm sure she has lots to do today. Can we get a quick photo, though?"

"Of course! Bring it in, Addie." I opened my arms to her.

We were now besties, so the little girl snuggled up against me and pressed her cheek to mine, beaming.

"Aw, that's a good one," the woman said when she glanced at the image. She held her phone out to show me. "You look like twins!"

My throat caught when I saw the photo. It did indeed look like I was hugging the childhood version of myself. My hair had been the same color as Addie's until my mom decided that I'd be more memorable as an icy blonde, We'd started coloring it when I was twelve.

I was surprised at my almost feral urge to protect this little stranger. She'd already been pulled into the "beginner with raw talent" current, so I had to toss out a lifeline.

"Addie, I want you to make me a promise, okay?" I said to her as she started to slide off the bench.

She paused to nod solemnly at me, eyes wide.

"Make sure that you *always* have fun skating. And when it's not fun, remember that it's okay to take a little break."

It was a risky bit of advice if she had a limelight-starved parent like mine. If I could do anything for the next generation of skaters it would be to make them remember the feelings that got them on the ice in the first place, before the politics and deprivation could steal the joy from it. I now knew firsthand that it was possible to find balance in the sport, but I felt like the exception.

Addie nodded as if she understood, but my message wasn't just for her.

"Thank you so much, Quinn," the woman said. Her broad smile signaled that she was in fangirl mode and couldn't process what I was saying. "Good luck in Italy! We'll be watching every second of it."

"Thank you." I smiled back at her. "And good luck to *you*, Miss Addie."

She was too busy pirouetting back to her booth to hear me.

I watched the two of them fuss with each other once they were both seated again, so wrapped up in trying to gauge their dynamic that I forgot to be vigilant about scanning the parking lot. I glanced out the window to watch for the most obnoxious rental car one could get from Hertz.

"Hey, you."

I jumped at the sound of the voice. *Damn* it, he'd managed to sneak in without me seeing.

Ben slid in the booth across from me. He smiled, and every little thing I'd worried about bubbled up to the surface.

The most annoying?

That despite everything, I still wasn't immune to him.

Bennett Martino was one of those people who probably came out of the womb with a spotlight on him. He had an aura that went way beyond his looks, which meant that it didn't matter if people knew who he was or not, he was still going to attract attention. He vibrated at a different frequency, especially when he had eyes on him. I'd had a front-row seat to his media-savvy side, but I'd also been lucky enough to meet the *real* Ben.

For one night, at least.

I hadn't seen him in person since the last Games, and the years had woven a couple of strands of gray in the dark hair at his temples. The gap between us felt even wider when I spied the beginnings of crinkles in the corner of his eyes. He was only nine years older, but it felt like he had an entire lifetime on me.

Ben had one of the most expressive faces I'd ever seen, even when he was just sitting still and staring at me. His thick eyebrows had a life of their own, which meant they telegraphed how he was truly feeling at any moment, despite all the media training he'd been through. They were almost as hypnotic as his black-brown eyes, which never strayed from your face when he was talking to you. He came across as so damn *likable*, a mix of mischief and focus that guaranteed a good time.

"Miss Quinn Albright. It's been too long," Ben said. He tipped his head winningly, like I'd be as powerless as the rest of the world when he unleashed the charm. "Really good to see you."

It took all my emotional-regulation practice to keep from freaking the fuck out at him for implying that we were just old friends catching up.

I glanced around the restaurant to make sure no one was close before speaking. "You're a fucking asshole. Do you know that?"

He jerked his head back, but I could tell he wasn't shocked. "Whoa. We're going there already?"

"Do you think I asked to meet you just to hang out?" I hissed, because I noticed that Addie and her mom were now watching the gold medal speed skater and the Olympic hopeful trying to play nice. "I have some things I need to say before I pretend to tolerate you for the next week."

The teenage waitress sidled up to our table despite not even stopping by to refill my coffee as I'd waited for Ben.

"Ohmygod, *hi*, Ben!" She gave him a little wave. "Total stan here."

"Aw, thank you," he beamed at her. "If you're a skating fan then I'm guessing you must like this one too?" He pointed at me.

It was just like him to share the spotlight as a way to try to make nice with me.

"Of *course*, who doesn't love the Swan?" she replied, glancing at me for two seconds then back at Ben. "I already fangirled over Quinn when she got here. So what are you two doing together? Like, a collab or something?"

He adjusted himself to take up more space in the booth, kicking one leg up and draping his arm over the back of the bench.

"You could say that. Stay tuned."

He winked at her and she immediately blushed and turned on her heel. She stopped herself after four steps and jogged back to us.

"Duh, I'm sorry, can I get you coffee? And do you need a menu?"

"Definitely," Ben replied with a winning smile. "One of us needs more than egg whites for breakfast."

"Because one of us is still competing," I added in a saccharine voice. "You haven't been back out on the ice in *how* long, Ben?"

He winced ever so slightly, and I knew my stinger had found its target.

"Not in a while. I've been too busy expanding my empire. Which is what brings me to Woodspring to meet with this one."

The waitress's eyes jumped between us. "Oh wow, this is so exciting! Can I get a picture with you guys before you go?"

"Of course," Ben answered for me.

We both knew that a photo of the two of us together would crank the rumor mill into high gear. The single dim photo with us clinched in the background behind the downhill team on that fateful night had been enough to send the internet into two days' worth of speculation about what exactly was going on between us.

Which was absolutely nothing, thanks to Ben.

And then there was the black-and-white photo that *I'd* posted in the desperate weeks after we got home as a bat signal for him. A reminder of what we'd shared. I'd only left it up for a few hours before mortification had set in and I deleted it, but by that time the post had already racked up eight thousand likes and a couple of hundred comments that said some variation of "Is that Ben?????"

I pretended that I had plausible deniability on my side since you couldn't see his face in the shot, but our joined hands with his ankle tattoo blurry in the background definitely told a story.

"I'll be back with some coffee in a minute," the waitress said, eyes still on him.

"And a menu," he reminded her with his toothpaste-ad smile.

"*Right*, a menu."

Ben and I leaned back against the bench simultaneously, like we both wanted to keep some distance between us. It was hard for me to believe that he thought he could waltz back into my life and I'd be fine with it.

"So, is this like a peace summit, or . . ." he trailed off.

"No, this is an 'air my grievances so I don't murder you' talk. I have plenty I need to say to you, and if you're not willing to hear it I suggest you crawl back to your producers and tell them exactly why I'm refusing to do the show."

His face went white. "Whoa, whoa, hold on. This is happening, Quinn. Everything's confirmed. The rest of the crew arrives tomorrow."

I shrugged a shoulder and felt delightfully petty. "Yes, but you know firsthand how critical it is for me to stay focused right now. I mean, what if I get so worried about you guys interrupting my training schedule that I accidentally injure myself during practice tomorrow?" I widened my eyes and held my hand over my heart. "Oh my goodness, *no one* would question me pulling out if that happened, right? And what's crazy is that all of a sudden my knee's feeling a little wonky." I rubbed it and grimaced like I wanted people in the cheap seats to see the show. "Who knows what might go wrong. Can't you just picture how terrible that would be for you?"

"You *wouldn't*."

The naked fear in his voice tickled me.

I shrugged again.

Ben scooted closer and leaned closer across the table. "You don't understand. It *has* to happen. We're doing this."

"We?"

"Damn straight," he replied. I could tell he was aiming for levity but it came off a little nervous.

Something in his expression snagged me. Despite all our baggage I was still a sucker for a hard-luck story. "Why?"

He glanced around, looked down at his hands, then finally back at me. "I actually need this gig."

"Okay, well, you're here. You've obviously already got it."

He shook his head. "I don't," he said softly. "This is a conditional hire, based on how Italy turns out. And your piece. I've done some spotlight interviews for them and it's a big deal that they gave me an assignment this big as a final trial. I've obviously, uh, gone through some dicey scenarios over the past few years. That means the producers aren't sure they can trust me."

I love how he spun his bad decision-making as something that happened *to* him, like unexpected speed bumps in the road.

"So . . . yeah," Ben continued, "I need everything to be perfect. I'll beg if I have to. *Please*, Quinn."

He clasped his hands under his chin.

I'd suspected that I had a little leverage in the scenario but I never imagined that I was driving the whole damn tow truck. Rather than putting him out of his misery I let him dangle for a bit.

I didn't respond until I was convinced that he was suitably stressed out.

"If that's the case, you need to shut up and listen," I gloated.

Chapter Five

*W*e both fake-smiled at the waitress when she came back with coffee.

"Okay, I'm listening," Ben said softly after she walked away.

And that was a big part of the problem. For all his good-time party-guy vibes, I knew firsthand that Ben was a phenomenal listener. Once he was locked in, it was too easy to crack open your heart and reveal the messy contents to him. And his advice? Nearly as good as my therapist's.

I'd always hoped that I'd get this reckoning with Ben. I'd envisioned it would play out like we were in a movie, with music swelling as I made point after devastating point, until Ben looked suitably regretful for what happened between us.

Or *didn't* happen.

The vintage diner setting with a bipolar jukebox spitting out Gwar one minute and Britney the next didn't exactly set the mood. And then there were the eyes on us . . . Most folks were used to seeing me around town, but our combined star power seemed to be attracting more attention than usual.

I cleared my throat. I *thought* I was prepared, but I'd crafted my speech without considering how it would feel to be sitting across from him again. I wasn't sure which part was safe to focus on—his unwavering stare, the set of his angular jaw, or the mouth that looked like it was seconds away from curling into a smile despite the tension.

Not the mouth. Definitely not the mouth.

"Do you know how much you hurt me?" I began, trying to keep my voice steady.

He finally broke off eye contact to glance down at the mug clutched in his hands. "I do." Ben looked up to meet my eyes again. "And I'm sorry."

I'd expected excuses, not him copping to being a dick right away. I had reams of supporting evidence to make my case, but here he was, apologizing right at the jump. Admitting that he'd been wrong was the equivalent of a bucket of water on my five-alarm fury.

"Good."

It was all I could come up with as I recalibrated my approach.

"I've thought about it a lot over the past few years, and I came close to reaching out, but you seemed like you were doing well," Ben said.

"No thanks to you," I shot back at him. "And it took time for me to get to that point. I went through hell."

"Yeah, I figured." He sighed and fidgeted with his mug again.

"That night, you told me not to worry." I hoped the tremor in my voice wasn't obvious, because I didn't want him to think he had access to that part of me again. "Your exact words were "I've got you." And I *believed* you, Ben."

Saying it out loud made me feel needy, but of course he already knew I was.

After our time in Switzerland, Bennett Martino knew every single one of my secrets.

Now I had to make sure he wouldn't be sharing any of them with his viewing audience.

"Why did you act all invested in me?" I demanded. "I told you *everything*. From the bullshit with my mom, to the way Carol treated me." I leaned across the table to hiss-whisper the next part. "I told you about my fucking eating disorder!"

He winced.

"If you were so worried about me, then why didn't you reach out once we got home, when I *really* needed you?"

It felt so good to pin the question on him like he was a bug on corkboard. Ben frowned at me.

"I know this might sound hard to believe, but it was for the best," he insisted.

My mouth dropped open.

"*Wow*." I nodded my head when I finally snapped out of my shocked haze. "Okay. Really patronizing. Leaning into the age gap thing, huh? Mr. Been There Done That knows all."

"No, it's not like that," he said. "Not even close. The stuff we talked about that night . . . I don't know. In a way I feel responsible for what you did when you got home."

"You mean quitting?"

He shifted. "Yeah. I was terrified that I pushed you to it."

"Please. Don't give yourself so much credit for my good decisions," I mumbled as I fiddled with a sugar packet.

"You were spiraling that night. I was worried about you, and when you started talking about which competitions you were going to plan for next, and how you and your coach—who you *hated*—could rework your routines . . . Quinn, you sounded . . .

robotic. There was no passion for your sport, just this zombielike drive to win again. Like you had something to prove."

"You think?" I asked sarcastically.

"Come on."

I hugged my arms to my chest and scanned the room again. Thankfully, everyone was focused on their food, not us. I watched a group of teenage girls laughing and downing waffles and felt a twinge of jealousy. Did they consider calorie counts, or was it possible for some people to just . . . eat? Because at that age I'd forgotten what waffles tasted like.

"I felt bad for even *implying* that you needed a break," Ben continued. "When I heard you'd quit I felt . . . I don't know . . . sort of responsible for it."

"Shame you didn't think to check in on your young patient."

"Quinn, I'm trying here, okay? Or should I not bother?"

He looked genuinely upset, and it almost swayed me. But I had years of built-up anger fueling me, and I wasn't about to get lulled by his handsome sad face.

I remembered every minute of our conversation that night. We'd sat huddled together for hours while I cried and ranted about the state of my life. It got to the point where I'd nearly hyperventilated, and that was when Ben had pulled me close and wrapped his arms around me. I cried against his shoulder until I felt okay to keep talking.

That hug felt different from any others I'd gotten during Switzerland. I'd been falling the whole time, desperate for someone to grab on to me and tell me that I was still worthy, but only Ben had *really* seen me. The way he'd held me, pressing himself to me like he could ground me with his body, made me feel safe in a way I'd never experienced.

It was no surprise what happened later that night.

Before that point, Ben gave me the space to rant, and offered me his perspective without judgment. He never came out and told me that I needed to consider quitting, but he didn't have to. Little by little, through examples from his own career and a thoughtful examination of mine, the answer became clear to me on my own.

It felt like we were at the beginning of something real and important. Being so open had left me feeling bruised *and* free, like Ben was going to help me carry my load now that he knew it was crushing me.

"And I'm sorry, Quinn, but I need to remind you that I came back to the States dealing with my own shit. I won gold, and it was amazing, but I was also retiring. I had sponsorship commitments I needed to fulfill, and so much press." His brow knitted as he broke off, like it was his turn to stop himself from saying too much. "Let's just say there's a lot you don't know about that period. You were in my thoughts, all the damn time, but I needed to deal with my own shit first."

It was a bucket of water on my fury, although being busy with his many gold medal commitments wasn't exactly a rough go compared to what I'd dealt with when I got home.

He deserved a thimbleful of grace and nothing more.

"You're right. I'm sorry," I admitted quietly.

But still . . . how hard would it have been to send me a quick text? Just an "I'm thinking about you, stay strong" message would've been enough to make me feel less alone as I took an arcade rifle to my life and picked off the parts that were no longer working for me.

"No need to apologize," he said quickly. "I'm sure from the outside it looked like I was having the time of my life. And I was, for a little while. Then reality hit, *hard*. And let's just leave it at that for now." He took a long draw of coffee, still watching me over the rim of the mug. "I wanted to reach out to you, Quinn. I did, I swear. But you were sorting through your entire career, questioning everything. I thought I'd be a distraction. Plus . . ."

"What?" I pushed.

When he finally refocused on me I felt a tremor pass through my body.

"I was closing in on thirty. You were a child."

I snorted. "Oh *gross*. Don't make it sound so Lolita."

"But you get what I'm saying," he said in a strained voice. "The whole thing was complicated, given where we both were in our careers."

I hated that he was making sense, but his logic couldn't erase the pain I'd carried in the years since. Even an "it's not you, it's me" text would've been better than the ghosting he subjected me to. And I'd gotten a little unhinged as my unanswered texts piled up.

I still cringed thinking about some of the stuff I'd said.

"We're both coming to this taping with baggage," he said.

I snorted in response. His was a carry-on, mine was a steamer trunk.

"But we *have* to make it work. You'll get to tell your story the way you want, and I'll get my contract with the show."

I allowed a single nod in response.

"So with that in mind, I was hoping we could lay out some ground rules for this interview," he said.

"Please." I spread my hands and swept the air in front of me. "Enlighten me, oh wise elder."

"You're so fucking annoying," he said and chuckled.

"Childish, you might say," I countered.

He ignored me. "We both have a lot riding on the next couple of weeks. I need your episode and then my coverage of the Games to be flawless. After a bunch of false starts, this job feels like a fit for me. I can envision an actual future with the show, so I need everything to go smoothly."

I ignored his bossiness. "Future? What's that?"

"Yeah, my point exactly," he said. "So what I'm asking is for us to enter into an agreement. We'll forget about our past and focus on making something inspiring together. Remember, this interview will help you, too, Quinn."

"Fine," I agreed. "But you're not the only one who gets to lay down rules, so it's my turn."

"Go for it."

I forced myself to ignore how willing he seemed to hear me out, because it was only for selfish reasons.

"I expect this to be one hundred percent professional. That means you have to forget everything personal I told you in Switzerland. Don't even *hint* at it. I opened myself up to you, not your viewing audience. You can't act like we have any shared history. And don't try to be my buddy. As far as anyone knows, we were both at the Games four years ago, and that's the extent of our relationship. Distant teammates."

A quiet settled over the booth as we considered the fiction I was proposing, because there was still gossip residue about exactly what had happened between us in Switzerland, and doing the show would resurface it. The last thing I wanted was to be considered nothing more than one of Ben's conquests.

"You probably don't even remember half of what happened that night," I scoffed at him. It was how I'd consoled myself when he didn't reach out to me. Maybe he'd been drunk for twenty-four hours? It was the only acceptable explanation of why he'd let me twist in the wind once we got home.

Ben went still, his eyes locked on me.

"I remember every second."

My stomach dipped like I was on a small-town carnival roller coaster.

I'd shared the ugliest parts of myself with him, and he'd accepted me anyway, at least for that night. Would it even be possible for Ben to forget all the crap about my mom if he got the chance to interview her? And when I talked about how pumped I was to be going to the Olympics again, would he know that it was an act, and that I was actually terrified of blowing it for a second time?

Of course he would. After that night of truth telling I felt like Ben knew all the parts of me I tried to keep hidden. That the burned-out gifted kid was still fighting for her chance at gold.

He'd heard it all and acted like none of it mattered. That night, all he'd cared about was making sure that I was going to be okay.

In another life, Ben and I would be soulmates. In this one, we were nothing more than temporary colleagues.

Chapter Six

I still had one more question for Ben before we started our week-long game of make-believe. I waited for the waitress to finish refilling his coffee before asking.

"Why *me*?"

Ben froze, and his face tightened as if I'd slapped him. But his serial dating wasn't exactly a secret.

"You knew all of Team USA was chasing you," I continued. "Hell, *every* athlete that was there wanted you. So why did you pick the one person who was crashing out? You could've had a shit ton more fun with someone like Nari Choi or Deanna Wilcox instead of wiping my tears all night."

I hadn't even wanted to turn up at the impromptu gathering of athletes—we weren't allowed to call it a party—after what I'd been through on the ice. I felt so ashamed, like I'd let down the entire country, let alone all my teammates. Our plans to dominate the figure-skating podium were crushed, all thanks to me. I wasn't exactly in a great headspace for having fun, but my teammates Alyssa and Charlotte convinced me that being around other humans might take my mind off my many failures.

I wanted to forget about everything I'd done wrong for the night. My falls during my long program, the many close-up photos of my tearstained face afterward, Carol's obvious disappointment that she didn't even try to hide from me. I didn't need anyone else to make me feel bad for my shitty performance, I was doing an amazing job of it all on my own. Still, both Coach Carol and my mom were more than happy to point out in excruciating detail where things had gone sideways.

It felt impossible to get away from my sadness. My *grief.* I'd been training for the moment for my entire life, and I'd blown it. One of the headlines actually said THE SWAN GETS PLUCKED. That night, I tried to fake being okay with the rest of the gathered athletes. I wasn't the only one with a black mark next to my name after competing, but it felt like the spotlight was harshest on me.

We'd been outside under the stars, gathered around a firepit in a common area, hiding our beers in the sleeves of our official country parkas like high schoolers. At just nineteen, I was happy that I was legal in Switzerland. I didn't *want* to get drunk, but it felt good knowing the option was available to me.

The night wore on and everyone started scream-singing the goofy Olympic theme song "Striving," which had lyrics in our host country's languages, including German, French, Italian, and English. I retreated into the background, clutching my still-full beer as tears slid down my cheeks.

And that's when Ben finally walked over to me.

At first I thought he was just passing by on the way to get more alcohol, but he wound up in front of me, clutching my elbows as I quickly swiped away my tears. But his nearness—*the* Magic Martino was asking me how he could help me—only made me cry harder. I was mortified, but I just couldn't stop. The mix of embarrassment that he was witnessing my breakdown combined with my bottomless grief meant that I couldn't morph into a cool girl. I was fully inhabiting my mess.

I wound up nearly hyperventilating with snot running down my face, until he offered me a crumpled napkin from a kebab house and pulled me into a tight hug.

I finally managed to calm down thanks to a breathing exercise he suggested, until the two of us inhaling and exhaling in tandem, staring into each other's eyes, started to feel a little tantric. That's why it made total sense when he reached out to cup my cheek and gently draw me to him.

"Why you?" Ben repeated. He stared at the table for a long time, which made me worried about what he was going to reveal. "I can't explain it. It just . . . I don't know. In that moment it made sense."

"What did?" I pushed.

Ben finally raised his eyes to meet mine and it hit me like a jolt of static electricity. I forced myself not to look away.

"You and me."

Something tightened in my stomach. This confessional stuff was derailing my plan. I was supposed to be in charge of the inquisition, not fighting for air.

"I don't believe you," I shot back, trying to douse the pilot light that flickered on in my heart.

"I figured you wouldn't, which is partly why I didn't mention it."

"And what about the next day?" I demanded.

Ben looked incredulous. "Hold on, you don't want to talk about that night?"

It sounded like the hum of conversation in the diner dipped at the mention of our night together, but I knew it was just my imagination. I leaned closer to him, just in case.

"What's there to say?" I hissed.

I wasn't about to be forced into admitting that I still conjured up memories of our night together in my fantasies. That every spot he'd touched on my body had left a brand on my skin.

Ben fidgeted. "I just thought if we're taking time to hash everything out, that should be part of the conversation?" He leaned closer. "We didn't sleep together—"

"Yeah, I know, I was there." I narrowed my eyes at him.

I remembered everything that had happened on his cardboard bed, including the way I'd begged him not to stop. When he'd claimed there wasn't a single condom in his room, I volunteered to get dressed and track down one of the free condom vending machines spread throughout the village. I was still mortified at how obvious my need for him was, but it made sense, because Ben's hands on me erased everything else. Nothing mattered as his kisses found new ways to shift my focus from my body's failures to the delights it was capable of.

And holy shit was it delightful. I didn't have a ton of experience at that point, just a couple of flings with male skaters, one of whom turned out to be gay, but I could tell even in the moment that what happened between us wasn't normal in the best way possible.

Ben had *worshipped* me. No part of my body had escaped his attention, so that night I'd learned that a kiss behind the ear meant goose bumps down my arms, and a kiss between my legs meant fireworks. I'd wanted to return the favor but it was like my orgasm was a sedative. I'd woken up the next morning still nestled in his arms.

"If you're okay with everything that happened that night then I am too," he said. "We can move on."

I wasn't okay with it, because no one I'd been with since had come close to making me feel the way that Ben had. But I wasn't about to give him the satisfaction of letting him know.

"And as for the next day, it just made sense to hang out, you know?" Ben continued. "I was worried about you."

For a second I thought he was going to reach out to take my hand, but he diverted to his coffee cup instead.

"I thought it was important for us to have fun," he added.

It was another truth about our time together that I wasn't going to admit to him. Somehow Ben had pulled off a miracle and managed to keep me laughing for the day despite, well, *everything*. I'd ignored my mom's and Carol's frantic calls and boarded a train to Lugano with him, and because it felt far away in the Italian part of the country I'd pretended that I was just a normal person enjoying a Tuscan getaway. Ben and I had braved the winds at Lake Lugano and filled up on piadinas and amaretti in a cozy grotto in town.

That day he'd more than lived up to his nickname, because for nine hours he'd magically made me forget that I was a loser.

I realized that I'd been staring at him and now he was waiting for some sort of confirmation that I was still listening.

"It was a long time ago," I finally said. "And it's about to be forgotten history. Yes?"

His mouth went tight as he nodded. "Agreed."

Even though I'd spent the last few days steeling myself for the showdown and visualizing all the ways it could play out, I'd never given him the grace of thinking that he could topple a few bricks from the walls I'd built. But his willingness to abide by my rules meant something to me.

The week with Ben wasn't going to be pleasant, but at the very least I could now trust that *I* was in control.

Chapter Seven

$\mathcal{I}$ didn't dress differently for practice the next day because I knew that Ben was going to be watching, but I *did* put some extra thought into my outfit. I was in my usual black Lululemon leggings, black zip-front fleece, gloves, and ratty black legwarmers. But underneath, for when I no longer felt the cold? A strappy, open-backed, ridiculously complicated black leotard that looked like something a dominatrix would wear. And makeup. Just a little, so I didn't look as exhausted as I felt.

I think I'd slept four hours total the night before, reliving every second of our conversation at the diner. Our surface-level truce was the only way to make the show happen. I'd have to bottle up all my unresolved bullshit for the week.

Easy.

I'd woken up to a text from Mel this morning letting me know that the four-person camera crew that was supposed to be arriving later in the day was going to be delayed a few hours, and reduced to two people thanks to a biking doping scandal that had just hit the news. I tried not to feel offended that my story had been one-upped by human growth hormones.

That said, I *still* didn't know how the week was going to play out. For as long as I could remember, my life was basically mapped to the minute, especially when competitions were on the horizon. Once again, Ben had muscled his way back into my life and flipped it upside down.

Even though I wasn't due on the ice until eight, like always I'd padded in forty-five minutes to stretch, foam roll my body, put pads on my blisters, and tape myself back together in the locker room before I even looked at my skates. I tried to focus on what my body was telling me in the moment, without getting obsessed about the new twinges I kept feeling as I stretched.

Ben was already at the rink when I made it out to the ice, chatting with Mel in her usual spot in the players' box. I skated across the ice to them, hoping that the stuff I'd picked up in my acting classes was making me look convincingly nonchalant. They continued their conversation but eyeballed me as I got closer.

"Damn," Ben said, staring at my feet. "Black boots *and* blades? You're gonna be starting a new trend at rinks all over the country."

I swiveled back and forth to show them off, a little surprised that he hadn't seen them yet. I'd been wearing them in competitions for the past year, and they were a symbol of my new "fuck tradition" attitude. How good a reporter could he be if he hadn't done his research?

"Aren't they great?" Mel asked. "I was against them initially but Quinn wore me down. And when you think about it, she has a point; if she's wearing a dark costume why wouldn't she cap it off with black skates? Would you wear a black gown with white shoes?"

"I haven't worn a gown in a while, so I'm not sure what the trends are these days," Ben joked.

Switching up my skate color was one of the many changes I'd wanted once I had the freedom to actually have opinions. I knew it was a risky choice given how traditional and stuffy my sport was, but I was banking on my skill to take the focus off my costume choices. The judges couldn't have a problem with skates that were helping me nail every jump.

"It's an evolution," I said with a shrug.

If the cameras had been recording our little prepractice chat I would've come up with some sort of sound bite-y response. For now I could still lean into my petulant teenager vibes.

I glanced down at Ben's feet. "*You* brought skates?"

"Well, yeah." He looked between his skates and me, confused. "Why wouldn't I? I thought it might be fun to get some footage of us out there together."

"As long as it doesn't interrupt my practice, fine," I said as I squeezed by him to drop my stuff on the bench.

"Such a great idea," Mel said. "Love it, Ben."

I could tell that she was already under his spell. I wasn't the only one looking all shiny and cute for practice; Mel was in her fancy competition jacket with lipstick on. She was happily married with two kids, but clearly we were all powerless to resist the Martino Magic.

"I'm warming up," I said as I stepped back on the ice.

"Sarah will be here in two minutes," Mel called after me.

I nodded and tried to ignore the fact that everything in my body felt extra tight this morning, from my shoulders down to the balls of my feet. My power pulls were choppy and it wasn't because of divots in the ice. Frank would never allow them, so I reluctantly took the blame. I actually tripped doing a simple backward jump swizzle, but Mel and Ben were too busy gossiping to notice.

"Hey you," Sarah shouted from the far side of the rink as she pulled off her guards and sped across the ice to me. "Sorry I'm a little late."

I hid a laugh as she skated to me, because Sarah had gotten the "look cute" memo as well. She was in a white parka that I'd never seen, and her blond hair was blown straight and half pulled back, the way she used to wear it when she was competing. She was an ice dancer who'd done the circuit in the early nineties in the shadow of Tonya and Nancy, and the era still had a hold on her.

She caught up and skated backward in front of me as I continued warming up, glancing over at Ben. "What's he like? Is he nice? Is there anything I need to know?"

"He's fine, and you already know that the rest of the crew is running late. That's it."

Sarah looked over to where they were watching and waved. "Damn, he's even hotter in real life."

"I think he looks older."

She made a face at me. "Get your eyes checked. He's sex on skates, now and forever."

"I've got bigger things to worry about," I said as I rolled my neck. "I feel like the Tin Man. I'm tired. And a little grumpy."

"Yikes," she laughed. "I'll give you a few more minutes and go say hi, then let's get to it."

I went through the rest of my warm-up, avoiding going back to where Ben had my coach and choreographer laughing their asses off.

At least someone was having fun.

The first quiet notes of my short program song echoed through the rink and I felt myself relax a little, until I remembered that Ben was going to hear Sarah yelling at me to remember my sex appeal. As much as I loved our new direction, the old training that had been pounded into me was tough to short-circuit. Sometimes I defaulted to my "placid princess" face when what I needed was to bump up my smolder.

Sarah skated back out on the ice and paused a few feet away from me. While Mel and I worked out the critical technical aspects of my programs, it was Sarah who brought the artistry.

"Okay, it's time to woo me, Miss Albright," she joked as the music started again from the beginning.

I looked over to the players' box and found Ben leaning on his elbows, locked on to me. Mel was beside him with her phone ready to record.

Showtime.

I rolled my shoulder and did full-body undulations in time with the opening, then began my step sequence. The song was a slow burn of a ballad that started off quiet, allowing me to slowly bloom with my spins and jumps as it built to the first crescendo. Then, at about minute two, the song built to a gospel-like swell that gave me the tempo to clear the length of the rink for the more impressive, score-heavy jumps to come.

First up? A flawless triple flip toe loop combination.

"Take your time . . . and *good*!" Sarah yelled and clapped as I landed. "Gorgeous."

I loved skating the piece because I was finally able to show off a side of myself that audiences had never seen. Sweet and soft had left the building.

"Let's see that sexy melt," Sarah yelled. "Give me *face*."

It sounded like nonsense but I knew exactly what she meant. In this program, I was stepping into my power.

"Yes, *seamless* . . . gorgeous, Quinn . . . and there's that *one*, two, three," Sarah said as I went into my spin combination. "Nice!"

I smiled because I knew I was nailing it. When I glanced over at Ben he was practically drooling.

More jumps, spins, and general perfection. It felt like Ben was my lucky charm, because I was skating like I was being scored instead of doing my first run of the day on achy joints.

"Bah, bum-bum-bum," Sarah sang along to the final few beats of the song. "*Yes*. Love it."

I grinned as my audience broke into applause.

Sarah and I skated over to the box and Mel immediately went into a slice-and-dice debrief of my performance, which was mostly positive. I'd *always* have issues to address—perfectionism was a disease without a cure—but I sure liked it when the praise outweighed the criticism.

I tried to ignore the fact that Ben was more focused on taking notes in an actual notebook than paying attention to the feedback. I'd expected some sort of reaction from him, but he kept his head down, scribbling away. He finally glanced up at me.

"Well, that was fun."

I couldn't keep from scowling at his word choice.

"Seriously? All of that," I gestured to where I'd just melted the rink, "was *fun*?"

It wasn't like I'd skated to a Disney tune. Suddenly, I felt silly for leaning into my sex appeal, especially if it didn't translate.

"She's been competing with this program for a while," Mel explained. "Was that the first time you've seen it?"

I wondered if the weight of three sets of eyes would impact his answer.

He bobbed his head and grinned, clearly immune to our glares. "Yeah, it was. I wanted to come to this week without preconceived notions about your new programs, so I wouldn't be influenced by what the media has been saying so far."

Mel, Sarah, and I scowled in unison.

"Back in my day, reporters prepped for important interviews like this with a packet of information about their subject, so they'd have a framework for the story they want to tell. They usually did a ton of research beforehand. Is that something that . . ." Sarah trailed off.

"Yup, I get that," Ben replied good-naturedly. "I'm taking a different approach, and my team at *The Score* is okay with it."

It felt like he was a student getting called out for not doing enough work for a presentation. *Why* was I trusting him to chart my comeback?

Then again, Ben knew more about my origin story than anyone. He knew nearly all the truths I'd never shared, and despite agreeing to come to this week with a clean slate, there was no way he could truly avoid incorporating everything I'd confided in him. He didn't need a packet filled with media-friendly pull quotes, because he'd gotten the real story directly from the source.

My pageant queen, borderline-narcissist mother; my absentee, workaholic father; my struggles with disordered eating triggered by abusive coaches; my disdain for the system that valued medals over mental health. I'd spilled it all to him.

And now the regret I'd felt at a low simmer since Switzerland was about to boil over.

In the months after the Games, once I realized that Ben *wasn't* going to be the lifeline I so desperately needed, my anger shifted to embarrassment. I'd exposed my soft, white underbelly to him and he'd rejected me. I was needy, and weak, and a disappointment to the entire world. His rejection of me validated every negative feeling.

Until therapy. With the help of my counselor I was able to re-frame what had happened between us. It didn't make me hate Ben any less for drop-kicking me when I needed him most, but it did prove that his actions weren't a reflection of my value.

"Okay, let's go again," Sarah said, breaking me out of my self-doubt tailspin. "You're on a roll."

I nodded and glided back out to the center of the ice. *Fun?* Allow me to expand your vocabulary, Mr. Martino.

My second run-through was even better than my first. Rather than trying to seduce an entire arena, my focus was solely on Ben. His pen hovered above his notebook while he stared at me.

The fleece came off right before my third run-through. The notebook sat on the boards, untouched.

More feedback from Sarah, some refining, a few laughs, and I was feeling even better than normal. We wrapped up as more skaters started to dot the ice. I prepared for the squeals of recognition when they realized that the mighty Magic Martino was at our humble arena.

Ben seemed to sense it as well and pulled on a baseball cap.

"I'm going to cool down now," I said to Mel and Sarah, even though they already knew what came next.

"Hold up," he replied quickly, frowning at me. "Can you and I go skate for a bit? Please?"

Chapter Eight

*W*hy bother? The cameras aren't here," I said to Ben.

Plus I had zero desire to spend any more time with him than necessary. Mel and Sarah picked up on my vibe and quickly packed their things and left us alone.

"I thought it would be fun," he shrugged.

"If that's the case we definitely should save it."

"Are you saying we can't have fun off camera?"

I pursed my lips and glared at him. "Yes, that's *exactly* what I'm saying. Have you forgotten everything we talked about yesterday?"

"Yup, got it." He stood up and walked to the edge of the ice. "You can do what you want, but I'm skating. I don't get the opportunity much these days. I feel like an addict staring at a pile of cocaine. I *need* this."

I watched him pause at the edge then step onto the ice one foot at a time, deliberately, like he was a newbie afraid of slipping.

"Home at last," he sighed as he glided away from me.

I debated grabbing my stuff and leaving. There was no point in hanging out with him any longer, and I needed to stick to my daily routine.

Then he turned and beckoned me, smiling that irresistible smile as he did effortless backward crossovers.

Damn it. I couldn't be a total dick to him, especially since it looked like a few skaters had recognized him and were watching us.

"Fine," I said to myself with a sigh.

I caught up and fell in line beside him. We slid into a natural rhythm, like pairs skaters.

"I like this rink," he gestured around it. "It's homey."

"Is that a compliment?" I asked, preemptively offended on behalf of my turf. "Because it doesn't sound like one."

Ben used to train at a state-of-the-art arena in Utah that had every amenity, on-ice and off. While my arena was more advanced than a basic neighborhood rink, it certainly wasn't the Olympic proving ground that he was used to, with a full gym, video analytics lab, dance studio, and rehab center all on-site.

"Definitely a compliment," he nodded. "There's community here. A rink like this is where the journey begins for a lot of these kids. They have this vague idea that skating is fun. Combine that with natural talent and they're off."

I didn't have to ask if that was how it happened for him because I already knew his entire backstory, like the rest of the country. An art dealer father and opera singer mother from California who had no background in sports, but recognized and supported Ben's drive. His move to the Utah facility at thirteen, and then his ridiculous winning streak.

"Listen, I wanted to talk about something with you, before the rest of the team get here," Ben said. I could feel him watching me. "When your mom confirmed everything, she obviously green-lighted the home visit and gave us a bunch of dates that work for them. Now, I know that's going to be a challenging part of the—"

"Nope." I shook my head vigorously as I interrupted him. "I have zero time to fly home. Every minute between now and when I leave is accounted for. Doing this interview is enough of a distraction."

"Yeah, when Kim asked me about going to Connecticut I tried going to bat for you, because I had a feeling you wouldn't want to do it based on everything you told me in Switzerland. I couldn't come out and give Kim the full story, so I was stuck. I tried coming up with excuses for why it won't work, but it turns out your mom has an ace up her sleeve to get you home."

"I'd love to see her try it," I said and fumed at her overreach. I picked up speed, so that Ben had to do the same to keep up with me. "There is absolutely nothing that I need in Connecticut."

Ben did a quick turn to skate backward in front of me, expertly weaving through the two tween girls hovering nearby with just inches to spare.

"She asked me to tell you. Your driver's license is going to expire while you're in Italy, and you're still registered in Connecticut."

I sputtered for a few seconds. "How do you . . . how does she . . ."

But I didn't have to ask how my mom knew when my license expired because she used to micromanage every aspect of my life. What shocked me is that *I'd* let it slip through the cracks in the time since I'd gained control.

"I'll renew online," I said. I skated a little faster still.

"Can't," Ben replied, still gracefully navigating his way backward through the other skaters. "She said that you need to have a new photo taken. You could probably move your primary residence to Colorado to avoid the trip back, but that opens up other challenges."

I hated to admit that there were tax implications for me having my family home still listed as my primary residence. I'd untangled as much as I could four years prior, but there were still elements that tied me to my parents.

"I have my passport."

"You need two valid forms of ID at Olympic Village. Security is tight as hell," Ben replied, sounding apologetic.

"Fuck," I muttered as reality sunk in.

"Honestly, it might help to have us with you as backup, if you have to go," Ben suggested. "I can run front for you."

He had a point. My spotlight-obsessed mom would probably focus all her energy on looking perfect for the camera instead of criticizing me. My dad would just show up and be country club charming, as usual.

"This is the *last* thing I need."

"I know," Ben agreed. "It sucks, but think about how shitty it would've been if you'd gotten to a checkpoint and discovered it was expired then?"

"Yeah, thanks, Mom," I said wryly.

My stomach twisted at this latest addition to my schedule. I felt like the control I so desperately needed was slipping away at the worst possible time.

"When?" I demanded.

"Kim is working on the exact timing with her, but it looks like it'll be two weeks from now."

There was no good time to go home, but doing it so close to my departure was downright criminal.

Ben fell in line beside me again. "Do you want to talk about it?"

I shook my head. I'd already given him plenty of access to my dumpster fire backstory; there was no need to add more kindling.

From this point on I was all sound bites, all the time. They might think I'd granted *The Score* an all-access pass to my life, but I was pretty good at micromanaging as well.

First step? Redirecting the conversation.

"How do you feel?" I asked, pointing to Ben's feet.

I knew I had an advantage over him since he wasn't in his native skates, and I wanted to hear the many ways he felt hobbled without them.

"It's always an adjustment when I go back to these. They don't feel natural to me. But I bet I can do some of the stuff you do wearing them."

There was no end to Ben's confidence.

"Oh, you think so? Please grace me with your figure-skating skills."

"I'm sorry, did you say jump?"

Ben paused then did the tiniest, shakiest waltz jump ever executed in the Greater Woodspring Skating Arena. I managed not to laugh at him, until he finished with a graceless, stiff-armed pose.

"Sad." I shook my head.

"Okay, watch *this*."

He attempted it again and managed to get a little more air, but nearly fell when he landed it.

"It's your arms," a little voice echoed out.

We both turned to find a young boy nearby, watching us with his hands on his hips and the furrowed expression of someone who'd been coaching newbies for thirty years. I recognized him as a promising ten-year-old figure skater named Nathan who'd been putting in plenty of hours at the rink with a private coach.

"Oh yeah?" Ben asked him. "What should I be doing instead?"

"Arms out for balance, like this."

The boy executed a flawless jump and we both broke into spontaneous applause.

"Now you," he said to Ben. "Don't be afraid, you just have to believe in yourself."

"Great advice. I'll do my best." He grinned as he shot me a look.

Ben paused, skated a few steps, then managed to get air *and* land without wobbling.

"See? You're a natural," the boy said proudly. "Just keep practicing and you'll get even better."

Ben hid a laugh. "Well, thanks. I sure will."

"Hold on . . ." the boy said, eyeing Ben as he skated closer. "I know you."

I expected Ben to whip off his hat with a flourish, but he waited quietly for the boy to continue.

"You're *Magic Martino*! Oh my god," he cried after a few more seconds of staring at Ben.

Ben laughed. "I am. What's your name?"

"Nate," he answered in an awed voice. "I can't believe you're here!"

"In the flesh," Ben said.

I rolled my eyes.

"Can you show me some speed-skating stuff? Please?" Nate asked excitedly. "My coach isn't here yet, I have time."

"Heck yeah, let's do it. Quinn, you want to stay for a lesson?"

I frowned at him from behind Nate. "Hard pass."

"Okay, I'll text you when Neil and Hailey get here and we can finalize the flow of the rest of the week. I think Mel and Kim have worked out a rough game plan."

"Might be nice if you looped me in," I grumbled.

Ben skated closer to me. "We thought it would be best to work around your current schedule and slot us in wherever it's least annoying. Don't worry, you can swap out anything you don't like."

"Oh trust me, I will."

Nate was swiveling between us with wide eyes because it probably seemed like I was being mean to his hero. I faked a smile for his benefit.

"Nate, have fun and be careful, okay? This guy likes to go really fast." I pointed at Ben, and he winked at me in response.

"I *know*," Nate replied, still awestruck. "Me too."

I skated back to the players' box to grab my things then headed for the locker room. Zoey was on her way out.

"Aren't you supposed to be lifting right now?" she asked me.

We knew each other's schedules by heart.

"I'll give you one guess why I'm just finishing up," I smirked.

Zoey brightened despite my negative tone. "He's *here*? Still?"

"Oh yes, giving a speed-skating lesson to an admirer. Do you know Nate?"

"Of course, he's the cutest. And a real daredevil." She paused. "Ben's working with him? I can guarantee that means he's going to switch sports now."

I'd never considered that what was unfolding on the ice could redirect a young skater's entire career. Getting a free lesson from a three-time Olympian would probably rewire Nate's brain, and before long he'd be less worried about his jump height and more focused on speed-induced adrenaline.

"Would it be weird if I introduced myself to Ben?" Zoey asked.

"Not at all. Just remember whose team you're on," I joked, but not really.

Because I knew firsthand that no one was immune to the many charms of Magic Martino.

Chapter Nine

I couldn't deny it. My left ankle was aching. I'd tried mind-over-mattering the pain as usual, and I'd already downed more than the suggested maximum daily amount of Advil, but the throb radiating up the front of my thigh was unmistakable. It didn't help that I'd lifted heavy at the rink gym, with a focus on my quads. I texted my massage therapist to see if she could slip me in the next morning.

Hours later I was back at the rink to meet with Mel, Ben, and his two-person crew. As much as I wasn't excited about doing the show, I *was* a little bummed that I didn't even merit a full team to cover my story. Especially since Ben didn't seem like he'd put much effort into his research. I was sort of hoping for a producer sitting just out of his sight line when the cameras were rolling, who could rein him in when he went rogue or supply supporting details when he lost the thread.

Hopefully the people who did the editing on *The Score* could make up for any of Ben's shortcomings, because how exactly was he qualified to bring my story to life? He wasn't even a real reporter.

I walked into the observation room above the ice to find everyone already chatting.

"The woman of the hour," Ben said when he saw me. "Quinn,

please meet Neil Pappas and Hailey Burkhart, our shadows for the next week."

I shook hands with Neil first, a tall skinny guy in a black knit cap, two sleeves of tattoos, and black-rimmed glasses, then Hailey, a petite blonde with a pixie cut in jeans and a black Western-style chambray shirt.

I was shocked by how young they were. Was my comeback being handled by an all-newbie team?

"Big fan," Hailey said as we shook hands. "I'm so excited to be with you throughout this journey."

I managed to give her a smile even though I didn't love the sentiment. Ben and Co. weren't going to be *with* me with me for the run-up to Italy. We had a week carved out of my insane schedule to get the primary footage for the show, and then they'd be doing standard coverage of everything and everyone once the Games began.

I switched on my public persona. "Agreed, this is going to be fun!"

"Yeah, we're honored to be here," Neil said. "Normally we'd have a bigger crew, but bio-identical human growth hormones are tough to beat, in more ways than one."

I grimaced. "Yeah, that sounds like a mess. I can't believe Andre Levins got caught doping."

Actually I *could* believe it. I'd seen plenty of the dicey stuff that athletes did to tip the scale in their favor.

"Oh, not just Andre." Neil raised an eyebrow. "The scope of it is crazy, hence us needing to throw all our firepower at the story. But don't worry, you'll never know the difference. I have a hidden third arm in the middle of my back, I can do it all."

"It's true, I've seen it myself," Ben laughed. He pointed at Hailey. "That one over there can hold a camera, key light, and a boom mic all at the same time."

"Eh," Neil said. "Hailey's in more of a production assistant role this time around. I'll be in charge of our cameras."

"Hold on, that's not what Kim said." Hailey frowned at him. "She said I'm ready to be on cam two."

"Well, Kim's not here," Neil replied smugly.

The room went quiet as the pair shot daggers at each other. Awesome, *more* tension on what was already going to be a hell of a week.

"Hey, as long as you make me look pretty, we're fine," Ben joked.

Mel brayed out a laugh. "Oh, you *always* look good," she said in a flirty voice I'd never heard.

"Thanks for noticing, I'm blushing," Ben flirted back.

Hailey caught me rolling my eyes.

"Let's sit," Ben said. "I know Quinn is busy, so time is money."

"At this point, the only time she's not working is when she's sleeping," Mel said as we took our spots at the table."

I shot her a grateful look, because she was still trying to level set them about my availability.

"Mel, I know you and Kim talked quite a bit as we were sorting through schedules," Ben said. "I wanted to confirm that we're all still on the same page. And please forgive me in advance for any hiccups, because this is my first time running the show."

It was a rare moment of humility, the last thing I expected from a man who once told a reporter that he was going to write a book about his life story, which was destined to be a *New York Times* bestseller. Bennett Martino always assumed that his force of will would make what he wanted to happen, happen.

I paused. I'd sworn I wasn't going to do the interview, yet here I was, sitting across a table from the man. Maybe Ben was more powerful at manifesting than I gave him credit for?

I pulled out my phone just as a text from Zoey came through, which included a photo of her and Ben arm in arm on the ice. Another ally down.

"As we talked about, we're doing one master interview, where the two of us will sit down and go over my main questions. That'll be the meat of the show. At that point we can also address anything else we uncover during our time together," he continued, his eyes drifting to me.

I felt preemptively itchy at the thought of it. There would be zero uncovering happening with Ben. He'd never get access to that part of me again.

"Did you send us the questions?" Mel asked, once again running front for me.

Ben shook his head. "I didn't. I know firsthand what happens when you get the questions in advance—spin city. I prefer to have a few guideposts for the conversation rather than a strict script."

Mel frowned at him. "But you said you haven't really been researching Quinn's comeback, so how do you know . . ."

He broke out his gold medal smile. "Please trust me, we're good, I swear. I might be new in the interviewer's chair, but I've sat through enough of these things to know what to do and not do. It's going to be great, I promise you."

"It's just that I've been burned before," I finally spoke up, giving Ben a pointed look.

"Exactly. We need this to be a feel-good story." Mel picked up the thread even though she didn't catch my subtext. "Not too much focus on the past, okay?"

"Understood." Ben nodded and turned to me. "I'll take good care of you."

He said it softly, and just for me.

I felt like I was on a boat, fighting to keep focused on the horizon so I didn't get seasick, because the way he said it made me want to believe him. But I knew better. I had to stay vigilant, because Ben had figured out how to make me feel at ease, and I wasn't about to open up and let him pick through my brain again. Getting me to confess to my traumas on camera would all but guarantee a juicy show, which was exactly what he needed.

"I want to point out that we currently have that interview scheduled for the *end* of the week," Neil said.

Ben nodded. "That's not normal, I get it. Listen, I've been the subject of what feels like thousands of these types of interviews, so doing it this way makes sense to me. The interviewer and the subject are in a much better place for intimacy after spending time together doing all the other stuff."

Ben caught me frowning at the word "intimacy."

"Remember, Quinn and I have a lot to cover," he added. "We're basically strangers."

He shot me a pointed look.

"But you did some research, right?" Mel asked hopefully.

Ben gave her his get-out-of-jail-free smile, which if the TMZ reports were accurate, was something that occasionally worked on the men and women in blue.

"Sure, something like that."

Mel glanced at me and we shared a moment of worry.

"Are you guys going to talk about that photo that leaked from the last Olympics? The hugging one?" Hailey asked. "I'm sure people want to know the details."

Ben laughed. "Nothing to tell. We were at a, uh, gathering of athletes outside in the dark and this one tripped. I grabbed her and kept her from face-planting, that's it. Now, would I also add that perhaps Miss Albright drank a few too many Feldschlösschens that night? Not on the record, I wouldn't. But if that's implied . . ." He shrugged adorably.

Neil and Hailey laughed, but Mel didn't. She knew I hated beer. I appreciated that Ben was putting distance between us, but I needed to pull him aside and tell him not to fictionalize my life if he was going to be so careless about the details. A gold medal winner overdrinking was just celebrating. A loser doing the same thing was drowning her sorrows.

"Can we finalize the rest of the schedule?" I asked, glancing around the table. "I want to make sure that my training isn't interrupted, but I also understand that you guys have shots you need to get."

"Right, let's dive into the specifics," Ben said as he pulled out his phone. "Okay, so we're going to be doing a tour of the arena with you, like a behind-the-scenes look at a day in the life that our viewers eat up. Mel forwarded us a list of folks here at the rink who we can interview. Easy stuff, I think we can grab that on Tuesday after you finish your morning practice." Ben paused to look at Neil. "Make sure you add the Zamboni guy, Frank, to the list. I met him this morning and he's a trip."

Neil nodded toward Hailey. "Write that down."

Her face went crimson at his bossy tone. *Oof.* The week was shaping up to have plenty of minefields.

"We'll obviously want to record a few practice sessions," Ben continued. "Do you have a preference which day?"

"Never?" I said with a laugh, even though I meant it.

"I was thinking we could do it later in the week as well. I'd also like to chat out on the ice, after your session is over." He pointed at

Neil. "The good news is this one played hockey for the Buckeyes, so we can get up close and personal out there."

"Not too close, I hope," I joked.

Not that it mattered. I was used to camera angles so close that they captured the hairs in my nose.

"Please, you're perfect," Hailey said as her eyes traced around my face. "Do you even *have* pores?"

There were a few topics I hated discussing on the record, and the way I looked was one of them. I noticed that reporters never asked the handsome male skaters about their skincare routines, or if their fellow skaters got jealous about the attention they received. Stars on the red carpet were starting to push back on those types of questions, but I wasn't in a position to make waves. While my mom considered her beauty the be-all and end-all, I preferred to focus on my skills.

"Ha, give my primer all the credit," I finally answered.

By this time of day I knew that most of my makeup had all rubbed off. For everything that my mom had stolen from me over the years, from my self-confidence to a positive body image, I would always credit her for my clear skin and symmetrical features.

"Kim said something about going to a dance class, and the gym with Quinn, and a costume fitting as well?" Mel asked, bringing us back to the topic up for debate.

Ben nodded. "Yup, I know the gym session is an easy get, but what about the costume stuff?"

Mel and I exchanged a look, because my costumes were currently getting tweaked. We'd made a few adjustments to my short program costume thanks to unofficial feedback from judges during Nationals, who seemed scandalized by my new selections.

I'd spent my early career skating in long sleeves and fluttery skirts that hit below my butt, in various shades of pink, white, yellow, and baby blue. This time around I was as close to naked as the rules allowed, with flesh-colored illusion mesh and crystals doing the heavy lifting to keep my kibbles and bits covered. My "Bulletproof" costume was black with fierce oxblood accents that looked like it had shattered onto me, and my "Movement" one was a gold number that seemed like it was fighting to cling to my body as I performed. I'd always be a shiny girlie for competitions, so the Swarovski gems were still in full effect on both costumes.

I had no problem wearing either one out on the ice in front of the world, but I knew that being in a confined space with Ben watching as I tried them on would feel like foreplay. Like I was modeling lingerie for my boyfriend with my chaperones looking on.

"Lucky break, because we're heading to Quinn's final fitting on Thursday." Mel turned to me. "Is it okay with you if they tag along?"

We all knew that the only answer was yes.

"Sure, why not?"

"Perfect," Ben said with a satisfied nod. He tapped on his phone. "I'll add that to our schedule for the day. Whew, we're gonna have a busy week!"

I shifted in my chair but managed to keep my performance smile plastered on my face. As challenging as the background with Ben was, I had the added stress of making the public understand I was in a better place now. That my history didn't define my future.

That I was a winner and *nothing* could bring me down.

"The last thing we need to hash out is the home visit," Ben said, sliding his eyes to me.

Okay, maybe one thing could.

Chapter Ten

*W*e stood in the rink parking lot debating our food options. The last place I expected to wind up after finishing our schedule for the week was picking a dinner restaurant with *The Score* team, but they'd all cajoled me into joining them. Neil mentioned a couple of beef-and-grease spots, but Ben finally suggested our town's lone vegetarian restaurant, Dalla Terra.

"You don't eat meat on certain days, right?" Ben asked me.

I never talked about my dietary preferences in the press, so I wasn't sure how he'd uncovered it. But then I remembered my extended food rant that night in Switzerland. I'd told him things that *no one* knew. It was yet another bit of my soul that I'd sliced off and handed to him, and now I was going to pay for it with cameras watching.

I sidestepped his question. "Dalla Terra is amazing. It's classic Italian food with a vegetarian twist."

"You're speaking my language," Ben said with a hand over his heart. "My Nona Rossi used to make a killer eggplant parm."

It was impossible to forget that Ben was a second-generation Italian American, since it came up in almost every interview. He even had a tiny Italy flag tattooed on his ankle, the tell in the photo I'd posted of us then quickly deleted. I had a feeling he'd lobbied hard to go to the Games given the location.

"Eh," Neil grimaced. "Vegetables for dinner? I don't know . . ."

"Then go to Burgerville by yourself," Hailey said a little too forcefully. "It's not like we can mess with Quinn's meal planning, you know? And she doesn't strike me as a loaded tots kind of person."

"Yeah, you're free to go wherever," Ben added. "You can take the rental if Quinn drives us."

Neil glanced at the three of us. "Okay, *fine*, I'll go eat like a bird with the rest of you."

"No complaining," Hailey scolded, wagging her finger at him like an old-timey schoolmarm. "I'm not in the mood to listen to you bitch."

"I don't complain, I express strong opinions," he replied. "I'm not allowed to have opinions?"

Ben ignored their bickering. "Where are we parked? I'm starving, let's go."

The restaurant was busy, but the minute they spotted Ben they cleared a spot for us that was meant for three. Our knees were inches away from one another's beneath the rustic table.

"Should we get a couple of bottles of organic wine?" Neil asked as he scanned the drink menu. "Our per diem isn't even close to maxed out yet. The dollar goes a lot further in rural Colorado than in Manhattan."

"You guys can, I'm good with water," Ben replied.

I was happy he'd opted out first, since the rare nights I was able to be social I was usually the one refusing alcohol. Ben's struggles with drinking had made plenty of headlines over the years. I wondered if him staying dry was part of his plan to get hired, or was it a bigger life directive. Whatever the case, it was a personal decision and I wasn't about to ask him for details.

Orders were placed, and then it was time for the awkward small talk. I prepared for the spotlight, only to discover that I was going to be a supporting player for the night.

"Whatever happened with that hurdler chick?" Neil asked as he took a massive scoop of sun-dried tomato hummus. "You guys wound up hanging out for a while after you interviewed her for that first trial episode you did, right?"

I could've sworn I saw Ben flinch at the question. "Oh, that was nothing."

"Seriously? Because I felt like you two needed to get a room during the interview," Neil snorted out a laugh.

I hadn't watched the show but the split-screen stills from it had wound up on my timeline, and even the photos looked scorching. Elli Andreson was a gifted athlete from Finland who also happened to be drop-dead gorgeous, which made it easy for audiences to speculate that Ben had been flirting with her during their interview.

From what I'd heard, it was very mutual. Like, the BookTok girlies went feral for their chemistry. There were dozens of videos showing Ben using the "triangle method" on Elli, which was an eye contact technique that supposedly made people fall in love with you.

"I thought you guys dated for a while?" Hailey asked.

Which was exactly what I'd turned up when I definitely wasn't deep-diving on her in the hope of accidentally finding more details about what was going on between them.

"Maybe for like a minute," Ben replied. He seemed to fixate on getting the perfect pita-to-hummus ratio. "It was nothing."

The vibe felt too heavy for what wasn't a big reveal. Ben was a known flirt and heartbreaker—present company one hundred percent included—so I couldn't figure out why he was acting like a youth pastor caught kissing a high schooler.

Neil turned to me. "You better be careful or you might be next. He has a way with the ladies. No one can resist the power of Magic Martino." He wiggled his fingers like he was casting a spell on Ben's behalf.

"Seriously?" I laughed in Neil's face. "Watch me."

Ben deflated half an inch at my response, but I knew better than to think that it had anything to do with *me* specifically. It wasn't that he wanted another chance, it was because he couldn't believe that a human female wasn't tripping over herself to impress him.

Or *any* human, because Ben had a huge gay fanbase. He knew how to walk the line and be just flirty and receptive enough to score him a "Favorite Ally" pass.

"Yeah, and maybe you need to remember that this is work?" Hailey said. "Ben doesn't need you to be his pimp, Neil. He does just fine on his own."

I swallowed down a laugh. Hailey was growing on me.

"Whoa, stand down, Captain Feminism, I was just having some fun," Neil replied. "He gets it. Right, Ben?"

Ben's face went stony for a moment as he finished chewing.

"Listen, all I'm worried about this week is capturing a great story," he replied. "And staying out of Quinn's way."

It was the last thing I expected him to say. Ben lived his life on fun mode, and even though I'd encountered a different side of him that night in Switzerland, I figured it was the exception and not the rule.

"Thanks," I said softly. "Appreciate that."

He met my gaze and for a moment it was just the two of us, confessing our feelings by the distant glow of a bonfire. Something in my chest toggled toward the warmth and safety I'd felt that night, but I smashed the sensation before it could spread.

The server interrupted my delusion to deliver our entrées.

"Yay, time to eat weeds," Neil joked.

"For someone who keeps shitting on the food you sure did some damage to that hummus," Hailey said.

"*And* the arancini," Ben added.

Neil didn't answer because he was too busy downing stuffed peppers, which I was pretty sure he didn't realize were vegan.

I was hungry, like always, and the spaghetti squash casserole with way too much parmesan sauce was a blissful change of pace for me. I forced myself to eat slowly. I was on guard now, because even though the meal seemed pleasant enough, they were still trespassing in my life during a critical period. And they were *watchers*. Anything I said could and would be used as content, even unofficially. I was under a spotlight even when the cameras weren't on me.

Yeah, this was going to be our first and last group dinner.

"Fan club alert," Hailey said under her breath. She jutted her chin toward a group of six women across the restaurant who were doing a terrible job of pretending not to watch us.

I looked over even though I knew they weren't staring at me. They'd been busy taking photos of their food but they'd finally picked up on the force field radiating from Ben, and now they couldn't stop glancing over. I caught one of them pretending to show her friend a photo but I could tell she was filming us. I shifted so my back was to them.

No sense in cranking up the rumor mill early.

"Anyone want to bet on how long it takes one of them to come over here?" Neil asked. "Given the nonstop staring and empty bottles on the table, I say it's fifteen minutes."

"We'll deal with them when we have to. How's everyone's food?" Ben asked.

"Passable," Neil answered as he scraped up the last bits of his meal, way before the rest of us were even close to finishing.

"Amazing," Hailey sighed and gazed down at her mushroom flatbread. "I think I'm coming here every night. I mean, it's all healthy, right?"

That's what I told myself when I cheated and got takeout, but the cheese sauce and pasta were just as devious as the stuff from Olive Garden.

"Close enough," I agreed.

Neil refilled Hailey's glass without even asking, and her nod and quick sip suggested a level of comfort that didn't compute with the way they acted. Maybe that was just how it was with long-term colleagues?

"How long have you two worked together?" I asked Hailey.

She and Neil squinted at each other. "Uh . . . this is like month three?"

He nodded. "Yup. She's a newbie and I'm showing her the ins and outs."

"I'm new with *The Score*," Hailey corrected him quickly. "I've been in production since I graduated. I started as an intern on the *Today* show, then they hired me full time. Live morning TV is a different animal. I'm happy I got out."

"If all goes according to plan we'll be doing some live feeds from Milan," Ben said. "It'll be my first time going live and asking the questions instead of answering them."

Neil turned to him. "Hold on, did they finally make you an official offer?"

"Not yet, but it's coming," Ben said with the same bravado he used to have when he talked about winning medals.

I had to wonder what the producers were waiting for, and what their contingency plan was if they decided that Ben wasn't a fit. *And* what he had to do to prove to them that he was the right person for the job.

Not that it was my concern. All I wanted was for him to remember our rules and keep our time on camera light and fluffy. People who watched my segment needed to come away from it thinking that my life was a mix of passion for my sport, hard work, and plenty of sunshine.

It actually was, now. As long as we focused on the present and future, the profile would turn out fine.

"Hiiii, you guys." A pretty ponytailed brunette waved both her hands at us, standing a few feet away from our table like there was a force field around it. "Sorry to interrupt . . ."

"Not at all," Ben replied with a huge smile. "Hi there!"

This time I could almost feel the shift in him. From regular person trying to finish his dinner to celebrity.

"Um, my friends and I were hoping that you might take a picture with us." She glanced around the table and her eyes rested on me for a beat longer, like she was processing whether Ben and I were together. "Would that be okay?"

Neil and Hailey were already moving out of the way before Ben could answer.

"Of course, happy to," Ben said as he slid out of his chair.

The whoop that went up from the table when Ben walked over was loud enough to get the whole restaurant staring at them.

I watched as Ben did his thing. A few regular photos of him with his arms draped around the women, saying stuff that had to be compliments based on the way they giggled in response. One of them filled a glass of wine and handed it to him so they could all toast, but he put it down before anyone could take a photo.

"Hey Ben, help me make my ex jealous," a woman in a sparkly sweater cackled.

"Okay, let's do this," he laughed.

She jumped out of her chair and Ben waited as she hitched her skirt down her thighs.

"Hug me," she commanded as she swung herself against him like she was Tarzan and he was the vine.

She wound up in his arms, probably too drunk to realize that everyone could still see her butt cheeks despite her skirt wrestling. Ben seemed to sense it immediately so he angled her privates away from the camera and the rest of the restaurant.

I watched him dividing his attention as the other women pawed at him. I'd had my share of uncomfortable fan interactions over the years, particularly when I was younger and didn't feel like I was allowed to assert myself. Even now, when a kindly looking grandpa insisted on hugging me, I had a hard time maintaining my boundaries. Part of it was the innate desire to please everyone all the time, and the other was the weight of being a public figure who couldn't afford to piss off a fan.

"One more," the woman drunkenly pleaded as she clung to Ben. "But this time kiss me!"

A chant started. "On the mouth! On the mouth!"

Ben smiled like the pro that he was. Hell, he probably *liked* it.

"Ready?" the unofficial group photographer asked. "Kiss countdown! Three . . . two . . ."

Ben demurred and glanced over at me. It looked like he was trying to gracefully get the woman off him, but she turned into a python.

"One!"

The last thing I saw was his pained expression as the woman grabbed his face and kissed him square on the mouth, as dozens of cameras flashed.

Chapter Eleven

$\mathcal{T}$he two places where I felt most at home were on the ice and in front of a mirror in a dance studio. Today, though, my studio was way less hospitable than usual thanks to the camera crouched in the corner and mic wires tucked into my leotard.

And Ben getting ready to watch my every move, notepad in hand.

And my teacher Justin's focus on the trespasser and not his student.

We were supposed to start fifteen minutes ago but Justin couldn't stop fawning over Ben. Everyone was set up and ready, with Neil on the camera and Hailey poised to do whatever her job was—so far it had involved feeling me up so she could get the mic attached to my thin leotard—yet Ben was still fielding eager questions from Justin.

"I swear, that waltz you and Violetta did on *Dancing with the Stars* was revolutionary," he said. "I think it rewired my brain."

Ben threw his head back and laughed at Justin's hyperbole. "Why, thank you. We had fun with that one."

"Seems like you two had a *lot* of fun," Justin answered, wiggling his eyebrows. "Was that a showmance, or . . ."

"A gentleman never tells," Ben said with a wink that did all the telling for him.

I'd seen a second or two of videos from the show that I couldn't swipe away fast enough and heard all sorts of commentary about their partnership as I scrolled, but I never paused to watch any footage of them. At least not for more than a few seconds, and yes, the little that I saw proved that he was fucking phenomenal, and that there was real heat between Ben and his smoke show Russian partner.

But who *didn't* Ben have chemistry with?

"You looked so smooth, but that was some complicated choreo," Justin said.

"You think?" Ben frowned at him. "You could totally do it. Let me show you."

He reached out his hand and my lanky, six foot four, redheaded dance teacher went concave, like Ben had shot a lightning bolt at his chest.

"Seriously? The show was like three years ago. You still remember it?"

"Every second is etched in my brain," Ben answered, tapping the side of his head. "Put me in front of the judges and I'll score another perfect thirty right now, even without practicing."

I couldn't frown any harder at him.

"C'mon, let's do it," Ben continued. "Can someone play 'Love Story' by Indila? If not I can count it out."

Of *course* he could count it like a dance teacher. Ben could do everything.

He was still standing in the center of the studio with his arm outstretched, in perfect dance posture. The familiar one-two-three waltz rhythm filled the room, probably thanks to Hailey, and even though I was a few seconds away from getting pissed off at the time wasting, I sort of wanted to see what the two of them could do together.

"You don't mind a quick detour?" Ben asked me.

I shook my head. I was an excellent fibber.

Justin stepped over to him and took his hand tentatively.

"I'm leading," Ben joked.

Justin had about two inches on him, but he somehow managed to compress his body enough to look like a convincing follower as they began moving together. It was a fast Viennese waltz with a woman singing in French over dreamy piano and strings. I half expected the two of them to ham it up as they danced, but Ben was deadly serious, staring at Justin with the same intensity he'd had when he danced with Violetta.

It might've been the sexiest thing I'd ever seen. Ben had chemistry with *everyone*.

The pilot light in my heart flickered on yet again, and it wasn't just because the song moved me. I was awestruck that sporty-guys'-guy Ben had zero qualms about gracefully spinning Justin across the floor. They moved perfectly in sync, Justin thanks to his years and years of training, and Ben because he seemed to have a natural gift for movement and the muscle memory to recall the choreography.

Unlike Justin in his black tank top, dance pants, and bare feet, Ben wasn't dressed to move. His button-down shirt, jeans, and dress sneakers should've handicapped him a little, or at least left him squeaking his way across the floor, but Ben still glided like he was on skates.

He made it impossible to look anywhere but at him.

I glanced over to Neil and Hailey and they were equally mesmerized by the show. Justin was a trained ex-Broadway dancer, so it was no surprise that he could fake his way through it, but Ben was obviously a good enough leader that they even nailed all the little flourishes.

I swear I caught Justin's fair skin going pink every time he whipped his head from the awkward side-angle dance position to gaze at Ben. Ben beamed back at him.

They finished and they bowed in tandem. We applauded so long that they both took a second bow.

"Holy *shit*," Neil called out. "That was insane, you guys. Glad I turned the camera on."

Justin hugged Ben quickly. "Oh my god, that was so fun. Thank you!" He turned to me. "*You* need a turn with this one next. He's amazing."

The thought of Ben's hands on my body, expertly leading me through choreography, was enough to make me hold my breath for a moment. I definitely hadn't agreed to touching him.

Thankfully, I had an ally on my side. I pointed to the clock mounted above the mirrors. "We need to watch the time."

"Aw, crap, sorry." Ben's forehead furrowed. "We'll disappear into the background now and leave you to it."

The lesson went well despite the unblinking eye in the corner recording my every move, along with Ben taking notes. But dance was my safe space, my original obsession before I ever touched a skate. Ballet, jazz, tap, ballroom . . . my skating foundation was strong thanks to everything I'd learned on a parquet floor as a child.

It felt like Justin worked me harder than normal, partly because February was speeding toward us and probably also because he wanted to impress Ben. We ran through a ballet warm-up, then some free-movement exercises, a couple of dry-land run-throughs of both my performance pieces, and then we finished with some new hip-hop choreography, just for fun. I'd never danced better, and by the time I finished I was a sweaty mess.

And now I was going to have to be on camera. Perfect. I wasn't my mother's daughter in that respect, because I never even considered asking to do the interview *before* I sweated my face off.

"Do you have another class right after or can we stay in here for a bit, just to finish up with a couple of quick interviews?" Ben asked Justin. "First you, then Quinn. No problem if not. We can find another space."

"We're good for the next hour," Justin answered. "And I would be honored to say nice things about Miss Albright on the record."

"Fantastic, appreciate it. Hey Quinn, do you mind stepping out for a few minutes? It's a more candid conversation when the subject isn't watching."

I was grateful for the chance to do a quick touch-up in the bathroom while they chatted. I wasn't concerned about what Justin would say about me because we were each other's biggest fans. I *didn't* love not getting to watch Ben in action before sitting down with him for our first official interview.

I was used to quick blot-and-brush primp sessions thanks to the interviews that usually happened right after finishing a performance. My sweaty hair was fine in a topknot, and a little mascara and lipstick made me look human again. I threw my fuzzy white shrug over my gray leotard since the sweat wasn't drying fast enough.

Hailey walked into the bathroom. "They're ready if you are."

I turned around to face her. "Do I look okay?"

I was surprised that I even cared, but the specter of my mom would always haunt me, especially with a trip home on the horizon. Plus, I knew she'd scrutinize every second of the show to find negatives to point out to me and anyone else who'd listen—always disguised as concern, of course. If I looked too pale, she "worried" about me getting sick. If my smile was anything less than neon white, she scolded me about the negative health effects of drinking too much coffee.

"Gorgeous, as usual." Hailey smiled at me. "Let's go."

"This'll be quick," Ben explained to me as I walked into the studio. "It's supplemental."

"Okay," I said, even though I wasn't sure what he meant.

Hailey tested my mic again, and we were off.

"We're not doing an intro or anything since this'll be slotted into the piece," Ben continued.

I nodded and actually watched the switch happen in Ben as we waited for Neil to get into position with the camera. His incandescence got even more vibrant, like someone turned up his brightness setting. Ben marked the beginning of the interview to camera, then focused on me.

"Let's talk about your dance background, because what I just saw out there was next level," Ben said.

His opener was gift-wrapped with a bow, his way of proving that he was going to abide by our agreement. Ben knew exactly how and why I'd gotten into dance, or at least he had four years ago.

He could've said something like, "Your mom was your first dance instructor, correct?" It would've made for a better story, and teed up the home-visit portion of the show. Instead, he left it up to me.

"I've always loved dance," I began tentatively. "Since I was really young. You could say it's in my genes."

I assumed that I had some hereditary skills thanks to my mom, plus the years watching her teach classes from my pack and play probably helped with my timing and rhythm. When I heard certain old songs I was instantly brought back to that big mirrored room that had been my second home. I could almost *smell* the place, and hear the wood floor creaking beneath dozens of feet.

I'd accidentally given him a thread to unravel by mentioning genetics though.

"So you took classes as a child." Ben nodded at me in a way that made me feel like I was already doing a good job. "What age did you start?"

"As soon as I learned to walk, basically," I laughed. "My baby shoes had taps on them."

I realized that I had to come out and talk about it, high level. I knew she'd bring it up, and it would look weird if I didn't corroborate it.

"My mom is a dance teacher," I explained. "I lived my dance lessons every day."

His mouth went tight when I admitted it, but I noticed that Neil wasn't swinging the camera around to capture Ben's expressions. He didn't have to disguise his knee-jerk negative reaction to me talking about her.

"Do you have a favorite style of dance?" Ben asked. "Because I'm guessing that you're good at everything."

I wanted to hug him for the blatant pivot. Ben was already working hard to help me feel safe, so even though it was risky, I relaxed a little.

I wasn't about to let my guard all the way down, but I decided that it would be okay to crack the window for Ben.

Chapter Twelve

"You good, sweetheart?" Frank asked me. He was standing near the pit with a hose, melting the pile of snow the Zamboni had just scraped off the ice. "It's early."

He was used to me sneaking in the back door before the rink officially opened. It happened more frequently when competitions loomed, and obviously there was no bigger one than what I was about to face.

I gave him a quick squeeze on my way past. "Yup, just hoping to steal some alone time to clear my head before the rest of the world shows up. Lots going on lately."

"Well, I just finished out there, so it'll be nice and smooth for ya. Have fun." He pushed his glasses up his nose with the back of his hand.

No one worked harder than Frank, and even though we had a half dozen guys willing to step up and take over the Zamboni duties, he wasn't ready to let go yet. He'd been a hockey player back in the 1960s, which meant that he had ice in his veins as well. Unfortunately, thanks to his sport and the lack of support for players back in the day, he also had a pronounced limp from osteoarthritis in his hips.

Things were better for athletes now, but not by much, which was why I had a team of people helping to keep my own machine in top form.

I ran through my off-ice warm-up quickly with a focus on my ankles and feet. The pull to get out on the ice was stronger than usual, probably because it was the only place where I could forget about the rest of the world. For all the pain I faced daily thanks to falling in love with a sport that was all hard edges and frigid temps, the rink was my home. My skates gave me wings. My heart was free on the ice.

Even during the dark years, I never stopped loving my sport.

I dropped my stuff off, put in a single earbud, and headed out to the center. I wasn't going to skate any of my programs, I just wanted to let my body respond to whatever music came on my random Spotify playlist.

First up? "Slave to Love" by Bryan Ferry. The perfect song for a languid, dreamy start to my six a.m. session. I fished my other earbud from my pocket, because I wanted to hear every note of it. I'd learned the hard way that earbuds became projectiles during spins, but I wasn't ready to break out the big moves quite yet. For now, I just wanted to let the music wash over me.

I closed my eyes, arched my back, and let go. This floaty, weightless feeling was my reason for being. My *love*.

The song came to an end. I opened my eyes, did a half turn, and screamed.

"Ben?! What the *fuck*?" I fumbled with an earbud.

He was right behind me. My entire body went numb, half from shock and half from the way he was staring.

Like I was naked.

"Sorry! I thought you saw me," he said as he skated even closer.

"I don't have eyes in the back of my head, so *no*, I didn't see you," I said, clutching my chest and trying to will my heart rate to slow down.

I realized that he'd probably witnessed all my sexy improv and felt my cheeks go hot. I wasn't skating to be perceived in this moment, and it pissed me off that he'd intruded. I spent most of my time being watched, judged, graded, so the moments when I could skate just for myself were precious.

"Hey, you folks okay out here?" Frank called from the edge of the ice. "I heard a scream."

"We're *fine*," I yelled back, waving one hand over my head while glaring at Ben.

"Okey doke. I'm heading out for a quick bite," he yelled back before he disappeared into his cave.

I refocused my attention on Ben, so mad that I was nearly fuming.

"Why are you here?" I demanded.

"Heads Will Roll" by Yeah Yeah Yeahs kicked up in my remaining earbud, which felt like the right sort of hype song in the moment.

"This." He pointed to the ice under his skates. "I forgot how much I miss it. I had no clue you'd be here too, I'm sorry I scared you. Frank let me in. Anyway, I thought I had your full schedule nailed down. You didn't mention that you do early morning skates."

His expression looked so believably worried that I could *almost* forgive him. I fished through my pocket to find my phone and turn off the music.

"Well, sometimes things change. And I didn't think you needed to know every *minute* of my day."

"Maybe now I should? Fill me in." Ben tried to hide a grin. "So this never happens again, of course," he said quickly.

"Should I set up a shared Google calendar?"

"Yeah, that would actually be super helpful, because then—"

I narrowed my eyes at him.

"Right. Got it. Anyway, I'm sorry I intruded, but I'm really happy I got to see that. It was beautiful. Different," he said softly. "You are just . . ." He shook his head, like he couldn't find the words.

We stared at one another silently, his dark eyes doing to me exactly what they did to the rest of the world.

Seducing.

I skated away from him under the pretense of needing water, but it was actually because I felt that urge rising up in me again. The swift current of need that I could spend all my energy fighting, only to end up exhausted and overpowered by it anyway.

I hated that, despite everything, I was starting to trust him again. Our first interview at the dance studio had felt like a conversation with a friend. He knew where my land mines were buried and he managed to avoid every single one of them. He'd made me feel so safe that when we finished I had to hold myself back from hugging him. Not that we talked about anything major, but still.

"Do you want me to leave?"

"No," I sighed. "You can stay."

Inexplicably, half of the overhead lights went out with a mechanical *ca-thunk*, leaving the rink with dim mood lighting.

I understood Ben's pull to get back on the ice, because here I was, heeding it as well. And I skated every damn day. I couldn't imagine how deprived he must feel after going from a life on skates to . . . I wasn't even sure how he filled his days now, and it was time to find out.

"What do you do, when you're not being my shadow?" I asked Ben. "You said you're on a trial run with the show, so like, how have you been keeping busy up to this point?"

I braced myself for a fire hose of impressive side hustles, but his expression went momentarily pained, like I detonated one of *his* hidden land mines.

"My focus right now is on *The Score*," he answered. He skated away and I followed him.

I sped up and moved in front of him, so I could watch his face. "Okay, so what about before? Like, for the past four years?"

"Why does it matter?" Ben scowled.

Rather than retreating I decided that it was *my* turn to be the interviewer.

"Why are you being so defensive about a simple question?"

I could tell he was trying to lose me, moving into his crouched skating position and picking up speed. But he was at a disadvantage in regular skates. I had no problem keeping up with him.

"Because my life is an open book. You know about *Dancing with the Stars,* and my stupid reality show. You've seen my billboards for Powerade and Toyota. I'm financially stable, if that's what you're wondering."

I shook my head. "Nope, I don't care about your bank account. I'm talking about how you *literally* fill your days. Do you even skate anymore?"

Ben's brow furrowed a little more deeply. "Not as much as I'd like."

"Okay, so like . . . you wake up and then you . . ." I rolled my hand in front of me to encourage him to fill in the details.

Something switched on in him, and I watched him unfurl and then recenter himself like he was getting ready to deliver a talking point on camera. "I hustle. That's what I do. Okay?"

Mr. Sunshine was really good at keeping his mask on. As much as I wanted to continue chipping away at his walls, I figured I should return the favor and respect his boundaries.

We skated side by side with just the sounds of our blades on the ice filling the silence, until I pulled out my phone to tap into the rink speakers. Loud music would kill the confusing vibes in the air. I scrolled through a few songs that echoed around the rink.

"Hey, can you play *My Heart Will Go On*?" Ben called after me.

I made a face as I spun around to him. "Um, *no*?"

"Come on. You got a problem with Celine?"

"Of course not, she's *uhmazing.*" I said it with her dramatic accent and hand gesture. "But I'm *so* sick of it since someone always skates to it. That song, *Carmen*, *Bolero*, and *Swan Lake* all need to die in a fire."

"But I really want to show you something." He did backward crossovers in a circle around me. "Consider it payback for me spying on you."

He did prayer hands under his chin.

"Fine," I sighed and cued up the song.

The flute opener echoed around us.

"Are you ready for a show?" Ben grinned at me, and I was relieved that the good-time version was back.

He skated to the center of the rink with his arms outstretched dramatically then posed with his hands off to one side, like he had an invisible partner.

"What are you doing?" I asked.

"Watch."

As if I could do anything but.

He was in black track pants that were clingier than they needed to be, and I guess stalking me across the ice had warmed him up, because he was only wearing a black short sleeve T-shirt on top.

Biceps peeking out from beneath the sleeves, and thick forearms. Yup. There they were. Fine. Whatever.

Ben went into a basic forward glide with his arms spread as Celine started singing, wearing a gigantic, cheesy smile.

"Oh no," I said when I realized what he was doing.

"Yup, you're getting a private performance from the first-place winner at the Little Gems Juniors Winter Classic. I had a partner but I'll do it for you solo."

"Hold on," I said. "You were a *figure* skater?"

It was a part of his history that had never made it into the many profiles he'd done over the years.

"Damn straight," Ben said as he did a little bunny hop. "I got conned into figure skating for about a year and a half. I didn't love it but I was really fucking good, so they wouldn't let me quit."

I sputtered my exasperation at his humble brag.

"I loved going fast. I thought about trying hockey, but then I saw speed skating and I was a *goner*," Ben continued. "Addicted at minute one."

I realized that he'd probably just sent young Nathan down the same path.

"You like this performance?" Ben teased, doing exaggerated backward wiggles. "Totally worthy of the gold."

It was a routine for a baby skater, with one foot glides, tap toe jumps, and lots of what I assumed was vamping to give his partner time to show off. I wasn't surprised that he was graceful, but it was clear that his skating skills now outpaced the choreography and he was dumbing himself down.

"How old were you?"

"I was seven, my partner was six." He did some forward crossovers. "Oh, this is the part coming up where we did a waist lift."

"At *seven* years old?"

He chuckled. "I was strong for my age and Bella weighed about twenty pounds total. A bent arms lift, not over the head. Our coach really pushed us."

I snorted. "A pushy coach? Wow, I'm shocked."

"Get over here, lemme see if I've still got it." Ben reached out to me.

I wondered if I physically recoiled from him.

"Oh, no way, I'm good," I replied quickly, because I didn't want to be reminded of how it felt to have Ben's strong hands gripping my waist.

"C'mon," he pleaded.

He attempted a toe loop that I could tell wasn't in the original program because he nearly fell on his ass.

"This is the part where it's supposed to happen," he mimed, holding someone in front of him and lifting ever so slightly while eyeballing me. "I could totally do it. You're tiny."

The old me would've pocketed the throwaway comment to be dissected later, because the *t* word was always my goal. Now I knew that the scale didn't reflect anything about my overall health. Or worthiness.

"I'm heavier than I look."

"Okay, biceps," he said admiringly as he did easy two-legged spins. "I see those muscles. But I still think you're basically a feather in human form. So let me try." He paused. "Wait, have you ever done a lift?"

"Yes." I frowned at him. "Of *course* I have."

Only goofing around with Zoey, but still. It counted.

"I don't believe you," he teased. "I don't think you have the skills to be a partner, Miss Independent."

"Negging doesn't work on me," I said as I skated over to him and snowplowed a thin layer of ice at his skates. I turned around in front of him and we moved in tandem. "Fine. Lift me."

I didn't have to ask him twice.

"*Yes!* Ready? Keep your core tight," he said as he skated behind me.

I gawked at him over my shoulder. "I'm sorry, are you *seriously* mansplaining figure skating to me?"

"Sorry, just a safety precaution. Okay, let's do this."

Celine hit some high notes right as I felt Ben's surprisingly warm palms close around my waist. I'd already peeled off my fleece, leaving just a thin Lycra layer between my skin and Ben's hands. When he connected I jumped as if he'd singed me.

"Sorry," he repeated. Ben adjusted his grip and I could've sworn his thumbs slipped down a little lower than required, to graze the top of my ass.

No, that was just him making sure that he had a good hold. It wasn't like he could risk dropping me given my Fabergé egg status until after the Games.

I felt him dip slightly, to ready his quads.

"Split legs, not stag," he coached. "Move with me."

I nodded and tried to focus on the mechanics of skating backward with Ben holding me, and not the feverish heat spreading through my body.

"And up she . . . *goes*."

His hands went tighter as he raised me into the air, pausing when my skates were about a foot off the ice. I felt like a toddler being helped up to a water fountain.

"Higher," I demanded over my shoulder. "This doesn't look cute at all."

"Well okay, then. Going up," Ben said as he lifted me so my head was just above his.

I leaned back and extended my hands gracefully. Ben wobbled from the fulcrum shift.

"Why are you doing stag legs? I said split," Ben huffed from behind me.

"Because it's *prettier*," I snapped back at him, defiantly raising my knee even more, so that I was fully inhabiting the deer-jumping-a-fence pose.

Celine warbled on as we found a position that was comfortable enough for Ben and elegant enough for me.

I think we both felt the moment when we dissolved into a single unit. Instead of fighting against gravity and each other we became helium, trying to stay tethered to the ice so we didn't float up to the rafters.

We were effortlessly perfect.

Ben raised me higher still, and I took advantage of the extra airspace by arching my back even more. I could've kept improvising with him forever, but when he gave me an extra squeeze I knew he was about to lower me. I did Vaganova arms one last time as he brought me down, until my skates connected to the ice, so gently that I could've been landing on a pillow.

"Big finish," Ben said softly, still holding me by the waist. "Now turn to me."

I did an abrupt spin and wound up crushed against his body. He placed one hand against my head and gently drew it to his shoulder then circled the other around my waist, clutching me tightly. Our chests rose and fell in tandem, partly from the exertion but mainly because being pressed together felt like a terrible idea.

Terrible or not, there was no way I was moving out of his embrace. The only time I'd ever felt as safe was four years ago, in the exact same position. It was almost like Ben's strong arms *belonged* around me, and we both knew it.

"I can smell you," Ben murmured against my hair.

I wasn't even sweaty yet!

"*Excuse* me?" I put my hands on his chest to push him away but he tightened his grip.

"It's a sense memory. It reminds me of that night in Switzerland," he continued. He inhaled deeply. "I've caught traces of you in a springtime breeze, and now I'm finally getting a full hit. It's you, but mixed with blossoms and fresh air. Let me enjoy it for a second, please."

His confession left me breathless. Ben had cataloged my *scent*? The thought of him tilting his head back and trying to catch whispers of me in the wind made me cling to him a little tighter.

The finale of a performance was supposed to be the period at the end of a sentence. An obvious stopping point. But our embrace with our hearts pounding in rhythm felt like a line on the first page of a very long story.

Despite that, or probably because of it, we silently agreed to remain pressed together, clinging to each other until the overhead lights flipped on again.

Chapter Thirteen

*O*f all the places for me to get a flat tire, my trusty Volvo had done me a solid and crapped out near a scenic overlook pull-off. Much of the drive to Thornville was on a road that was cut into the side of a mountain above the Clear Creek River, with about six inches of shoulder on either side. Changing my tire in any other spot would've been a death wish.

Although if Ben had his way, I wouldn't even be getting out of the driver's seat.

I hadn't wanted to carpool the hourlong drive with him to my costume designer, Greta's, showroom, but there wasn't enough room for him in the equipment Subaru with Neil and Hailey, and everyone agreed that it was a waste for us all to go in separate cars. It was bad enough that Mel was meeting us there a little late thanks to an unexpected trip to the pediatrician first thing in the morning.

Add in the sexy little pairs skating session with Ben a few hours prior and I was fighting to keep things professional between us.

"It's my car, let me do it," I insisted as Ben fished through my trunk to find the spare. We'd quickly figured out that I'd run over a nail that had been slowly leaking the entire drive. "I'm fast."

He shot me a look. "I've got this. It's cold out."

"Do you *really* think the cold bothers me?"

"Doesn't matter. I'm a gentleman."

"C'mon, I'm *serious*," I bitched at him. "Mr. Chen showed me how, and he made me and Zoey race to see who was better at it."

It was typical of my surrogate father, teaching us a useful life skill and then turning it into sport. It was how I'd learned to read a map—who can find the quickest route to Salt Lake City?—and jump-start a car—the loser gets electrocuted.

"We'll split it. I'll take care of the jack and pull the old tire off." He paused. "And maybe I'll put the spare on."

"Oh, so all I get to do is take care of the lug nuts? *Move*."

I hip checked him hard enough that he stumbled a few steps away from the trunk, then hoisted the spare out.

A car sped by and honked at us.

"I can take care of myself," I said as I lowered it to the ground and started rolling it toward the flat.

"Yeah, but isn't it nice to know that you don't always have to?" Ben asked. He grabbed the wrench from the kit and knelt down in front of the flat tire. He started spinning the thing on the first lug nut.

"Only *half* a turn before you jack it up," I scolded.

"Sorry, sorry, you're right," he said as he moved on to the second one. "Been awhile."

I tried to ignore the way the bright sun brought out the hidden copper in his hair, and how his forearms flexed as he spun the wrench like a pro. And those hands . . .

Ben glanced over his shoulder and caught me staring.

"What? Am I still doing it wrong?"

"No, no, not at all," I sputtered as my face went hot. "Should I get the jack?"

He reached for it. "I'm right here, let me do this part."

"Fine," I sighed. "But you have to put it in a specific spot under—"

"Thanks, AutoZone, I know that."

Then he had the audacity to *wink* at me.

He bent over to look under the car, which made his jeans slide down enough to expose the waistband of his boxer briefs. The red, white, and blue Ralph Lauren logo on the band proved he was Team USA forever.

Ben had the front of the car suspended in record time, way faster than I could've done it. Not that I'd ever admit it to him.

"*Madame,*" he said with a flourish. "You're up."

"Thank you. Now watch how it's done," I boasted.

I moved quickly, like I was on a NASCAR pit crew, because that's the way Mr. Chen had taught us. He'd lectured us about the hidden dangers of breaking down on a busy road, so I maintained a healthy fear even though the mountain pass had been pretty quiet so far, and we had a decent buffer from any cars that drove down the rural road.

I got the tire off, rolled it to my trunk, and then ran back.

"And the crowd goes wild," I intoned with the cadence of a sportscaster. "Quinn Albright is about to set a new world record in flat changing."

Ben applauded as I tried to lift the spare triumphantly, but I misjudged my grip and the thing slid out of my hands.

And speed-bounced directly toward the drop-off to the river.

"No!" we screamed in horrified unison.

Ben unfroze first, tearing after the runaway tire. The observation spot was basically a sloped dirt pull-off littered with stones, which made the tire move unpredictably. Just when it started to slow it would hit a rock, bounce into the air, and recharge.

"Careful," Ben shouted when I tripped on my own feet.

He finally chased it down at the last second, kicking it onto its side just before it was about to bounce over the guardrail and into the river.

"Oh my god, that was almost a *tragedy*!" I breathed, clutching my chest and dropping to my knees.

Ben laughed as he squatted down to collect himself, keeping one hand on the tire. "You're right. A double tragedy—littering in a pristine waterway, plus without this tire we'd be stranded here together for all eternity." He gave me a winsome grin. "I'd have to build us a cabin on the mountainside."

"Oh yeah?"

"Yup," he answered confidently. "And you'd have to forage for all our food. Berries and mushrooms, mainly."

"Okay, I get it." I smiled back at the thought of it. "We'd also adopt some baby animals to keep us company, like a possum. Maybe a raccoon too."

He nodded. "Exactly. And the fireflies would be our string lights. Every night we'd sleep beneath them on pillows made of foraged goose down."

"And we'd climb to the top of that mountain to howl at the full moon with the wolves every month," I added. "Wild and free."

Sensations I'd never experienced. Ben, on the other hand, had been the poster boy for both. We both gazed up at the mountain, squinting into the cold sunshine.

"Damn," he finally replied. He cocked an eyebrow, righted the tire, and pretended to roll it toward the river.

"I wish," I admitted.

"Hey, in a few weeks you'll have more free time than you ever wanted," Ben replied with a little more grit in his voice than necessary. "Maybe you should start planning some camping trips?"

"Oh? Just like you did post-Olympics. A quiet escape to Walden Pond for some introspection, perhaps?"

It was a dig, because his victory tour was headline-worthy. Seeing the photos of him stumbling out of clubs in sweaty, half-open button-downs in the months after Switzerland was all the proof I'd needed that I'd been a charity case for him.

"Mistakes were made," he replied with a wince. "I can be your cautionary tale. Do as I say and all that."

"But you did have fun," I insisted.

He took me in for a beat. "That's how it looked, huh?"

The whimsy of our fireflies-and-feather-pillows conversation evaporated.

"If I can do anything for you," Ben continued, "other than delivering a great episode, it's to make sure you don't make the same mistakes that I did. Because the one thing people never talk about is how—"

A gigantic black pickup slowed down to a crawl, then pulled in behind my car.

"Uh oh," Ben said under his breath. He placed the spare back on its side and stood up in front of me.

I spied a young girl in the passenger seat as the driver opened the door and stood on the running board.

"Hey," the guy in a baseball cap called out to us. "You folks okay?"

Ben gave him a wave. "All good. Just changing a tire."

The guy glanced at my stopped car and us hovering near the edge of the drop-off. "Need any help?"

He sounded skeptical.

"I dropped the spare," I explained. "It rolled over here."

"Ah. So . . . you're okay?"

I realized that we probably looked pretty shady, like we were throwing tires down the hill for sport.

"We're about two minutes from hitting the road again. But thanks," Ben answered.

The other car door opened and the little girl hopped out, clutching her phone. "I know you! You're Quinn Albright!"

I felt my cheeks go hot. I could never predict where I was going to get recognized, which meant I was never truly alone.

"Yup, it's me," I gave her a little wave, still unsure how to respond when people told me my name.

"You're the reason I started skating lessons," she said excitedly.

"Oh, no way! Are you having fun? Because that's the most important part."

"She better be," the man laughed. "They cost enough."

"See that guy?" I pointed at Ben, eager to share the spotlight. "That's a three-time gold medal speed skater."

"Oh, *yeah*," the guy answered for her. "You're that Blake guy."

"Close," Ben answered good-naturedly. "Bennett Martino."

"Yup, that's right! Bailey, you should get a picture with the two of them."

My stomach clenched. A photo of the two of us meant more Ben and Quinn lore that could muddy my comeback story.

"Can I? Would you mind?"

"Of course," Ben answered. "Happy to!"

"I'll take it for you," her father said.

We squished together and I made sure to put Bailey in between us, as a buffer.

"Say 'gold medal,'" the man coached.

We all laughed, but I shouted the two words in my head as he snapped the photo. I was used to manifesting my future medal every chance I got.

"Is this okay?" Bailey asked, holding her phone out to show us.

It was an adorable photo, with Bailey's braces taking center stage. Somehow Ben's hand wound up grasping my waist, and mine was clutching his shoulder.

"It's perfect," Ben said. "You two look like models."

Bailey blushed. "I'm going to post it!"

I had to face it; the narrative of what was happening between me and Ben was out of my hands already. Pictures would be posted— I'd seen plenty of cameras pointed our way at the diner and out on the ice—so assumptions would be made, long before the show was broadcast.

But no matter what the world thought, I knew there was no way I was going to wind up as Ben's latest romantic roadkill.

Chapter Fourteen

"This is *not* what I was expecting," Hailey said as she helped Neil get set up in Greta's showroom. "I thought we were going to be in someone's kitchen."

"Greta's one of the top figure-skating and dance costume designers in the country," I replied as I gazed around the familiar space. "She's got a team of eight under her, from an airbrush artist to a woman whose sole job is applying crystals to the costumes. She is *big-time*."

"Well, business must be booming." Neil snapped a camera onto a tripod. "Because this is impressive."

Greta's studio took up three floors in the airy loft, and I felt like I'd financed a big part of it. I glanced over to where Ben was laughing with the woman of the hour. Greta Bouchard was a stunning Canadian gold medal ice dancer who'd never been able to find the types of cutting-edge costumes she wanted when she was competing, so she set out to make her own, using influences like Samba dancers from Brazil and drag queens. Greta not only understood how to bring a shred of a concept to life, she also knew firsthand how a seam in the wrong spot or an uncomfortable arm hole could ruin a skater's headspace before they even set foot on the ice.

Ben called me over to where he was chatting with Greta. "We were just talking about how we should capture this and we both agree that sitting back and letting the magic happen will work best. I might shout some questions to you as you go through the fitting, but we're not going to do a formal sit down Q and A. You're both too busy."

"I'm back-to-back all day," Greta agreed. "But this is going to be quick. Just a final modesty check."

"Oh?" Ben suddenly looked very interested.

Greta snorted. "Yeah, the judges at Worlds thought Quinn looked too, um . . . *naked* in her short-program costume, so we need to Amish her up a little."

"What, like put a turtleneck over top?" Ben laughed.

"Close!" Greta replied. "The chest area needed some additional beadwork, and we added some extra coverage in the tail region. You've seen her costumes, right?"

I expected him to go a little sheepish at the question, but true to form, Ben acted like his lack of preparation was no big deal.

"I actually haven't," he said cheerfully. "By design."

"But how could you miss them?" Greta pushed, clearly a little shocked. "The gold one we're fitting today was *everywhere*."

It had been my very own "J.Lo in the green dress" moment. Jaws dropped, scandal followed.

I loved that my outfit sparked a debate, because I knew my mom was hating every second of it. She didn't give a shit about how revealing it was—the only reason she'd dressed me in pastel princess dresses was because it was the brand she'd decided fit me best, not for any modesty reasons—it was the fact that I'd cultivated this genre-shifting look all on my own.

"Sorry I'm late," Mel burst in, weighed down with half a dozen bags of god knows what.

"How's Caleb?' I asked.

"Fine. He stuck a bead up his nose and I couldn't get it out. My little genius. Are we good to go?"

Everyone turned to look at me. "Yup, I'm ready. Back in a sec."

I could hear them all chattering away as I went into the fitting room. I was used to an audience of three people max when I did fittings; Mel, Greta, and maybe one of her seamstresses. Now I felt like I was about to be on *Say Yes to the Dress*, with a camera crew and everything. I could hear them putting a mic on Greta and figuring out the lighting.

I stripped down and worked the surprisingly thick costume up my body. My mom had always told me that I looked better in silver. Oh, the irony to be claiming gold for myself.

I studied Greta's changes to the costume, which thankfully weren't too obvious. A wave of gold crystals now splashed a little higher on my chest, and the seat area was wider, so no scandalized grandmothers in Topeka could claim that I was wearing a thong on the ice.

I pulled on the fingerless gloves dripping with gold beading, which made me look like I was controlling raindrops when I moved my hands through the air. From a distance, I was basically nude and gleaming. The crystals scattered across my breasts and from my hips down looked like dew that might fly off if I moved too quickly. There were strands of the same beading that cascaded down from various parts of the costume, so that when I went into a spin they flared out around me, flapper dress–style.

I took a steadying breath and padded out to where everyone was waiting, purposely not looking at Ben.

"Absolute perfection," Mel said from her spot just beyond Greta. "Incredible."

"Thank you." I did a little curtsey.

"*Wow*," Neil said in a low voice.

"Marilyn Monroe!" Hailey chirped. "The *Happy Birthday* dress!"

Greta nodded as she strode toward me. "Yup, that was definitely part of the inspiration, along with Britney in the sparkly nude *Toxic* bodysuit. But Quinn's main vibe was Mitzi Gaynor's nude illusion dress."

"Who?" Hailey asked.

"An old-timey singer and actress," I answered as I got up on the little podium in front of the three-way mirror. "Look up the dress, you'll see how close we came."

Hailey dropped the equipment she was holding and whipped out her phone. "Oh, damn. That woman is *naked*."

Greta started fussing with the butt area of my outfit. "Yeah, her dress was very sheer, but this costume is all an illusion. Everything that looks like skin is stretchy flesh-toned fabric. Quinn is more covered up in this than in a bikini, but you'd never think so because the color match is so perfect."

"Hailey, the boom please?" Neil said in a pissy voice.

"Sorry," she said as she shoved her phone in her back pocket and held the mic on a stick over our heads again.

"We didn't want to put a mic on your outfit," he explained. "Ben said that we can't risk any beading damage."

I finally allowed myself to glance over at him, to give him a grateful nod, but froze when I saw the way he was watching me.

The hunger in his expression was so unmistakable that I was almost embarrassed, like I needed to cross my arms to cover up my newly embellished boobs. He didn't even try to hide it when our eyes snagged. My body sparked to life, like he'd just lit a fuse in my chest.

I wanted to look away but I couldn't, because we were having a conversation without words from across the room. I didn't have to ask if my revised costume was okay. Ben's face told me everything I needed to know.

"Quinn?"

I jumped and refocused on Greta. "Sorry, what was that?"

"Can you bend over? I want to check coverage from the back."

Neil snickered.

"Hey Neil, swing the camera around front, please," Ben said, anticipating the shot before Neil could get a close-up of my seemingly nude and sparkly ass.

He did as instructed.

"Three steps back," Ben instructed. "You're in the way."

Neil sighed and moved.

Mel started plucking at the beaded strands hanging down. "Swear to me that these aren't going to fly off, Greta."

I'd already competed in the costume without a problem but Mel was a worrier so I didn't have to be. Not only would we get hit with a deduction if any part of my outfit dropped onto the ice, there was the very real possibility of tripping over anything that fell off.

I could tell that Greta was in her own world, running her hand down seams to check for any strings that might be poking me. "My première d'atelier Manon would sooner hang up her scissors after forty years of sewing than let one of her pieces fail. They're triple reinforced."

Greta and Mel walked me through a series of poses to check for comfort and possible wardrobe malfunctions, all while the camera captured every second. I'd expected Ben to be more involved but he hovered in the corner like he was uninvited. I opted to ignore him.

"Can we put the music on for a second?" Mel asked.

Two seconds later Hozier's "Movement" flooded the room, and I reflexively started going through my choreo, watching myself in the mirror.

"*Fuck*," Ben said softly as went into a languorous backward arch.

"How does it feel?" Greta asked me, pulling my focus away from whatever Ben was going through. "Anything pinching?"

I stepped off the platform, readied myself, and did a quick double-double. "Nope, all good."

"Damn! On dry land," Ben exclaimed. "Did you get that?"

"I'm not missing a thing," Neil answered. "Don't worry."

Ben was warming up to producer mode. He wasn't bossy, but he seemed to have a vision for the piece despite his lack of preparation.

"And you're still good with the gloves?" Mel asked me. "They're not annoying?"

I swizzled my arms over my head. "There's no way I'm giving these up. The *drama*."

"A hundred percent," Hailey quietly agreed.

"Okay, so I think we're set with this one," Greta said as she turned off the music. "I'm glad you're pleased. Next."

I gave myself one last look in the mirror. It was *my* vision, and it was perfect.

A few minutes later I was back on the little podium in my other costume, basking in more fawning.

"It's like Versace and McQueen had a baby," Hailey said with awestruck reverence.

Her on-the-nose take shocked me, because she didn't look like she cared about fashion. But then again, she was dressed for work that involved crawling on the floor and standing with her arms over her head for extended periods of time. The unisex Henley and cargo pants with a million pockets were probably a job requirement.

"You nailed it," I replied. "We were going for Versace's safety-pin era mixed with McQueen's overall fierceness."

Ben was now standing beside Neil, more focused on the shot than me.

Which, rude. I might not be as naked, but the "Bulletproof" costume was just as hot.

"Do a slow pan down," Ben coached in a quiet voice. "Make sure to get all the detailing in close-ups."

There were plenty of amazing stylistic decisions to take in. While the gold one was over-the-top sexy, this one was sexy in an angry way, like I was a dominatrix and my black skates were my weapons of choice. The slashes in the bodice made me look like I'd been in a knife fight, and the remaining costume was barely being held together with swatches of sparkling oxblood red whipstitching. My left arm was encased in black illusion netting from my shoulder to my wrist, while my right had strips of black fabric crisscrossing around it. The bottom of the costume consisted of tatters of fabric, dotted with black crystals that reflected the light. The effect of the thing was that I'd been through a battle and lived to tell.

Which was basically my life story.

"I added some detailing on the train," Greta said as she fussed with the trailing pieces coming off the back. "A few more layers of sheer fabric, plus extra crystals. Does it feel okay?"

"Honestly, I can't even tell the difference."

I smiled as I studied myself in the mirror. I liked this version of myself too. A soldier facing one last skirmish.

"It's perfect," I said. "Thank you."

Greta moved closer to me. "Did you see the little addition in the bodice of both pieces?"

"No, I didn't notice anything new," I said, staring down at the front of the costume in the mirror.

"It's on the inside, right here," she said, crossing both of her hands over her chest. "I stitched a little heart in each one, cut from my Turin costume. For good luck."

My eyes welled, and I tried not to look at the camera because it would make me feel self-conscious. "You destroyed your Olympics outfit for me? But it's *iconic*. Greta, you shouldn't have."

She swished her hand at me. "The pieces are dime size, I didn't destroy a thing. Just a little good luck token, so you'll know that we're with you."

I sniffled and nodded. I hated that I was already breaking down during what was only my second official taping with *The Score*. And at a freaking costume fitting, which wasn't even dicey territory! How the hell was I going to act when Ben was firing questions at me during the sit-down portion? And the home visit?

I knew shows lived for this kind of weepy content. I could already envision the promo shots featuring a close-up of my brimming eyes.

But damn it, I couldn't stop the tears.

"Thank you," I said in a shaky voice. I reached out to grasp her hands. "What a gift."

Greta's chin trembled. She squeezed my hands. "You're not just doing this for yourself. Your win is a win for all of us. And we believe in you, Quinn."

I hope that I managed to look stoic for the camera, because her offhanded comment woke up the doubt monster inside me. I knew all too well that I had the world's expectations on my shoulders once again. My country. My teammates. My coaches and support team. The skating governing organizations. I knew exactly what was expected of me, and how it felt to leave all of them disappointed by my performance.

"Hey, hey," Greta chastised as she stepped up on the podium to give me a hug. "It's okay, you've got this! Dry those eyes."

I squeezed her back and turned my face so the camera couldn't capture just how emotional I was feeling.

"You guys are making *me* cry," Mel said. "Group hug!"

She ran over and we embraced on top of the podium, which was too small to fit the three of us comfortably. Our tears turned to giggles as Mel fell off.

I tried to be in the moment, to laugh with the rest of them so I looked like I was having fun. I was victorious Quinn now, not weeping Quinn.

But I couldn't drown out the voice in my head, reminding me that if my win was a win for all of us, then so was a loss.

And I couldn't let that happen again.

Chapter Fifteen

*N*eil was disappointed by my restaurant choice once again.

We'd finished up with Greta and decided to do a quick group lunch before making the drive back to Woodspring, and they'd all deferred to me to pick the spot thanks to my dietary requirements.

We stood in a line, staring up at the options on the menu board.

"Salad, salad, and oh look, *more* salad," Neil complained.

"You haven't eaten at a Green Street before?" Hailey asked him.

"Do I look like I fit in here?"

She paused to eyeball him. "Actually, you do. The cap and tattoos are sort of the vibe."

"They have paninis," I added. "And you can do a custom built salad and make it like, all of the meats if you want. I'm definitely going heavy on the grilled chicken in mine."

I'd learned that Neil's grumbling was performative. Despite the fact that the three of them were interlopers in my life, it already felt like we were a team. I wanted everyone to be happy.

"Meat salad? Now you're talking," Neil answered.

I moved to the end of our group's line, to get a temperature read from Mel.

"How do you think it's going so far?" I asked her under my breath. "Did I do okay back there?"

"Oh, totally. This profile is going to be amazing," she reassured me. "I could see the monitor and it looked like Neil knows his shit."

"At least one of them does," I said glumly.

"Hey, don't sell Ben short, he asked Greta some really insightful questions while you were changing. He has a vision, I think."

"I hope it's more than 'watch this loser try again,'" I joked.

"Okay, *stop*," she scolded me. "Don't even allow those types of thoughts into your head. And there's no way that's going to be their angle, if Ben has anything to say about it." She gave me a raised eyebrow look that begged me to ask what she meant.

The line moved so I ignored her.

"You haven't noticed?" Mel craned her neck and leaned closer to me. She lowered her voice. "He looks at you like he's in love with you."

I swiveled to make sure no one could've overheard her. "Mel, *don't*. Okay? I'm not in the headspace to even think about going there again—" I broke off abruptly.

She jerked back, eyes wide with shock. "I'm sorry, *what*? Going where again, and with whom? What are you not telling me?"

It was the shrillest whisper-scold I'd ever heard. I tried to come up with a juke as we inched forward in line.

"Entanglements," I sputtered with my hands in front of me like it was obvious. "You know I can't lose my focus. And *Ben* of all people? Ew. No thank you, I'm not one of his conquests."

She watched me skeptically. "Agreed that you need to stay focused, but methinks you doth protest too much about him. He's a really good guy."

"Okay? And?" I shrugged a shoulder and pretended to study the menu even though I knew what I wanted.

"Fine, point taken," Mel said. "I just thought you should know that he's looking out for you, so you can relax."

"I'm *totally* relaxed," I snapped back at her.

Ben, Neil, and Hailey glanced at me in unison. I ignored them.

I was the last person to join them at the table, because I'd purposely ordered a green smoothie that took longer than the rest of the menu items. When I got there, Ben was talking to someone on the phone. He and Mel gave me tight-mouthed smiles that telegraphed their stress.

"What?" I asked Mel in a quiet voice as I sat down beside her.

"He's talking to your mom. About the home visit."

Hailey was fully dialed in to what was happening, unlike Neil, who was downing a surprisingly green salad like it was his last meal. I wasn't sure if she was paying close attention because Ben had hinted that there was drama with my mom, or because he was being weird during the call.

Which, talking to my mom, wasn't that hard to do.

"Right." He glanced at me with an apologetic look. "Of course, I totally understand that you also have a very busy schedule. But I thought we had a date nailed—"

He broke off to listen and I could just make out the contours of her voice bleeding through the phone. It was enough to make me lose my appetite.

The four of us stared at Ben as he tried to get a word in.

"No, Kim *didn't* mention your upcoming vacation. What an itinerary! First the Maldives then Italy for the Games. Take me with you!"

My mom's laughter was loud enough to be heard over the neo-soul soundtrack in the restaurant.

"Okay," Ben nodded. "Yup, we're sticking to the schedule we agreed to, so I'm glad it still works for you. We're all very excited for this part of the show."

I moved my fork through my salad like it was an oar in the water. It was one of my old tricks, to make people think that I was actually eating.

"You want to talk to Quinn?" Ben's face clouded over. "She's uh . . ."

I gave him an imperceptible shake of the head then stood up. "I need to grab more napkins."

"She *just* left," Ben said. "Should I have her call you back?"

I took my time at the utensil station, waiting until Ben's phone was facedown on the table again.

"What did she want?" I asked when I rejoined them. "And how did she get your number?"

I couldn't tell if the haze of tension around the table was real or just my overactive imagination. After all, my mom did a great job of performative caring, so most people had no idea why I'd left her in the dust for my comeback.

But of course, Ben knew everything. And Mel knew plenty about her, so 50 percent of the table understood that a call from Tricia was a Trojan horse.

"Kim gave her my number so we could finalize the details of the home visit. She wanted to check in to make sure we knew about their upcoming vacation, in case there was a conflict." Ben raised an eyebrow at me.

"Okay," I replied. "Did the schedule change?"

"Nope," Ben replied. "Everything is set in stone, so you have nothing to worry about. Zero deviations from what we all agreed to."

I gave him a grateful smile, because I could tell that he was trying to keep me steady. He knew firsthand how critical it was to stay sane and scheduled in the lead-up to the Games. Of course, the trip home was going to cancel out the first half of the equation, but at least I felt like I had an ally in Ben.

"That's when again?" Hailey pulled out her phone. "We need to watch flights since the weather is getting dicey."

"In two weeks," Ben replied. "We'll be flying in from Manhattan and Quinn will meet us in Hartford."

"Aw, it'll be a mini reunion before Italy." She tapped out the details on her phone.

"Something like that," I muttered.

"I'll be with you in spirit," Mel added. "Childcare didn't line up for me to take the time away. Sorry."

She bumped her shoulder against mine because she knew how challenging the trip was going to be. It wasn't lost on her that her skipping the trip was probably better for all of us, so she wouldn't be subjected to my mom's jealous sniping-with-a-smile.

Neil finally looked up from his phone. "Anyone want to see the rough footage from today? Because what I shot is god-tier."

"What you shot was under Ben's direction," Hailey corrected him. "Give him some credit."

Neil's mouth twisted as he considered it. "I mean, Ben has a vision, sure, but he's not DP on this shoot or anything. I went to film school, you know."

"Yeah, as if you'd let us forget it," Hailey griped quietly.

"I'm not trying to block your creative impulses," Ben said

quickly. "It's just that I've been where Quinn is sitting and I know what *I* think works with this type of storytelling."

Neil sniffed. "Kim not being here is giving you a lot of leeway. Normally the host is just a talking head."

"Yeah, but he's *way* more than a host," I said, insulted on Ben's behalf. "He's an athlete, plus being on the other side of the camera for years and years gives you a unique perspective."

"I guess?" Neil laughed. "So when Ben tells me he wants you in focus and the background hazy, at least *I* know he's looking for a shallow depth of field shot with a wide aperture. Kim would be able to tell me what f-stop to use. This guy doesn't even know what one is."

I held my breath and watched Ben's expression as he considered how to respond. My baggage was more than enough tension on the shoot. We didn't need to layer crew drama on top of it. He took a full thirty seconds, chewing slowly with his eyes trained on Neil.

"You're one hundred percent right," he finally said. "I'm an athlete who's out of my depth, you're the auteur."

Neil gave him a satisfied nod.

"But I *do* know how it feels to be filmed with shitty light or weird angles," Ben continued. "I know how it feels to fight back during aggressive gotcha interviews with hosts who have an attitude about me. I've gotten the most ridiculous, invasive questions during what were supposed to be puff pieces. And you can bet I've had plenty of villain edits that totally distorted my perspective, especially after some of my questionable stuff with the authorities. So no, I didn't go to film school, and I'm not exactly sure what an aperture is for, but I know firsthand that this interview is a gift to our audience from Quinn, during a critical time frame. That means I'm going to do everything in my power to keep her happy, safe, and protected."

No one said a word, or even *moved* after he finished his soliloquy. I didn't realize that my jaw was hanging open until it snapped shut of its own accord.

"Well, we appreciate it, Ben," Mel finally said. "As you know, focus is critical in the lead-up."

"Yep, I do indeed. That's why I've got three gold medals hanging up in my office," he said.

He'd flipped from the Ben I'd encountered by the bonfire in Switzerland to the one the rest of the world was acquainted with in seconds. I wasn't sure if it was a flex for Neil specifically, or just him settling back into his true form.

It didn't matter, because I was slowly coming to realize that maybe both sides could exist within him.

Chapter Sixteen

Our gym at the rink wasn't ready for prime time. Unlike the state-of-the-art gym at Ben's home rink in Utah, our humble Woodspring offering still had a late 1980s turquoise-and-pink paint job, a sock odor that never went away, weight benches with cracked vinyl, and an incomplete barbell set that stopped at thirty pounds. Not that I was lifting super heavy, but still. My training facility and Ben's were worlds apart.

It didn't matter to me, because I could easily work up a sweat off-ice with nothing but my sneakers. I did wonder if the optics of the gym would make me look like some poor, scrappy little underdog from a backwoods training center when that wasn't the case at all. Woodspring consistently turned out incredible athletes, so the powers that be subscribed to the "if it ain't broke" theory of managing the facility.

"I can't believe you get up this early every day." Hailey rubbed her eyes and yawned.

"Because she's got a winner's mindset," Ben said. He clapped his hands like he was trying to get everyone amped. "Let's do this, team."

"Where do you want me to set up?" Neil asked Ben.

It was a tiny but important power shift that meant that Ben's little speech the day before had landed.

"Let's talk to the woman of the hour," Ben replied as he turned to me. "Can you walk me through your routine and we'll figure out how to shoot it without getting in your way?"

My heart expanded a little at the question.

I scanned the empty room. "First I warm up, then I do some jumps in front of the mirror, then resistance band stuff, wall ball, box jumps, balance stuff on the Bosu ball, then hurdles. I stay in this area, mainly." I gestured to the open space in front of the mirrors.

"Okay," Ben nodded. "We can definitely work with that."

"I'm going to start warming up," I said.

"Do what you gotta do, don't worry about us. I just want to get some workout footage for b-roll, and I might ask you a few questions." Ben paused. "But only if it won't mess you up."

"It's fine, no problem."

I headed for my usual spot to start waking up my body with ankle and shoulder rolls. I skipped my earbuds because I wanted to eavesdrop on them as they set up, to see if there was any residual tension from the day before, but they seemed to be business as usual.

It took a few minutes for me to settle into a headspace that was okay with an audience during what was usually my private time. Admittedly, some of what I did off-ice looked pretty darn goofy, like power skips across the room and butterflies. But every athlete had their weird foundation exercises that support their real skills. I'd seen speed skaters doing "belt crossovers," which look like a slow-motion one-man tug of war.

Ben and Co. didn't move from their spot as I went through my workout, which helped me to lean into the exercises and even push myself a little harder. This interview was a chance for me to send subliminal messages about how much stronger I was now, so yeah, I showboated a little.

I pulled the Bosu ball into position in front of the mirror and started my balance exercises.

"I hated that damn thing," Ben laughed. "It looks like a toy but it feels like torture."

He was right, because the wheel-size blue half ball with the rigid platform on one side and a soft dome on the other looked like it belonged in kindergarten class. The way it trembled under my foot as I stretched my leg behind me in a Biellmann suggested that it was more deadly than it appeared. I was already feeling fatigued, so when I went into a pistol squat the thing really started wobbling.

"Did you ever try anything like this?" I asked Ben, holding position even though my thigh was screaming.

He stopped taking notes to watch me. "No, but it doesn't look too bad. I bet I could do it."

"Oh yeah?" I stood up, grateful for an excuse to stop. "Then get over here and prove it."

"Uh oh, let the games begin," Hailey said as Ben walked over.

Ben was wearing yet another navy checkered business-casual button-down and jeans, which would make getting into position even more challenging.

"Can we bet on this?" Neil asked. "Is that against company policy?"

"It's not a sanctioned competition, so the gambling rules don't apply," Hailey replied. "Yeah, let's make this interesting."

"What's your usual hold time?" Ben asked me as he shook out his legs and stretched his quads.

"Well, I just did a minute, so aim for that," I said, neglecting to mention that I'd doubled my usual time because of the camera.

"Ten bucks says he beats it," Neil said.

"Eh, I'm not so sure," Hailey replied. "I'm betting that he can't make it past thirty seconds."

"Ouch, Hailey, thanks for believing in me," Ben joked. "This is gonna be easy. Someone time me."

He was so cocky that I couldn't tell if it was blind confidence or if he actually *knew* that he could do it. I wasn't sure what types of workouts he did in his heyday, but I couldn't imagine that the figure skating–specific position was one he could nail. I knew his quads used to be strong, and even though he still looked as fit as he did in his glory days, time was a thief. If he wasn't consistently putting in the hours at the gym, achieving the awkward squat with one leg held out straight on a shaky surface wasn't going to be easy.

Ben got into position on the flat side of the ball without so much as a wobble. "Ready?"

"Three, two, one, *go*," Neil said.

I saw the switch flip in him again as he descended into position. The happy, good-time guy disappeared, and his expression went into Magic Martino mode. Dead eyes fixed on the distance, with nothing in his field of vision but *winning*.

"Lower," I coached. "You need to be in a full squat on one leg with the other out straight in front of you. Like this." I demonstrated the position again on the floor across from him.

"Yup," he replied, watching himself in the mirror across from us. He went into a deeper squat and I was happy to see the ball start vibrating beneath his foot, because it meant that he was already starting to feel weak.

No surprise, it was a passable version of a sit-spin position because Ben could do everything, but passable wouldn't do when
there was money *and* ego on the line.

"Now let go of your calf," I said. "I did thirty seconds holding
on and thirty seconds with a free arm."

He shot me a look before letting go. The ball jiggled dramatically at the weight shift.

"Okay, *ouch*," he groaned. "How much time left?"

"Fifteen seconds," Neil replied. "You got this."

The ball went into full earthquake mode beneath Ben's foot. I
wasn't sure if the muscle fatigue or diminishing balance would get
him first. His face was red from the strain.

"Yeah, uh . . . I'm not sure . . ." Ben grimaced and started to
straighten up.

"Eleven, ten, nine," Neil counted down. "Don't move, brother!"

Ben let out a pained sigh and dipped back into position, the ball
tipping back and forth like a rowboat in choppy water.

I knew *exactly* what was going through his mind. Forget about
the pain, focus on the goal. People are counting on you. Only
losers quit. Pain is weakness leaving the body. Get it done by any
means necessary.

"Four, three . . ." Neil counted down.

"*Fuck*," Ben exclaimed as the wobbling finally pitched him off
the ball and onto the ground.

"Aw man, you were right there," Neil scolded.

"Don't get old," Ben replied, and even though he said it in a jokey
way I could tell he was actually pissed at himself for failing so close to
the finish line. It was drive that united us; *every* competition needed
to be won, even if it was a round of pool at a bar or a three-legged
race at a family reunion.

"A little help, please?" Ben reached up to me.

As much as I wanted to make a crack about him being a senior citizen I refrained. I offered him my hand and pulled him to his feet. He held on for a few seconds longer than necessary before letting go, and gave me a final squeeze that felt like a thank you.

Which left me feeling like I was trying to find my own balance even though I was on solid ground. Was the blush that fired up my cheeks visible to everyone?

"Respect," Ben bobbed his head at me. "All I used to have to do was skate fast and turn left. You're a friggin' acrobat."

"Hey, you came close," I admitted.

I was happy he didn't make it. The guy already had three gold medals, let me have the Bosu ball moment.

"Horseshoes and hand grenades," he shot back.

I flinched. Carol used to fling the saying at me when I'd try a move and almost nail it. It took a real effort for me to stop uttering "Ugh, so close" whenever I fell, because I didn't want to hear her scolding me with the phrase.

I spotted Zoey, dressed for practice and hovering outside the door. I waved her in.

"Hi, guys," she whispered as she tiptoed in. "Am I interrupting?"

"I'm basically done," I answered.

"Yeah, she just humbled me on that thing." Ben pointed at the ball. "I need to leave and lick my wounds. But before we go I was hoping to ask a couple of questions, Quinn."

He gave me a hopeful look and I nodded.

"You two still good for dinner tonight?" Zoey asked, glancing between us. "Ben, my dad is super excited to meet you. He has a list of topics he wants to discuss with you. A literal list on an index card."

"Dinner?" I frowned. "What are you talking about?"

"I texted you but you didn't respond," Zoey replied. "And when Ben and I were working out the details he said he was pretty sure that your schedule was open for tonight, so . . . yay! It's a party!"

"I didn't see that text. And Ben doesn't keep my calendar, *I* do," I insisted.

I might've been a little too insistent, because everyone turned to look at me.

"Oh," Zoey pouted. "So you can't make it?"

I could feel Ben's eyes on me. I knew exactly how the meal would play out if I joined them; he'd charm every last one of them and Mrs. Chen would corner me in the kitchen to tell me how wonderful he was, and how handsome we look together.

As if I needed more people on Team Martino.

Still, if they were planning on me being there it would be rude if I didn't show up. And I hadn't spent time with the Chens in ages.

"Come on." Ben pushed me. "You have to eat."

He'd promised to leave my schedule unchanged, but little speed bumps kept popping up.

"And my mom is already making all your favorites," Zoey added. "Just in case you can make it."

I sighed. This was yet another Ben-induced deviation to my schedule, with a side of Zoey.

He stalked closer to me, like I wouldn't be able to say no if I was in his force field.

Which was half true.

"Listen, I get the need to stick to your routines," he began. "Discipline is everything."

"Which means that I can't—"

He put his hand up to stop me. "*Which means* that your discipline also allows you to shake things up now and then. If you're good ninety-five percent of the time, you can cut loose on that remaining five percent. Listen to your elder. I know things."

"And it's not like dinner with Mom and Pop Chen is equivalent to a night on the town," Zoey added. "They'll feed you and get you out the door in an hour and a half if you want."

They were double-teaming me into a dinner that I actually sort of wanted to attend.

"Fine," I finally replied.

Zoey yipped and Ben gave me a satisfied nod.

"Wait, if Quinn's going do I have to be there to shoot it?" Neil asked, looking panicked.

"Definitely not," Zoe grimaced. "My parents hate being on camera."

"Okay, good, because we've got tickets to a ScreenX show tonight," he said. "That new Marvel movie."

"'We' who?" Ben asked, clearly stirring the pot.

"No, I meant to say *I* have tickets. *I* do, not we," Neil sputtered.

I glanced at Hailey and she seemed very focused on unspooling mic wires.

Zoey chattered away as Ben helped break down the equipment, as cheerful as a puppy.

I sighed, because it was suddenly clear to me that the two were on the verge of forming an unholy alliance.

Chapter Seventeen

*T*he predictability of the Chen household never failed to comfort me. It didn't matter how many years passed, I could always count on everything staying constant in my surrogate home. Unlike my mother, Mrs. Chen didn't feel the need to switch out her perfectly good furniture every three years for a "décor refresh," which was why the place had a comfortable, well-loved patina.

The five of us were gathered around the dining-room table, which was reserved for honored guests, pushed back in our chairs and clutching our overfull stomachs. I'd worried that the mix of vibes would make the dinner awkward, but Ben's good-guy appeal and Mr. Chen's unabashed fangirling over him took the pressure off.

"I found this old interview of you," he said to Ben as he pulled his phone from his breast pocket. "You were very young. Just a boy. Maybe eight or nine years old?"

"Oh no," Ben groaned good-naturedly. "Those old clips are so embarrassing."

"No, this one is very good," he insisted. "Your drive was evident, even then."

Zoey snorted softly. Her father valued ambition and self-discipline over natural gifts, believing that anything could be achieved if you just put in the time. He had enough inspirational quotes to launch his own line of Hallmark cards.

Mr. Chen pushed play and we all leaned closer to watch. The small-town news reporter appeared on-screen talking about a local skating wunderkind, then the grainy footage cut to a very young Ben out on the ice.

"So cute," Mrs. Chen giggled when Ben appeared, doing a clumsy version of the glide stride that eventually won him gold.

I watched Ben watch himself, his mouth twisted in a half smile.

"*Terrible* form," he laughed. "This is painful."

"No, shh," Mr. Chen scolded. "Listen to what your mother and father say."

The footage cut to Ben standing in front of his parents, and I gasped at the resemblance to his handsome dad.

"This part," Mr. Chen pointed at the screen.

"We believe in him," Ben's pretty mom, Cynthia, beamed as she clutched his shoulder. "This is his dream, and we'll do everything possible to support him. When Benny sets his mind to something he achieves it, so we think he's going to go all the way to the Olympics, if we're lucky."

"Benny," I giggled and he made a face at me.

"And what happens when he grows a little bigger and decides that girls are more important than speed skating?" the reporter asked with an eyebrow waggle.

Ugh. I guess none of us were immune from stupid, sexist questions.

"I won't," Ben's little voice squeaked out before she could answer, and they all laughed. "Nothing is better than speed skating!"

I laughed as well, way too hard, because "Benny" grew up and learned how to juggle both.

The clip ended and Mr. Chen rested his phone on the table.

"Did your parents push you?" Zoey asked. She rolled her head to give her dad a pointed look.

Ben considered it. "No, not really. They *supported* me, but I pushed myself. It was a pretty healthy start, actually. They trusted my coaches, which allowed my parents to just be my fan club." He smiled. "They're still my biggest fans."

He'd transformed during the conversation about the clip from a regular guy enjoying postdinner conversation to his public persona. I swore I could see tension behind his smile, which didn't make sense considering we were discussing something positive.

"Why don't we go to the TV room and watch some of Zoey's old performances?" Mrs. Chen suggested. "She had raw talent at a young age as well."

"*Absolutely* not." Zoey stood up abruptly. "We're going for a walk. C'mon."

She stomped out of the room leaving us no choice but to follow behind her.

It was one of those typically weird Colorado weather days, with schizophrenic temps that could convince you that spring was right around the corner even though the calendar told a different story.

"Your parents are amazing," Ben said. "And your mom's cooking? Damn."

"Right?" Zoey agreed. "I'm pretty lucky."

"We both are," I added.

"Yeah, how exactly did you land with the Chens?" Ben asked me.

I kicked a rock out of my path. It was one of the few parts of my backstory that we didn't get a chance to cover in Switzerland.

"We figured out that Woodspring was the right facility for me when I was eight, and my mom and I moved out to a temporary apartment. She stayed with me for a year, but between her dance studio and my dad being helpless without her, she decided that she needed to split her time between here and Connecticut. Zo and I had become pretty close, so her parents stepped up and offered to let me move in with them, to continue my training."

Zoey threw her arm around my shoulders and pulled me in for a side hug. "And I got the big sister I always wanted!"

Ben watched us for a few moments, like he was cataloging the interaction. "Are you sure your parents don't want to do a quick interview, Zoey? It would really help round out the story."

Which my mom would hate. As much as she appreciated what living with the Chens allowed me to do, she didn't like sharing the credit for my ascent.

Zoey shook her head. "They worry about the language barrier. My mom thinks her English is terrible."

"Are you serious? Your mom quoted a Shakespeare sonnet to me. I think her English is better than mine," Ben said.

"Not happening, but obviously *I'd* be thrilled to participate," she countered with a wink.

"That's already a given," Ben replied. "I'm gonna sneak you in for an interview at some point."

"What about Friday night? We're having our annual showcase, so you could get some footage of me skating."

I laughed softly. Not only was Zoey an incredible athlete, her marketing instincts left mine in the dust. She was keenly aware of how to turn a throwaway moment into her chance to shine, and I loved her for it.

Ben watched me out of the corner of his eye. "I'll check in with Neil and Hailey to make sure they can do after hours, but no matter what I'd love to come. Are you going, Quinn?"

I nodded. "Yup, the showcase is a big deal at the rink, plus it's adorable watching all the beginner skaters."

"Okay, I guess it's a date, then," he replied.

I knew it was just an expression, but a lifetime of watching rom-coms lit a sparkler in my chest, despite not having the inclination or bandwidth to even *consider* dating anyone let alone the man who'd ghosted me when I needed him most.

"Speaking of dating," Zoey gave him a pointed look. "Let's get into it. I want the scoop on you, Ben."

"No," he groaned. "I'm not going there. I'm begging you."

That made two of us.

"I just want to get it straight from the source," she said playfully, skipping along beside him. "Because the whole universe was shipping a reunion with Violetta a few months ago. Is that true?"

He was shaking his head before she finished asking the question. "Nope. And if you swear to keep a secret, I can give you some insider info."

I tried to pretend that I was more interested in scanning the mountain range in the distance, not in getting the facts about who Ben might be fucking now.

"Ohmygod *yes*!" Zoey squealed and mimed locking her mouth shut. "Spill the tea."

Ben craned his neck to look around the neighborhood, like there might be paparazzi hiding out behind the Robertsons' mailbox. "Okay, this doesn't leave our little gossip session, got it?"

Zoey nodded while I maintained what I hoped was the right amount of disinterest.

"Violetta and I didn't date because she's already dating someone else. From the show."

"No *way*," Zoey replied, starstruck. "Who? Anatoly? Carlos?"

He shook his head.

"Vasily? Brian?"

Ben shook his head again as Zoey named every male cast member.

"Did he leave the show?"

"Nope, they're both still part of the cast."

"But I think I named everyone," Zoe muttered.

"Is he a she?" I asked, since it didn't seem like Zoey was going to connect the dots.

He touched one finger to his nose and pointed another at me. "Ding, ding, ding."

"Violetta is *gay*?" Zoey practically screeched.

"Shhh," Ben chastised. "Yes, she is. She's been with Elena since before my season, but they keep it under wraps. The show loves faking showmances with guests, and the two of them together reduces their options."

"Damn, you guys were incredible actors," Zoey's eyes were wide. "Did you talk about it beforehand? Like, map out how to be with each other? Because the way you grabbed her ass after you got a perfect thirty for the tango . . . that looked very real."

I pretended like I had no clue what they were talking about but yeah, I'd seen the photos from "AssGrabGate."

Ben chuckled. "We didn't sit down and negotiate which body parts were open for business, but we both agreed to play it up and make our time together look as hot as possible. And the social media team was obviously in on it as well. Those 'stolen moments' videos in the hallway backstage, where it looked like they were spying on us? Every single one was a set-up."

"No way! It's like finding out there's no Santa," Zoey said mournfully. "Was *anything* real?"

"Yeah, a lot of it is. Obviously the dancing can't be faked. And the frustration you see in the rehearsal videos is very real. But the stuff between cast members and guest stars can get the reality TV treatment if the producers think it'll collect eyeballs. I get it, though. There's so much media," he held up his phone and waved it, "that you need to do whatever it takes to grab attention."

Ben's dissection of what went into making the show sticky revealed more to me than he realized. I'd been taking him at his word so far, that he was looking out for me and would protect me during the shoot, but I knew that he was desperate for the job at *The Score*. There was a strong possibility that he could still do something unexpected to turn my episode into must-see TV. Especially with the sit-down still to come.

Did they have enough footage to fill an episode if I walked out in the middle of it?

"You've been awfully quiet," Ben bumped against me with his elbow. "Not a fan of the show?"

I managed a tight smile, because my overactive imagination had just recast him as a potential villain. "I never had the time to watch. Sorry."

"Do you still dance?" Zoey asked him.

I thought back to the beautiful moment at the studio with Justin. He definitely still had the skills.

"Not as seriously as when I was doing it every day, but yeah, if I go to a wedding I'll get out there and show off some moves."

"*She's* a great dancer," Zoey said, pointing at me.

"Well, she did mention during her first interview that it's in her blood."

My heart warmed a little at Ben sticking to the script. It wasn't my confessional in Switzerland that filled in my dance background, it was our interview.

But his acknowledgment of chasing ratings by any means necessary made me recalibrate how comfortable I felt with him.

"If I ever get the opportunity I'd love to dance with you, Quinn."

Ben was watching me, waiting for some sort of confirmation, but I couldn't bear to meet his eyes. I needed to keep my barriers up.

"Maybe someday," I finally replied.

A cold wind blew past us.

"Brr. I guess it's still winter after all," Ben said.

I started to close up my jacket but the zipper caught. "Damn it," I muttered as I strained to pull it up. "I can't . . . get it . . ."

"Here, let me," Ben said. He swung around in front of me and bent over to examine the thing, putting his face right at my crotch level. Zoe wiggled her eyebrows at me as he fussed with it.

"Your shirt is stuck in the zipper," he said as he tried to free it. "Hold on."

Before I realized what he was doing Ben had his warm hand beneath my jacket and pressed against the cotton of my T-shirt. He didn't seem to notice that he was rapidly heading for second base as he tried to pry the zipper open.

Zoey pulled her phone out of her pocket and snapped a photo, which I'm sure was ruined by my glaring at her.

Meanwhile Ben was totally focused on my zipper, not the fact that his knuckles were resting against my stomach. Of course today was the day I opted to skip my usual layers.

I forced my muscles from contracting at his touch, because it was nothing more than Ben being helpful. I was merely imagining that we were sharing a tender moment. He didn't wrench at the thing, he finessed it open, and unfortunately my body went along for the ride. Warmth radiated out from where his fingers kept grazing me, and even though I'd never been ticklish, I had to fight to keep from giggling.

"And she is . . . *free*," Ben said. He straightened, met my gaze, and smiled at me as he slowly zipped my coat all the way up to my chin. "Let's get you warm."

"I think she already is," Zoey gave me a shit-eating grin.

Ben pretended to be oblivious while I shot another glare at her.

It might've looked like a shared moment of silliness between friends, but my perimeter was now restored and there was no way I was letting him in.

Chapter Eighteen

So, I was hoping we could try something fun. It'll be quick, I promise."

Ben skated alongside me as we headed back to the players' box. We'd just finished up our early morning on-ice interview while Neil did a damn good job of filming us while skating backward.

"Remember, no off camera fun allowed," I wagged a finger at him as I came to a stop.

I realized after I said it that it was too late. Somehow, fixing a flat tire with him had been fun. Going for a walk and getting behind-the-scenes *Dancing with the Stars* gossip had been fun. Watching him eat up my studio time with my dance teacher had been fun. "Fun" was his level set, and when I was with him I had no choice but to partake.

"Oh, this is for the show. I would never force you to enjoy yourself, don't worry," he winked at me, and I found it unsettlingly sexy. "I thought it would be cool if you tried speed skating. It could be a silly little interstitial, you know? But no pressure to do it if you don't want to."

He looked so hopeful that I felt like I had no choice.

Doing the segment made sense from a show perspective, since it would allow the audience to see Ben in his element doing his thing and me making a fool of myself as I tried to keep up with him. Cute. Silly. I'd been so rigid about what I would and wouldn't allow in the piece that I sort of felt I owed him the favor of giving it a shot.

"Okay, but without the special skates it'll just look regular. I guess you can coach me on the posture and stuff, but it won't be as fish out of water without those long blades."

"Oh, ye of little faith," Ben said as he hopped off the ice and wobbled over to his duffel bag in the player's box. "Check this out."

He unzipped it and pulled out a pair of speed skates that looked well-loved but serviceable.

"Wait . . . are they even my size?" I asked, eyeing them suspiciously.

Suddenly I wasn't so sure about the impromptu lesson.

"Yep." Ben held them out to me.

"Where did they come from?" I asked.

"Don't worry, I know people," he replied. "Are you in?"

I looked at Neil as he skated over to us from where Hailey was on the other side of the ice with a camera on a tripod. We still had about thirty minutes before anyone showed up.

After micromanaging everything, I felt like I needed to let him have a win.

"Sure. I'm in."

"Let's *go*," Ben clapped. "Yes! This'll be cute." He paused. "Not like in a puppy who can't walk on wood floors way, though. In a 'Quinn's good at everything' way."

Neil came to an impressive hockey stop at the boards and balanced the camera on the edge of it. "We doing it?"

"We are," I said with a grimace as I took the skates from Ben and studied them. "Cut away when I fall, please."

"Oh come on," Neil replied. "You're not a total novice. You obviously have incredible strength and balance. You know your edges. You have spatial awareness, and you understand the ice. You'll be great."

I held up a speed skate–clad foot. "Yeah, but what the hell is *this*? The blade is so freaking long."

"And that's why we go so fast!" Ben laughed. "You'll see."

I paused. "Did you bring your skates?"

He shook his head. "I didn't. This isn't about me. I was worried that if I brought them it might turn into the Ben show, which is why I only have my regular skates. Don't worry, I can coach you in these."

It was so uncharacteristic of him that I had to fight to keep my mouth from dropping open in shock. Ben *lived* for the spotlight. Or at least the version of him that I used to know did.

I finished lacing them and stood up. "Okay, it already feels weird. Like I'm standing on two by fours."

Ben turned to Neil. "Can you get all this?"

He nodded and hoisted the camera to his shoulder.

I watched Ben shift into performance mode the moment the camera switched on.

"Before we get out there I'm going to let you in on a little superstition of mine," he said, pausing at the doorway. "No one knows, so consider it an exclusive. I always, *always* have to make sure that I step out on the ice using my right foot."

I thought back to our first morning at the rink, because I'd noticed that he'd seemed tentative.

"It's a little OCD, I know. But now it's so ingrained that it's non-negotiable. If I forget, I have to leave the ice, take my skates off, put them back on, and head out on the ice leading with my right foot."

Ben wasn't calling it OCD in a jokey way. I'd known many athletes who had to fight through versions of the condition, especially when it came to preperformance rituals. I knew better than to call him on it, especially since he'd just admitted to the world that even the great Magic Martino could be governed by intrusive thoughts.

"So are you saying that I should step out on my right foot?" I asked him.

"I mean, it works for me," he laughed.

"Three gold medals can't be wrong. I need all the help I can get." I did an exaggerated step out onto the ice using my right foot.

"Feel okay?" Ben asked the minute I touched it to the ice.

I moved my now gigantic feet back and forth.

"Absolutely not," I replied, trying to find a graceful way to stand but feeling like a duck. "My body usually goes into autopilot when I get out on the ice and I *can't*. It feels so weird! Like, where's my toe pick?"

"No toe pick, and you've got a seventeen-inch-long blade, which is way longer than you should be in given your size and your newbie status. But beggars can't be choosers, so we'll make it work."

Neil did graceful arcs around us a short distance away. I glanced over at Hailey and saw that she was filming as well.

"Okay, guess it's time for me to humiliate myself. I'm all yours, coach."

I went pink at the accidental implication, but Ben ignored it.

"Let's first get you used to the new sensation," he said. "Just move with me."

My body tried to react as it normally would but my feet felt sluggish. Still, I managed to come across halfway graceful as I glided along beside him.

"Okay," he nodded approvingly. "Looking good, Albright! We're about to hit a corner, are you ready for crossovers?"

I attempted to do the move that I could perform forward, backward, and upside down in my regular skates. Crossovers were a foundational move I'd been doing since I was a child, but when I tried one in speed skates I nearly fell on my ass when my front blade hit my rear one. I threw my arms out to the side for balance like a newbie on the ice for the first time.

"So close," he said encouragingly. "Try placing your foot down quicker and push through that crossover."

I did another slightly more successful version the second time around.

"Okay, there she is! Gorgeous," Ben applauded.

Praise from Ben did something to me even though I knew he was lying. I wanted to impress him. I wanted him to think that I was effortlessly good at the sport he'd dedicated his life to.

My crossovers continued to be shaky but I didn't fall, so there was that.

"Okay, straightaway time." He pointed down the rink. "Regular strides. Let's get some speed."

It was another move that was as natural for me as walking, yet in the speed skates I couldn't help the ridiculous little wobble after each push off.

I pointed to my feet. "That's a lot more real estate down there than I'm used to."

"Yeah, but you're a natural. You're already doing instinctive weight transfers. Now let's work that posture a little to make you look official. Watch me for a sec."

He sped up so that he was in front of me and hunched into the low, crouched speed skating position, which meant that I was being forced to stare at his ass. I hoped the camera angles didn't make it look *too* obvious. He turned around to face me.

"Now you. Deep knee bend, and get that back low, like you're a table."

I crouched in an approximation of what he'd just done.

"Lower, and flatten that back!"

My thighs reacted like I'd never done a squat in my life.

"Okay, now hold that and follow behind me," he barked.

Freaking *impossible*.

Ben started doing the ubiquitous shifting that speed skaters did on straightaways, swinging his arms in time. The up close and personal vantage point proved how graceful he was, and within a few seconds of watching I found my body adapting to his rhythm. My strides evened out, until we were nearly in perfect cadence, like we were waltzing.

He did a quick turn to watch me and I struggled to keep the same rhythm without him demonstrating it for me.

"Yeah! Look at you!"

"Is this right?" I asked, suddenly feeling awkward.

"One hundred percent," he said. "I'm really impressed."

Mission accomplished.

Ben went over some of the other basic skills, and I started to feel more comfortable in the skates.

He slowed down until he was beside me again and we fell back in step. "Now let's crank up the heat. Show me what ya got. Ready?"

For a couple of seconds it looked like he was running on his toes picks since he was in regular skates that actually had them, then the next thing I knew he was half the rink away from me. I could see Neil laughing so I took the bait and chased after Ben.

I was fast but obviously not as fast as him. I put up a decent if awkward fight until he slowed down for me.

"My *thighs*," I straightened up and glided beside him. "How am I feeling it already?"

"Yeah, it's an anatomically uncomfortable sport. You get used to it. Sort of."

"So are we racing or what?" I asked him.

His eyes went wide. "Hold up. You really want more smoke after what I just did to you?"

I hitched a shoulder. "Why not? I think you might be rusty now, old man."

"Whoo-hoo," Ben said and turned in a circle, addressing an imaginary audience. "She's trash talking! I was trying to be nice to you but not anymore. We're doing this."

He quickly described start position and the takeoff to me and we lined up side by side. Neil acted as our official.

"Go to the start," Neil called out. "Ready."

We lowered ourselves into the deep squat.

"*Go!*"

The sound of our skates echoed around the rink as we ran on the ice. My takeoff was shockingly strong, but everyone watching knew that I didn't have a chance at beating a three-time Olympic gold medalist at his own sport.

I wanted Ben to have a chance to show off. To remind the audience watching *The Score* that the kickass interviewer was also a peerless athlete. And I wanted to get close to the magic he made on the ice, like his winning streak might rub off on me.

I put on a sloppy, giggly show half the rink behind him. I could tell he hadn't even moved out of second gear in an effort to let me save face. When he glanced back at me, he was laughing too.

Yeah, I now had zero doubt that having fun with Ben was a given.

Chapter Nineteen

This might be the cutest thing I've ever seen," Ben marveled as a group of five-year-olds dressed as Minions skated to "Happy Together."

We'd met at the rink for the showcase, mainly because I'd been subjecting myself to way more Magic Martino than I'd signed on for and didn't want to do yet another date-adjacent activity with him. Hailey and Neil had to skip the event because they were union and getting close to hitting their hours for the day, which left the two of us without a buffer, sitting side by side in the packed arena.

I had my usual visceral reactions watching the adorable little girls—joy that they were blossoming in the sport, and worry about what they could face if any of them turned out to be like me at age six. All it took was one striving parent plus a driven coach to mine raw talent. The descriptors for a promising young skater sounded positive . . . small and strong . . . tiny and powerful . . . a fearless firecracker. The reality of what might await the girl possessing all those gifts was what stressed me out.

I understood all too well that talent and damage often went hand in hand.

"Do you know any of them?" Ben leaned over to ask me.

"Almost all of them, and I recognize the ones I haven't met," I said. "Like you noticed, we're a close-knit community."

He looked down at the program. "Zoey skates last."

"She's the rink's star."

"After you," he added.

Which we both knew was true, but there was no need to talk about it. It didn't help that we were attending the event together, because I usually attracted plenty of attention on my own. The parents and athletes I saw every day didn't give me a second glance, but the friends and family who came along to the event treated me like a celebrity. It wasn't fair to pull attention from the skaters, so I'd opted for my usual disguise of no makeup and a black knit cap pulled low. Ben had done his part to camouflage his star power in a baseball cap and a half zip with a high collar.

Still, I could feel eyes on us.

The little minions finished and glided off the ice to thunderous applause.

Ben studied the program. "My buddy Nathan is next. This might be his final performance."

I whirled to face him. "What do you mean? Is he injured?"

The corner of his mouth tipped up. "Not at all. I think it'll be because he found a new obsession. I gave him my number and he's been texting me all sorts of questions about speed skating. I gave him a couple of simple tests to try and he sailed through them. The kid has promise. I'm trying to get him hooked up with some folks I know in the area."

Ben sounded so wistful that I couldn't resist turning the tables and interviewing him.

"Do you miss it?"

"Fuck yes," he replied quickly. "Way more than I expected."

I stared at his profile, waiting for him to continue, but he busied himself with the program. An unfamiliar furrow appeared on his brow.

"Was it hard?" I probed. "Retiring?"

Ben stared out at the ice. When he finally answered his voice was a scrape of gravel. "Yeah. Devastating."

I didn't expect such a candid response, especially given that we were surrounded by people. I wanted to continue the conversation, to learn about the post-Olympic reality check that I heard could level even the strongest athletes, but Ben's expression didn't welcome additional questions.

I'd gotten a hint of what it was like when I quit. The mix of no rules and an empty calendar had been exhilarating at first, until it felt like a black hole that could swallow me up.

"Did you ever think about coaching?"

We paused to clap as Nathan skated to the center of the rink, dressed in black pants with a sequin stripe up the side and a bright blue silky shirt.

"I don't have the right temperament," Ben answered. "I don't want to create stars, I want to *be* the star. And realizing that has been the most humbling part of my comedown."

It was so self-aware that I had zero doubt that Ben had gone through therapy at some point.

We both went silent as "A Million Dreams" from *The Greatest Showman* began. I glanced at Ben out of the corner of my eye as Nathan skated, and I could tell he was trying to gauge how Nathan's power strokes and weight shifts would translate in speed skates.

Ben leaned closer to me, and the haze of his warm, earthy scent made me realize that he'd worn cologne for our nondate.

"I almost feel bad about stealing him, because he's *really* good."

"If it's what he truly wants then you're not poaching," I replied. "The decision is up to him."

Nathan finished his performance, and it felt like half of the people in the stands jumped up for a standing ovation.

"Quite a fan club," Ben whispered to me. "They're going to hate me if they find out I played a part in his decision to quit."

A hand reached between us to tap Ben on the shoulder. We both turned to find a mother and her preteen daughter seated behind us, grinning.

"I *told* you it was him," the girl said under her breath.

They both glanced at me and I saw their eyes go wide in unison. "And Quinn too? Oh my gosh," the girl said excitedly. "Bailey was right!"

We smiled back in the practiced way we'd cultivated when stopped by fans.

"Hi there," Ben said in his Prince Charming voice. "Are you enjoying the show?"

The little girl seemed nervous but her mom looked ready to jump on top of Ben. "We are," she replied. "My niece is the one who skated to *Bolero*. Wasn't she amazing?"

"*So* good," I answered.

The skater had put on a competent performance, but I could tell that her skating career would probably flame out in a couple of years. She acted like there was a checklist in her head, and each move she completed brought her closer to being finished. Her technique was decent but the passion just wasn't there.

"I'm sorry but I have to ask," the woman said as she glanced between us. "Are the rumors true?"

I tensed, but managed to keep my expression neutral. "Rumors?"

"Tell them, Julia," the woman urged.

The girl cleared her throat as she fussed with her phone, like she was nervous to suddenly be the center of attention. "So, I follow Bailey Harlow on YouTube, and she posted about how you guys got a flat tire while you were on a date and she and her dad basically rescued you two. Pictures and everything."

It was a struggle not to react to the revisionist history.

Ben laughed good-naturedly. "Pictures *plural*? Because I can only recall taking one."

"Yeah, look." Julia pushed play and thrust her phone out to us.

"Hey guys," the young girl we'd met spoke to the camera. "I wanted to hop on here because I've got a story time for you that you're *not* going to believe. Look who I ran into!"

The picture of the three of us flashed on-screen, then Bailey proceeded to talk about how her dad had helped us change our tire, and how we couldn't keep our hands off each other while we waited. She included a few photos that she probably took as they were driving away, including one where it *did* look like we were sharing a moment, with us standing close and staring into each other's eyes.

I choked when I saw that the views of the video were over two million. Who the hell was Bailey Harlow?

"So you're dating, right?" Julia asked excitedly.

The PA system screeched, making everyone flinch. It meant that they were getting ready for the next performer, which would end the teenage interrogation.

I opened my mouth to shoot her down but Ben beat me to it.

"I'm sorry to tell you that the influencer padded the story. Quinn and I are *not* dating," he said with a smile, to soften the blow. "We're working on a segment for *The Score*. I'm a new correspondent for the show."

I noticed that he skipped the "trial" part of his employment.

"But you guys are so perfect for each other," the woman pouted. "The skating thing . . ."

She trailed off, because that was probably all she knew about either of us.

"Agreed, we'd probably be quite the power couple," Ben said. "But right now Quinn's got gold on her mind. *That's* her focus."

The woman locked eyes with me and reached out to clasp my shoulder. "You're going to win this time, I know it."

The familiar weight of the world's expectations pressed against my chest, but I managed to find my smile for her.

"Thank you, I appreciate that."

The girl held up her phone, her expression hopeful. "Is it okay if I . . . ?"

Ben agreed to a photo before I could weigh in, but I realized that it didn't matter what I wanted. Our story was already out of our hands and being written by the rest of the world.

We turned so that we were both facing her as she snapped the photo. Ben left his arm draped around my shoulders for a few seconds longer than necessary.

The show rolled on until it was finally time for Zoey. The vibe in the room shifted as she skated to the center of the ice, looking stunning in an emerald-green costume. The whimsical "La Valse d'Amélie" from the movie *Amélie* began, and as usual, Zoey captivated the rink.

Ben leaned to whisper in my ear, and his warm breath against my skin made me want to lean closer to him. "She's so good it's ridiculous."

"I know," I said softly. "I'm really proud of her."

I noticed that Ben remained nearer to me than he needed to be, pressed up against my arm in a way that felt familiar.

"Is she going to get her shot to be a part of Team USA?"

"Not sure," I sighed. I glanced over my shoulder and lowered my voice. "Politics."

It killed me, because Zoey was a dynamic performer who married technical skills with a natural gift. But there were a finite number of spaces on the team, and despite our sport being merit based on paper, the reality was that it was subjective. Skaters had to deal with favoritism and questionable judges on top of all the hard work.

Ben pulled out his camera to film her. "For the show. It'll be good to intercut some of this footage with her interview."

"She'll love that."

I saw a text pop up on his screen as he filmed Zoey.

S.O.S., it read.

"Oh shit," he muttered as he stopped recording. "What now?"

A couple more texts came through, and I could tell by his expression as he read them that it was bad news.

"Everything okay?" I asked.

"Not sure. I need to call Kim to get the full story but I'll wait until Zoey's done."

I watched his expression out of the corner of my eye as Zoey nailed her final jumps. Brows drawn, his usually smiley mouth downturned. Whatever he was processing seemed major.

Zoey took her bows and Ben excused himself to make the call. I tried to intuit what could shake up the normally unflappable Magic Martino. Were they pulling my segment? Or worse, did they decide the show didn't need him after all?

Ben finally came back as the students skated out to do group bows and present their coaches with flowers.

And he was frowning. *Fuck.* Bennett Martino didn't frown.

"What happened?" I asked him as the audience around us stood up and started shuffling for the exits. "Are you okay?"

"I'm fine. This is about *you*," Ben replied. He heaved a sigh. "Your mom called Kim to tell her that the only time we can film with them is this week. For whatever reason, your parents are completely unavailable after that. More vacations, maybe?"

The tension between my shoulder blades released and I smiled reflexively. "Okay, this is *good* news! Now we can skip the home visit."

Ben still looked pained.

"I wish." He shook his head. "Kim said the higher-ups still want it, because it's an important part of your story."

I knew that it only mattered to them because it was juicy. "Daughter fires momager" was exactly the kind of high drama that brought in viewers.

"But . . . *how*?" I demanded. "We've blocked out our schedule for the week, and there's no way I'm sacrificing my training time to make this happen."

Ben paused to let a few people pass by him.

"They're literally checking flights right now."

I stared at him for a beat, fuming, then speed-walked away, threading through the crowd with my eyes down so I wouldn't have to greet anyone. The same burning anger I used to feel in my chest almost daily was back, like heartburn but worse.

It was just like her to gerrymander her way back into my life. It would've been hard enough dealing with her with my Italy departure date looming closer, but at least I would've had time to mentally prepare for it. Keeping me unstable was all part of her plan. Forcing me to come back was bad enough, but now I had to do it on *her* terms.

Ben caught up to me by a dark side exit that no one used. He grasped my arm, and I wrenched it away, glaring at him.

"Quinn, I'm sorry. I really am. I know how hard this is. I tried to beg off, I swear. I said we still had plenty we needed to film here, and the piece would be totally fine without the home visit, but they're not having it."

I fought to keep my eyes from welling. She didn't deserve my tears.

I squared up in front of Ben. "Doesn't anyone care that I don't want to do it? Like, do my feelings not matter at all? Your goal is content by any means necessary?"

He flinched. "You know that's not how I feel. I tried getting us out of it."

Us. Like we were a united front.

"I'm not going. I'm not ready to see her. I need time to get in the right headspace and you guys dropping this on me and expecting me to be okay with it isn't fair. So, no. Tell Kim it's not happening."

His expression tensed for a moment.

"I know this sucks. We're putting you in a tough position. But—"

"But all you care about is the show," I shot back at him. "And getting the job."

"Quinn, *no*, not at all." Ben's voice was wounded. "I was going to say that I'll be there for you. I know the backstory, so I think I know how to protect you."

I softened a little at the idea of having Ben shield me from my Mom's smiley jabs.

"No matter what, you have to go get your license, so won't it be a little easier with me by your side?" Ben asked gently.

As much as I wanted to, I couldn't argue with his logic. My

mom would be on her best behavior in front of an audience, and when she tried to slip in a zinger, maybe Ben would step up to deflect it?

He reached out to take my hands in his, and as much as I wanted to pull away, his warmth anchored me.

"I've got you, Quinn," he said, staring into my eyes. "Okay?"

I couldn't look away because it felt like he was peering into my soul, just like last time.

"Do you trust me?"

Damn it. It went against every primal instinct in my body, but I knew the answer was yes.

Chapter Twenty

*W*hat's going on with you?"

Ben was leaning forward in his window seat, eyeballing me as I clutched the armrests of my aisle seat. Considering how often I was on the road for competitions, you'd think my fear of flying would've decreased over the years, but it hung on, as stubborn as a grease stain on white cotton.

I shook my head, staring straight at the seat in front of me. "Nothing."

He didn't look away, and I could feel his eyes traveling up my body, cataloging every nuance.

"You're nervous."

"I'm *fine*."

He shifted, still watching me, and I could tell the inquisition was about to level up.

"Maybe we'll get lucky and no one will be seated between us. These early flights are usually less crowded."

"Yeah, I'm loving the six a.m. departure," I snarked at him.

"We have a shitload to do today, and I knew you didn't want to spend a second longer in Connecticut than necessary. Do you want the window? Where would you feel more comfortable?" Ben started to unbuckle his seat belt, poised to jump up.

A woman in a navy blazer came to a stop by our row looking just as unhappy as I felt. "Sorry, this is me."

She pointed to the middle seat, frowning.

"Of course," I said, doing an awkward half stand so she could squeeze by me.

"Before you sit," Ben began and the woman paused. He gestured toward me. "We're actually together, and my friend is a nervous flyer. Would you like to have my window seat and I'll take the middle, so the two of us can sit together?"

His unexpected kindness lowered my stress level by about 4 percent.

She glanced between the two of us and I waited for the inevitable spark of recognition, especially because she was within Ben's target demo; a middle manager–type clutching her laptop under her arm, who probably mainlined reality TV.

If she recognized him she didn't let on, which meant that we wouldn't be forced to make small talk with her all the way to Hartford. In any other scenario I enjoyed connecting with skating fans, but flying meant that I needed to focus. I didn't have the bandwidth to chat on flights because the only reason I hadn't crashed yet was the power of my visualization of the plane remaining in the air for the entire flight.

"Um, sure," she replied with an expression like she'd smelled something unpleasant. "But if you want to swap could I take the aisle instead? I get a little claustrophobic in the window seat."

"Done," Ben said.

The three of us shuffled our carry-ons and reading material and settled into our new seats, with Ben in the awful middle seat and me leaning against the window.

"You didn't have to do that," I said quietly. "But I appreciate it."

He bumped his shoulder against mine. "Happy to. I can be your human stress ball. If you're feeling nervous, squeeze this." Ben held up his hand.

"Have you been watching the weather?" I leaned forward to peek out the window at the gray sky. "Because it's looking dicey in Connecticut."

I started bouncing my leg and Ben gently placed his hand on my knee to stop it. "All I've seen is the *possibility* of snow. We'll be okay."

He sounded so convinced of it that I nearly believed him.

"Not if we get snowed in at my parents' house." I fell back against my seat and squeezed my eyes shut. "Oh my fucking god, this is a bad idea on so many levels. I swear, if I lose training time because Winter Storm Ronaldo strands us . . ." I trailed off because I wasn't sure what sort of punishment fit the crime, and who would deserve it.

I only realized that Ben's hand was still on my leg when he squeezed it. "Hey. Look at me."

I opened my eyes reluctantly and felt a wave of calm unfurl when I saw Ben's face, closer to mine than I was expecting. Capable. Focused. Trustworthy.

"If we get stranded—" Ben began.

I cut him off with a frustrated noise.

"I said *if*," he continued, squeezing my leg again, "I'll make sure you get a great workout somehow."

He seemed to realize the double entendre after it was too late, and we both wound up blushing, until he recovered and said, "You brought your sneakers, right?"

I nodded. "Running has always been my excuse to get out of the house."

"If all goes according to plan you won't need an excuse this time, I promise. We scheduled this trip like a military operation. We'll land, meet up with Neil and Hailey, who I think are back there somewhere," he jerked his thumb over his shoulder toward the rear of the plane, "grab the equipment and rental car, drive to your parents, set up, knock out the interview in a couple of hours max, then head to the hotel for the night. Tomorrow we'll wake up at the crack of dawn, go to the DMV—"

"You absolutely do not have to come with me to that hellscape," I interrupted.

He made a face at me. "Like I'm going to let you deal with it alone. I'm going. Anyway, DMV, new license with a killer photo, then off to the airport. And before you know it, you'll be back to the grind."

Which was exactly where I belonged. I'd get through the next thirty-six hours with the help of the accidental cheerleader and therapist beside me.

The flight attendants came out to do their show and my stress level spiked.

Takeoff was imminent. Three hours and forty-five minutes of hang time in the clouds. And at the end of it all? Not a tropical vacation. I was about to face more torture in the shape of Tricia Albright.

I closed my eyes and let out a long, slow breath through pursed lips.

"You've got this," Ben said quietly.

"I hate takeoffs. I feel like I've got a dozen rabbits in my stomach."

"Alive, or eaten?"

"Alive, and angry," I replied.

"Let's redirect that energy," he shifted in his seat. "Time for some guided meditation. I'm really good at it."

I cracked one eye to look at him and hoped it was enough to telegraph my disdain.

"I'm serious!"

"I meditate all the time," I replied. "And I do positive visualization of my performances. It doesn't help in this scenario. I've tried."

"Yeah, but have you ever visualized the medal ceremony?"

My sassy reply died on my lips. I'd been doing versions of cognitive rehearsals since I was a kid, but I'd never considered doing it for the medal ceremony. The reasons for the oversight lurked in shadows. I didn't like giving them air.

"No, I haven't."

"Okay, then let's do it now. Guided visualization, brought to you by me."

The plane started taxiing, and as much as I didn't want Ben chanting in my ear, I did sort of need a distraction. I put my hands in my lap and dug my fingernails into my palms.

"Go," I choked out.

He shifted a little closer, and his arm wound up pressed against mine. "Close your eyes." Was he *trying* to do a sexy voice? Because he sounded like a spicy audiobook narrator. "Now, picture yourself having just skated the most incredible programs of your life. You're finally done. The hard part's over. Every second of pain and sacrifice brought you to this moment. You won gold! You *deserve* to be here."

The plane picked up speed, and even though Ben's voice was a soothing focal point, I couldn't fully embody the scene he was describing. I could see the arena and feel the energy of the crowd, but picturing myself leaning down to accept a medal?

In my mind, my body looked like a mass of TV static. Unidentifiable as me.

"You step onto that stage and suddenly you feel the adoration of thirteen thousand spectators," Ben continued.

I cracked an eye. "Thirteen thousand? Are you serious?"

"Even more, thanks to the TV coverage, now close your damn eyes," he scolded. "As I was saying, you've never felt this way before. You're proud. Honored. *Vindicated*."

The last bit was specifically for me, because the only person Bennett Martino ever had to beat was himself. I, on the other hand, had plenty to prove to the rest of the world.

"The stage is *massive*. Normally the size of it would make you feel like a speck of dust, but it's impossible in this scenario because you're the *reason* for it. Every eye is focused on you. There's an energy in the air unlike anything you've ever experienced, and you're the conductor. The lighting is bright, so much so that you're almost tempted to squint, but you don't because you don't want to miss a second of what's happening. The two people on either side of you? Your former foes are now your allies, because the three of you have accomplished the impossible. You're the best of the best."

I'd experienced watered-down versions of what he was describing at various competitions, but I still couldn't visualize myself on *this* stage.

I let out a frustrated huff and opened my eyes.

"I can't do it."

Ben pulled back, his face drawn with worry. "Quinn, seriously? Why?"

Therapist Ben was back. I had to fight to keep from unloading my whys, because he already had enough intel on me.

"Old scripts," I replied. "Baggage. I'm working on it."

His eyes searched my face, and once again I could understand why every woman he came in contact with fell for him. In this moment I sensed that all that mattered to him was *me*. My hurt, my hope, my journey. It was the craziest juxtaposition; a man who seemed to have a bottomless well of self-love who could also pivot to completely focus on others.

"Do you want to talk about it?"

Yes, because I knew firsthand that Ben had the power to soothe me. But 100 percent *no*, because he didn't deserve more painful backstory from me.

I almost felt like an addict. Talking to Ben would make me feel better in the moment, but the comedown afterward would leave me bleary and broken. I had to keep reminding myself that his care was transactional.

He stood to benefit from my pain.

"I'll get there," I finally replied. "I'm fine."

Ben watched me for a beat longer. "One hurdle down. Look."

He pointed at the window and when I finally felt brave enough to peek out I realized we were at our cruising altitude.

"You can do hard things," Ben reassured me. "And when you feel like it's impossible, I'll help prove that it's not."

Chapter Twenty-One

*G*oing back felt like revisiting a crime scene.

The usual itchy-spiders-under-my-skin sensation intensified as we pulled into the neighborhood. The elegant sign read SERENITY SPRINGS; it had been anything but for me.

"Wow, nice 'hood," Neil said from the driver's seat of the car. He swiveled his head to take in the grand homes as we drove down the streets named Whispering Pines Way and Tranquil Glen Lane.

"Super pretty," Hailey agreed from beside me.

Ben remained quiet as we got closer to the house. He was wearing his focused prerace face, with his eyebrows drawn down and his gaze fixed on the horizon.

We both knew what we were walking into.

"Take the next left," I instructed.

We rounded the corner onto Harmony Circle, and there squatting at the end of a cul-de-sac was the lovely stone house where I'd spent my early years.

"*Stunning*," Hailey sighed.

I didn't answer her because I was too busy doing a final primp. I'd reapplied my makeup on the plane, so all that was left to do was make sure my forehead wasn't shiny and throw on some lipstick. I wasn't bowing to my mom's "always be pretty" directive, I was obsessing about how I looked as protective armor. I didn't want to have to listen to her cataloging my flaws in front of the team.

It was also a bit of a test. How long could I go before she found something that needed fixing?

We piled out of the rented Subaru in the driveway, blinking in the bright, cold sun.

"Sure doesn't look like there's a snowstorm coming," Neil said as he pointed toward the cloudless sky. "I think we're good."

"Yeah, but it's frickin' freezing here," Hailey complained. She pulled a hat out of her jacket pocket and pulled it down low.

"Cold and clear," Ben agreed. "Are we ready to get this done?"

"Yes, Chef," Neil joked as he popped the trunk to start unloading equipment.

"Hailey, I want you on camera two for today, to keep things moving," Ben continued as he helped grab carrying cases. "We're doing a three-shot for some of it and I don't want Neil bouncing around between cameras."

I glanced at Neil and he frowned briefly but refrained from complaining. Progress!

"Can I help unload?" I asked.

Ben shook his head. "We're good." He waited for me to meet his eyes and lowered his voice. "Worry about you, okay?"

We shared a moment of quiet solidarity, two soldiers preparing for a skirmish.

"*There she is!*"

The sound of her voice made me jump like the car alarm had triggered right beside me.

I could feel Hailey watching us so I locked into my stage persona. "*Hey*," I drew the word out, to avoid having to call her Mom.

Her kitten heels clacked on the slate walkways as she practically skipped to me.

The last time I'd seen my mom for a brief three-day break for Christmas, but we'd had a full house of aunts, uncles, and cousins, so we'd had minimal alone time. Now, I was about to be her sole focus, and in front of cameras no less.

My mom had never wanted to pursue acting, but she could have, given her natural gift for theatrics. I could feel Neil and Hailey pausing to watch our reunion, and the way my mom beamed at me and summoned a few tears really sold the happy Hallmark vibes.

"*Baby*," she cooed as she wrapped me in her arms, rocking us from side to side. "Welcome home."

I fought to keep from stiffening up. I pretended that we were ballroom dancing and I had no choice but to follow her lead, until I started to feel smothered.

"How are you?" I asked as I pulled away from her.

She looked perfect, as usual. I'd been cursed with a hot mom who'd had me young, which meant she loved it when men joked that we could be sisters. Her hair was a few shades blonder than mine, with a center part and smooth layers. She'd always avoided the sun, so her skin was flawless alabaster with just the right amount of pink on her high cheekbones. Every bit of her was calibrated to be polished, from the way her shoes matched her nails to her lashes curled in perfect crescents. She was wearing a hot pink cashmere wrap as a coat despite the frigid temperature, which was meant to look casual but I knew was planned way in advance.

"I'm *so* happy that you're here!" She turned to the team and waved both hands, pageant queen–style. "Welcome, everyone. I'm Tricia."

"Neil," he said, walking toward her with his hand extended.

"I hope when you leave you'll feel comfortable giving me a hug instead of this formal stuff," she flirted as they shook hands.

He laughed. "This is Hailey, and you probably already know Ben, because who doesn't?"

Hailey shook her hand as well, and then we all turned to see what Ben was doing, only to discover that he was missing.

"Where'd he go?" Neil asked, craning his neck to look around the yard.

We spotted him farther down the long driveway on his phone. He glanced at us without so much as a wave of acknowledgment and continued walking away.

It felt like his own bit of theatrics, to avoid getting mixed up in the homecoming, and I loved him for it. My mom wanted the world to stick to her choreography, and the fact that Ben wasn't falling in line for her welcome home performance was the perfect "fuck you" to kick off the visit. Not a big enough thing to cause real drama, but he seemed to intuitively understand that he needed to piss on her fence.

Gratitude warmed me, but I caught myself before I could get all moony over the man. He had a job to do. There was still a good chance that he could push on the bruise between me and my mom to drum up drama for the show.

"Is Mr. Albright home?" Neil asked as he pulled another case from the car.

"Call him Tim, sweetheart," Tricia replied in her honeyed voice. "And yes, he took today off but he's on a call in his office. He'll magically appear when we're ready to go."

I noticed that she kept glancing up the driveway, waiting for Ben to hang up and acknowledge her. Every second that passed felt like a win.

"That's everything. Is it okay if we go in and start setting up?" Neil said. He was clearly enjoying acting like the lead on the production in the few minutes Ben was pretending to be busy.

Tricia gave Ben one last, longing glance. "Yes, of course. It's so cold out here, let's get you inside by the fire."

My mom stood by the door like a flight attendant greeting passengers. She put her hand on my arm to stop me as I crossed the threshold. "Where's your overnight bag, honey?"

"Didn't they tell you? We're all staying at the Greeley Inn, so we can work on editing together."

It was a bit of fiction Mel and I had concocted to give me a valid reason to leave at the end of the day.

She frowned at me. "But you don't know how to edit."

"I, uh, I have editorial control on the program," I stuttered, throwing a nervous glance at Neil and hoping he wouldn't correct my lie. Thankfully he was too busy unpacking.

"Oh." She peered out the window by the door. "He's going to freeze out there. Should I tell him to come in?"

"Mom, he's used to the cold."

"That's right," she laughed. "Three speed skating gold medals means he's spent plenty of time freezing his booty off."

It didn't sound like a dig but I knew it was. I made a mental tally to keep track of how many times she mentioned his Olympic wins.

"Do you have a preference about where we set up?" Neil asked her.

"Ben will have thoughts about that," Hailey said under her breath.

He shot her a look then refocused on my mom. "Do you have a couple of options in mind? That way we can show Ben when he comes in."

"Yes, of course, we have lots of pretty spaces we can choose from. Follow me."

I remained in the front hall, waiting for Ben. For whatever reason, he felt like my touchstone.

He finally hung up and started striding toward the house. I leaned my forehead against the window, willing him to walk faster. I needed him to witness every second of the visit, so he could fully understand what I was up against.

"Well hello, pretty lady," my dad's voice rang out from behind me.

I turned to find him with his arms outstretched, ready for a hug.

He was still leading-man handsome, with a blocky jaw and the perfect amount of salt in his peppery hair. My father was basically a neutral stranger in my life, a member of the chorus who was always overshadowed by the lead. Not that he cared. It gave him the perfect excuse to lose himself in his work, and then on the golf course.

"Hey, Dad."

I relished the few seconds of connection as we embraced. It was the closest I'd come to true parental affection.

We pulled apart but he held on to my shoulders and studied me.

"You look really good, sweetheart. Healthy."

My heart warmed at the first part then dropped at the second. Healthy could be code for "not tiny enough to jump high."

It must've registered on my face because he quickly followed up. "You look *happy*."

I paused to consider it. I'd just come from a flight where I didn't feel terrified the entire time, I was hanging out with a crew I'd dreaded working with but who turned out to be okay, and the one person I'd spent the past four years hating was quickly becoming my strongest ally.

I smiled at my father. "I guess I am."

We were interrupted by a soft knock at the door.

I wasn't sure how my mom even heard it but she materialized in front of me to welcome the man of the hour.

She threw open the door dramatically. "Bennett Martino, *welcome*! You get in here right now!"

The intensity of her smiley greeting made him take a half step backward. "Uh, hello there."

"Come in, come in, everyone is waiting for you," she jokingly scolded him as she grabbed him by the wrist. "We were starting to get worried!"

He shot me a look as he crossed the threshold that told me he already understood.

"Yeah, sorry, lots of moving parts as we get closer to leaving for Italy, which I'm sure you understand with all your upcoming travel. We really appreciate your time today."

At least one of us did.

"Anything for our Quinn," she said, keeping her focus totally on Ben.

"Mr. Albright, it's nice to meet you." Ben stretched out his hand to my father, and they did the manly sizing-up thing as they shook hands.

"Big fan," he replied, which I knew wasn't true because the only sports my dad cared about were football and baseball. Even mine barely mattered to him.

Neil walked into the front hall. "Sorry to interrupt, but we have a few options for out setup. Want to come see?"

"I'll show you my favorite," my mom said, moving to the front of the group.

As always, the rest of us were left to follow behind her.

Chapter Twenty-Two

*W*e're ready for you," Hailey said as she peeked into the dining room.

It was the farthest spot on the first floor from where the team had set up to interview my parents on the sun porch. Ben had invited me to sit in on their solo portion of the interview, but I had zero desire to watch my mom fake-fawn over me. Besides, I already knew all her scripts. There was no need to give her the satisfaction of repeating them in front of me.

I stood up and stretched my arms over my head. I'd spent my time contorted in a highback chair, rewatching my old performances and texting Mel and Zoey for support. Anything to avoid hearing my mom's fake laughter echo down the hall.

"I love your house," Hailey said over her shoulder as I followed her. "It's perfect. Like a model home."

"That's exactly what she was going for," I said with a snort.

Not comfortable or warm. *Impressive.* Envy inducing. Like the room I was just in; the white oak table beneath the hand-painted wallpaper was so wide that you couldn't talk to the person seated across from you let alone comfortably pass the dinner rolls, and the chairs were cushioned, but the hard right angle felt like torture after an hour or so.

"It's going really well," Hailey continued. "Your mom is *so* good on camera."

I was well aware. "How about my dad?"

"Oh, he's great too. But it seems like your mom was more plugged into your career. He's letting her take the lead."

As ever.

I paused at the threshold of the room, marveling at the way the team had transformed it for the interview with big softbox lights and a maze of cords on the floor.

"Hey." Ben met me at the doorway and I caught the slightest furrow. He glanced at Hailey hovering behind him. "I'll get Quinn's mic on."

She frowned at him. "I can do it. It's sort of my job."

"Yeah, but I want to go over some stuff with her. Why don't you help Neil reset for the three-shot?"

Hailey nodded and moved on, leaving the two of us alone in the corner of the room a safe distance from where my parents were sitting. I could feel my mom watching us.

"How bad was it?" I asked softly, angling myself so my back was to her.

Ben handed me the mic pack and I shoved it in my rear pocket. "Well, I now know that you have the world's best mother, according to your mother. And that *she's* the one who pushed you to try a new direction. That about sums it up so far."

Instead of feeling angry, I deflated. There was no way I could refute what she'd said without blowing up the whole interview.

"Based on that," he continued, "I want to keep this group segment short. I can already sense how it's going to go. Here, you know the drill."

He handed me the mic and I threaded the cord down the front of my cashmere sweater. I'd worn a simple black turtleneck and pulled my hair in a ponytail, because it was the exact look she hated.

"Your poor nervous system," Ben said with a sad smile. "First the flight and now this. You holding up okay?"

I nodded unconvincingly, and he moved closer to me.

"Hey. We've got this," he said softly as his dark eyes held mine.

We. The word kept popping up, and I was starting to like what it signified.

"It's going to be fine," he continued. "But I want to have a code, for if you need to pull the plug. Just say 'spiral,' okay? Work it into your answer and I'll end the interview so smoothly they won't even know what hit them."

I glanced over my shoulder at my parents and then back at Ben. "I hate this."

He reached out to gently grasp my arm. "I know," he replied. "I'm here. I've got you."

We shared the moment in silence as I redefined the person I thought I had all figured out. I'd always considered Ben to be quicksand dragging me down, but I was learning that he was actually an anchor, holding me steady in rough waters.

"What are you two gossiping about over there?"

And the spell was broken, thanks to my mom.

"Just strategizing. We want to watch the time so we don't overstay our welcome," Ben answered breezily.

"Exactly, because the snow's about to start any minute," my dad said.

He pointed up to the glass ceiling of the sun porch and sure enough, the sun slid behind a dark cloud.

"Yeah, the Weather Service just changed it from a winter storm watch to a warning." Neil glanced up from his phone. "It's supposed to get really bad in a couple of hours."

"How far is the hotel from here?" Ben asked.

"It's close, like eight minutes," Neil answered. "I figured we wouldn't want to drive far."

I wished that he'd asked me where we should stay, because he'd accidentally picked a cozy little spot that was perfect for a romantic getaway.

"Let's get to it, then," Ben said. He locked on to me again. "Are you ready?"

I nodded and headed for the chair set up between my parents.

My mom slid her arm around my shoulders as I sat down. "This is so exciting!"

I noticed that one of the cameras was still rolling so I forced a smile. "Yup!"

We'd done plenty of interviews together but usually she did all the talking.

Neil moved in front of us and slapped the digital clapperboard with a guillotine chop. I was so on edge that I jumped, making my mom giggle at me. He slid on his headphones and took his position by the primary camera. I was happy to see Hailey behind her camera and ready to go.

"Okay, let's get started!" Ben sat down across from the three of us. "Quinn, your parents did a great job going over your origin story when you were little, so now I want to focus on what's next." He paused, to build in space for the edit between his overview for us and the first official question. He rearranged his face into a smile. "Tim, Tricia, how will you feel when Quinn wins gold in Italy?"

No mention of the messy middle of my Olympic journey four years prior, plus he was manifesting a win for me. Thanks, Ben.

My dad started to answer, but my mom stepped on his words.

"Sorry, honey, can I take this?" She beamed at Ben. "Hearing Quinn's name called will be a dream come true. The level of sacrifice we've dealt with to get her to this point has been extreme, you know? All those early morning practices, the expenses, the travel . . . it was a lot for me to take on." She leaned across me to tap my dad's hand. "Tim helped when he could, but he was busy keeping a roof over our heads and paying for her lessons, so it all fell on me. And I *welcomed* it, because I knew this young lady had a gift from day one. I can spot raw talent, and Quinn had it."

Finally. Half-hearted acknowledgment of *my* contribution to my sport.

"I'm sure a big part of it was thanks to my dance background," she continued. "Did I tell you that I was still teaching classes at eight-and-a-half months pregnant? Quinn was born with rhythm!"

My stomach twisted, because the woman couldn't even get past the first question without claiming some of my spotlight.

Ben nodded like she was making a valid point. "Yes, you did mention how long you danced while pregnant. Very impressive." He shifted to face my father. "Tim, talk to me about how you'll feel hearing your daughter's name called out at the medal ceremony."

He let out a whistle. "Oh, man. I'd call it a full circle moment. When she was just starting out I asked her what she wanted to be when she grew up, and I remember her answer clear as day. She said, 'Daddy, I want to be an Olympic gold medalist.' That was at eight years old! Her passion and determination have been there from the start. Watching her win will be really emotional for me."

I remembered that conversation. He'd said, "You can do anything," and I believed him. I knew that his support was there, even if he didn't manage to show it in obvious ways.

"Exactly," my mom added. "I really thought it was going to happen for us in Switzerland. How lucky are we that we get a second chance?"

Ben flicked his eyes to me and I gave him a tight-lipped grin in response. I was okay for now.

"I mean, I wish *I* was lucky enough to get a second chance, but it didn't work out for me. So watching Quinn live out her dream will have to do."

My heartbeat slowed. Tricia always had an angle that I could usually figure out, but it felt like this one was new.

"Well, you said your dance studio is at capacity with a waiting list, right? It sounds like it's a very successful business," Ben said cautiously, like he could tell that he was on unsteady ground.

"Yes, the Tricia Albright Academy of Dance is the most successful studio in the entire state of Connecticut."

An uncertifiable distinction, but who would dare question it?

"But there's more to the story," she continued coyly. "I guess you could call it an exclusive, just for you."

I swallowed hard. Where the hell was this going? I glanced over at my dad, but he was just smiling blandly with a blank stare, physically in the room but mentally on the golf course.

"Okay . . ." Ben said slowly. "Let's hear it."

My mom recrossed her legs and stared off into the distance. "This is a little hard for me to talk about . . . it was a long time ago but it still hurts, you know?" She managed to make frowning look pretty. "I've always been a gifted dancer. My goal was to pursue dance as a career, on the stage. I'd always wanted to be a Rockette. They're so poised and beautiful! So I auditioned. I knew I had a decent shot, but the competition was *fierce*. I couldn't quite believe it when I made it through the screening audition, then the next one, and the following, and then the final cut."

The *Rockettes*? As she spoke I felt my body starting to tremble. I thought I knew all her stories—I'd always been her captive audience—so what the hell was happening? I slowly moved my hands under my thighs, to try to stop the shaking.

"I couldn't believe that I made it. I was going to be a Rockette! You can't even imagine how excited I was."

She was never a Rockette. My dad reached over to squeeze her hand.

"Wow," Ben answered. "Quite an honor."

"Oh my lord, I was *thrilled*," my mom laughed. "A dream realized. But then . . ."

She trailed off and sniffled again. I could feel her staring at me, like we were in a play and I'd just missed a critical stage direction.

"Then I got an even bigger surprise; I found out that I was pregnant with this one." She slipped her hand over to cradle the side of my head and forced me close for a quick kiss on my temple. I had no idea what my face was doing in response but it probably wasn't cute.

"So my dream just, *poof*, disappeared." Her voice trembled but she smiled.

I felt clammy, like I was coming down with the flu as I figured out that I was my mother's dream stealer. My very presence was a reminder of everything she had to give up. In her eyes, I was to blame for her derailed future.

She'd had so many opportunities to let me in on this important part of her backstory but she'd kept it to herself, like she *knew* that she'd eventually have the perfect stage and spotlight for a dramatic reveal.

Her ability to direct my life would never end, it seemed.

"Replaced with a new dream, I assume," Ben replied. "A much more important one."

A beat, as my mom seemed to process that having a child was more meaningful than being a high-kick dancer.

"Yes, yes, of *course*," she insisted. "Quinn was my new life's passion. Her dreams became mine. And I tried my hardest to help get her to the top of the podium in Switzerland, but she didn't even win bronze. We were all *so* disappointed, me more so than her, I think. Mistakes were made—"

"But the good news is her chances for gold in Milan are strong." Ben interrupted her, like he knew exactly where the conversation was going. "America loves a comeback story, and Quinn is poised to deliver an incredible one." He focused on me. "Quinn, how will it feel to stand on that stage and see your parents out in the crowd, cheering you on as you're awarded the gold medal?"

I froze. Since the split with my old team, it hadn't even been a consideration, other than the feelings of superiority I knew I'd have for doing it on my own terms. I needed to manufacture a TV-ready, sappy response. The short interview already had me wrung out and buzzing on adrenaline at the same time, a nasty soup of emotions that didn't tee me up to be generous with my mother.

At least Ben had put me in control. I decided to use my Uno Reverse Card to end the torture.

"Oh my gosh," I began, trying to look appropriately awestruck at the idea. "I can totally picture that moment."

It was a white lie, and a nod to the visualization he'd led me through on the plane.

"It's tough to put words to the feeling," I admitted as both my parents stared at me. I focused on Ben instead, my surprise port in the storm. "I think I'll feel incredibly honored to represent my country. Relieved that all my hard work paid off. Joyful that I achieved a lifelong goal. And thankful that I had the support of my parents when I was just starting out."

I emphasized the time frame, because my mom's support morphed into intense pressure as the years rolled on, and that was nothing to be thankful for.

Ben nodded at me to signify that I was doing okay.

"I have *so* many emotions spiraling through me at the thought of winning gold," I laughed and hoped it didn't sound as fake as it felt.

It took a few seconds for him to make the connection that I'd invoked our safe word. I saw him snap out of interviewer mode to briefly acknowledge it, then just as quickly morph back into professional Ben.

"I can only imagine," he agreed. "The entire world is excited to watch your journey, Quinn. Tim, Tricia, thank you so much for sitting down with us today." He smiled at us and froze for a few seconds, then seemed to dim his wattage to normal levels again. "Okay, that's a wrap for the Albrights. Thank you so much for doing this, guys, you were great."

Neil and Hailey sprang into action, moving toward us to collect the mics.

"Wait, that's it?" my mom asked, sounding very disappointed.

"Yeah, you were perfect, we got everything we needed and then some," Ben answered. "And anyway, look." He pointed out the window to the snow just starting to come down. "The storm is here."

But what Ben didn't realize is he'd helped me weather an even bigger one.

Chapter Twenty-Three

I pulled my new license out of my wallet to obsess about the photo again.

"Was it the lighting?" I asked quietly. "The camera? Because this might be the best picture ever taken of me."

Ben dared to take his eyes off the icy road ahead of us for a second to glance over at me. "What are you talking about? You look gorgeous in every photo, and the fact that you can make a mugshot look like it belongs in a modeling portfolio proves it."

Despite the turmoil of the past few hours and the stress ahead of me, I actually looked pretty darn happy in the photo. Maybe it was because Ben had stood behind the glum guy taking it and made faces at me? How could I not laugh?

I slid it back in my wallet. "Thank you for making me go get it today. They're definitely going to be closed tomorrow if this keeps up."

The snow had started like someone upstairs flicked a switch. There was no slow lead-up to the heart of the squall; from the moment the flakes started coming down it was an intense, serious storm.

Which Ben was now expertly navigating despite the occasional black ice on the road.

I was wrung out after the interview with my parents but Ben had insisted we get my license before the DMV closed for the day, and we wound up making it minutes before they closed at five thirty. It was a scramble to get everything packed up and drop Hailey and Neil at the inn, but I appreciated that our rushing prevented me from having to go through a prolonged goodbye with my mom. The next time I'd see her would be in Italy.

"So can we talk about it now?" Ben asked me. "The interview?"

The rhythmic *thwack* of the windshield wipers filled the silence while I considered it.

"High level, sure. But I'm not in the mood for a therapy session." Even though I knew how good Ben was at it.

"Did you know about the Rockettes stuff?"

"Nope." I shook my head and fought off queasy feelings. "That was a bombshell that I'm sure she loved dropping on me."

"Does it bother you?"

I hadn't had the time to process it yet and I wasn't sure I'd ever want to. "Not that she had to quit, because it wasn't my fault. But if I'd known about it before it might've helped contextualize our relationship."

"It sure does explain a ton. Can I make an armchair diagnosis?"

I glanced over at him. "Are you qualified?"

He smiled. "I mean, I got my PhD from Reddit University, so not exactly. But based on my research I'd say your mom is a textbook narcissist."

"Yeah, thanks to my therapist I came to that conclusion as well. It helps to have a framework for her behavior, but it doesn't make living with it any easier."

Ben glanced at me again, his eyes soft in the fading light. "I'm sorry."

He watched me for so long that I worried we might drift into a snowbank and get stuck together forever.

Which wouldn't be the worst thing.

"Consider yourself lucky that you had normal parents," I said, trying to make light of my trauma. "Wait, you *did* have normal parents, right? That wasn't all for show?"

A single nod as he finally refocused on the road. "My parents were great. *Are* great. Zero complaints."

I wasn't going to let him sidestep my attempt to get him to open up.

"That must've been a huge help as you transitioned to regular civilian life," I said. "Having them in your corner."

I studied his profile and caught the frowning jaw flex.

"What?" I asked.

He answered with a long sigh. "It's complicated. There's just a lot you don't know about that period of my life. Talking about it makes me look . . ."

I held my breath as he searched for the right word.

"*Weak.*"

"Ben, no," I began, but I stopped myself just as quickly, because I didn't want to sound like I didn't believe his pain. "I mean, I get it. You're an incredibly strong person who was facing down an unimaginable challenge. Of course you faltered a little."

"Faltered," he repeated as he coughed out a laugh. "Oh, it was *so* much more than that. You probably think I just had a little too much fun, right? The gold medal playboy and his drinking problem." He opened his mouth to keep going then shut it abruptly.

"What?"

Ben looked over again and the pain in his expression made him almost unrecognizable to me. "Quinn, I couldn't get out of bed. For *months*."

It was my turn to flap my mouth open and closed like a fish on dry land.

"Disgusting, right?" Ben asked with another harsh laugh.

"No," I replied immediately. My hand snaked over to his shoulder reflexively and squeezed it. "Understandable."

"But it's *not*," he insisted. "I had everything. A great team and coach, amazing parents, financial security, and more gold medals than any human needs. Instead of celebrating it, I curled up in my apartment and tried to sleep and drink my days away." He shook his head. "Do you have any idea how embarrassing it was? But I was powerless against the black dog."

"I'm sorry? The what?"

"The black dog. Depression. I think the phrase started with Churchill. It's easier to call it that rather than what it actually was. No one wants to say, "I have depression.""

I was coming to understand that the post-Olympic dip was bigger and deeper than I realized.

"But you got help," I said quietly.

"I did. But not before my little breakdown put my entire career in jeopardy. I lost a couple of brand deals, my sports agent quit." Ben snorted. "Pretty shocking that more of it didn't end up in the press. The world just got the topline story of 'out-of-control athlete,' which is a hell of a lot more palatable than 'athlete undergoing a mental health crisis.' It's like a shameful secret that these superhuman machines have real feelings. We grieve, we bleed, but no one seems to give a shit about our feelings unless we win. Go figure."

I fought through my jumble of selfish emotions to find a response, because I totally understood what he meant, but I didn't want to make the conversation about me now that he was finally opening up.

"I had no idea. I'm so sorry," I said.

Ben's revelation had me rethinking everything I thought I understood about what happened, or *didn't* happen, after Switzerland. All I'd focused on was the way he was letting me down in my time of need without even pausing to think about what he was going through.

"Gross, right?" Ben said, like he was trying to play off the reveal.

"Ben, no. I wish I'd known."

"Nope." He shook his head. "You were dealing with your own demons. But now we're older and wiser. Some of us are *much* older."

"And we have the tools to process everything now? Yes?"

"I fucking hope so," Ben replied. "I never want to feel like that again."

He leaned closer to the windshield because the ice around the edges was encroaching despite the furious windshield wiping.

We drove in silence for the remainder of the trip, partly because I didn't want to be a distraction but mainly because I was trying to process what Ben had revealed to me. The light was fading and the bleak horizon made it seem like the snow was coming down even harder.

"Are you holding up okay?" I asked as we reached the final leg of the drive.

"I will be once we get there, which at twenty miles per hour, might wind up being tomorrow."

I squeezed my eyes shut. "Tomorrow. Ugh, I can't believe we might get stuck here. I did *not* plan for this."

Anxiety swirled up in my chest. I'd tried to ignore the possibility of an extra day in Connecticut, because interruptions to my routine felt like nails in my coffin. The countdown to Italy was now measured in weeks, not months, and each training day was meticulously planned to the minute. I'd been okay with an overnight, but the thought of being stuck longer meant I probably wouldn't be sleeping thanks to my training anxiety.

Which also stressed me out, because overnight recovery was critical.

"*Fuck*," I said under my breath as I pictured all the ways my progress would now be derailed.

"What?"

"Two full days off . . ."

"No, hold on, recalculate that. You didn't train today, but if we wind up getting stuck there's plenty you can do tomorrow. You've got your sneakers, and there's a conference room at the inn where you can work out. Sure, it's off-ice, but it still counts."

"Every day that I'm not on the ice is a setback that I clearly can't afford."

Ben adjusted his grip on the steering wheel. "If you keep telling yourself that you'll be correct. But if you reframe this little adventure as a chance to recharge and switch things up, then you'll be fine. Consistency is important, but so is a little novelty. Muscle confusion can benefit you."

The car skidded into the other lane but Ben righted it without missing a beat.

"I lost a full week of training time two months before Switzerland. Hip strain so painful that it made me want to cry. I was forced to focus on PT and mental training, which, if you listen to sports psychologists, is almost as important as the physical stuff.

The absolute *worst* thing to do in this scenario is freak out." He paused to swerve around an abandoned car parked haphazardly on the side of the road. "You know I'm right."

I chuckled. *There* was the Ben I knew.

We finally pulled up to the inn. Ben let out a long sigh and shook his hands. "That was really fucking stressful. I think every muscle is in knots."

"Well, now you can go to your room and relax," I answered as my brain conjured up images of Ben spread out in bed in his boxers.

Ben spread out in bed *out of* his boxers.

Yeah, I probably wasn't going to be sleeping much tonight.

Chapter Twenty-Four

*B*en's phone pinged and he paused to read it before getting out of the car. "Hold up, change of plans. We're going sledding."

"I'm *sorry*? We're doing what?"

Again with the assumptive "we."

He held up his phone. "Hailey just texted me, she and Neil said the manager gave them two sleds and they're on the hill behind the inn. She said they're having a blast."

I frowned. "Together?"

"I know, right? There's something weird going on between those two. Let's go investigate."

As much as I didn't want to do anything but go to my room and sulk about my trashed schedule, part of me wasn't ready to say goodnight to Ben yet.

"But I don't have boots," I protested. "My shoes will get ruined."

"Trust me. Come on."

We grabbed our luggage from beneath the piled-up equipment and headed inside, tiptoeing through the snow piled on the walk-way. Fifteen minutes later Ben had charmed the inn manager into giving us four powder-room trash bags and rubber bands to cover our shoes. We looked absolutely ridiculous, but I had to hand it to him; my shoes were totally protected.

I gave the cozy fireplace in the lobby a wistful glance, pulled my cashmere hat down over my ears, and headed back into the cold.

"There they are," Ben said, pointing to the top of the hill.

It was the perfect sledding spot, a wide-open space between two groves of pine trees, with a gentle slope and a long runway. Somehow the moon managed to fight through the snow clouds, casting an otherworldly glow on the area. I could hear Neil's and Hailey's laughter echoing in the distance as they raced down the hill side by side.

"C'mon," Ben said, grinning up at them like a kid. He grabbed my mittened hand and dragged me along behind him.

The drifts were already at my mid-calf, so that, combined with the makeshift snow boots, made for slow going. Ben didn't let go of my hand as we made our way over to where the two of them were waiting at the bottom of the hill.

"Hey there, glad you came. It's perfect snow for sledding," Neil said when we reached them. "I'd say we earned this fun."

The only thing I usually earned was rest and recovery, especially lately.

Hailey handed her sled to me, and the four of us trudged up the hill together. I pretended that the long walk up counted as part of my daily workout.

"Let's race," she said. "You guys against us."

I looked down the hill, which from the top was much steeper than I'd realized. "Is it safe?"

Ben was already getting in position beside Neil, his competitive spirit engaged. "*I'll* keep you safe. Get over here."

A chill raced up my back that had nothing to do with the

cold. Ben had issued an order and I felt like I had no choice but to listen.

I stared at the red plastic thing. "Should I be in the front or back?"

"My buddy Kevin was a Team USA bobsledding pilot and he told me that heaviest always rides in back, so that's me."

Ben dropped onto it and adjusted himself to make room for me.

I stared at him for a beat, because I was about to press myself between his legs. Not the worst place to be . . .

"Please don't crash," I said as I gingerly lowered myself onto the front of the sled.

"Never," he murmured as he scooted from side to side to accommodate me. "I have precious cargo."

If there had been a fainting couch nearby I would've collapsed onto it from the tenderness in his voice.

In my everyday life I would never, *ever* opt to go sledding in a snowstorm, but Ben kept gentling me into unexpected scenarios. It was an adjustment to shut off my training brain and allow fun to take the wheel for a change.

"Move back," he ordered. "We need to shift the center of gravity for maximum speed. I'm not letting those two dorks beat us."

I took a deep breath and pushed myself backward until I was pressed up against him. He braced his legs against mine, solid and strong, and then wrapped his arms around my waist. He gave me a squeeze.

"You hold on to the handles and I'll hold on to you."

I melted the moment he tightened his grip around me. I didn't realize how hungry I was for real, welcomed physical contact until I was embraced by it. Ben's arms felt as trustworthy as a seat belt, vital since I couldn't risk an injury.

Ben, for his part, seemed more focused on winning, which, no surprise. He and Neil worked out the timing of the countdown and I realized I was giggling before the sleds even moved, half from nerves and half from the sensation of being pressed against Ben's shockingly warm body.

"Ready . . . set . . . *go!*"

Ben let go of me to paddle his hands through the snow to give us an advantage, then circled me in a vise grip again as we started to descend.

And then we were flying.

I could not only hear him laughing behind me as we sped down the hill, I could *feel* his entire body shaking with it, which made me giggle along with him. His laugh was loud and from his belly, a full-throated, joyful sound that magnified the magic of tearing through the snowy darkness. We careered down the hill, coming close to running into Neil and Hailey.

She raised a fist at us as we pulled ahead.

The snow felt like little ice pellets hitting me in the face, which meant we were now dealing with a wintry mix. I forced myself to be in the moment and not think about what it would do to our travel plans the next day.

Neil and Hailey started to catch up to us so Ben let go of me to paddle again. The sudden weight shift made us fishtail, and when he tried to straighten us out he overcompensated, sending us flying through the air, ass over head.

We landed hard, but I'd spent my life falling on ice so the impact didn't even register. I wound up with a face full of snow as Neil and Hailey flew past us. The shock of the spill left me laughing and disoriented, until I realized that I was pinned beneath him.

"Are you okay?" Ben asked. He gently swept his gloved hand over my cheeks and eyes to clear the dusting away.

He was heavy on top of me, but I welcomed the sensation. His warmth grounded me, like he was a weighted blanket. But the way he was looking down at me made me feel like we were still cartwheeling through space.

"I'm fine," I agreed softly, even though my nerves were now humming with a need I'd been working hard to suppress.

"No injuries to report?"

His face was dangerously close to mine, scanning me with his usual ground-shifting intensity that never failed to leave me a little breathless.

"All good," I managed.

"I guess we lost," he said, still focused on me.

I no longer sensed the cold, and I wondered if the snow was melting beneath our bodies.

"Doesn't seem like it," I murmured, feeling bold.

I'd had the chance to study him up close once before, right as he leaned in close to kiss me by the bonfire. This time around I felt like I had the luxury of time to catalog his features, since there was little chance of a repeat performance of that fateful first kiss thanks to our agreement. In a few seconds we'd be back to sledding buddies.

But for now I could relish drinking in the way his beautiful face looked as he stared at me.

Ben's handsomeness was undeniable, but his real gift was his ability to mesmerize, like a sea creature that dazzled prey right into its mouth. I felt powerless to do anything but let him lure me closer.

"You're cold." He gazed down at me.

"I'm not," I insisted.

Our little puffs of icy breath air mingled between us.

"But you're trembling."

We both knew the real reason why. He was maintaining a boundary I now wished we'd never established.

I answered Ben with the tiniest shrug, like I was afraid if I shifted my body too much he might assume that I was trying to get him off me.

Neil and Hailey sounded very far away. We were basically alone in the dark.

Ben was doing to me exactly what he did to every other woman he encountered, and I was falling for it. The dark eyes locked on my face, the tiny smile that made me feel like we were sharing a private joke . . . every defense I'd built up was now in a pile of rubble.

What was going to happen next seemed obvious to both of us. Inevitable, even.

Normally, prolonged, silent eye contact would feel weird. With Ben, it was a prologue.

"What would happen if I kissed you? Right now?" Ben finally asked me, his voice soft and ragged. "Because I really want to."

My pulse sped to triple time.

"I think we should find out."

Chapter Twenty-Five

*H*e paused to scan my face again, like he wanted to confirm what I'd said, while every molecule in my body screamed *DO IT*.

It was a mistake, we both knew it, but the magnetic pull between our bodies was canceling out logic. I knew I'd regret kissing him, or letting myself be kissed by him, but I wasn't about to stop it from happening.

He leaned down to whisper in my ear. "I need you to know that I've been hoping for the chance to do this again for the past four years."

I couldn't blame my goose bumps on the snow.

"I don't believe you," I whispered back.

The moment stretched on while we both seemed to weigh what a kiss could mean.

After a lifetime on the ice the two of us were nearly immune to the cold, so it made sense that we could lay in snowdrifts like it was a day at the beach. My pulse thrummed in my ears as I waited for what was to come next. As much as I wanted to wriggle my body so that I could drape my legs over the back of his and lock my hands behind his neck, I was afraid to do anything that might break the spell.

"Are you guys dead?"

We'd been too wrapped up in each other to hear the unmistakable sound of footsteps crunching on snow. Neil's voice startled me enough that I somehow summoned the strength to push Ben off me with enough force that he landed beside me with a thud. I sat up and tried to pretend that I was a normal, functioning human and not someone dealing with near-kiss aftershocks.

"We crashed," Ben answered as he sat up next to me, totally unfazed.

"Clearly," Hailey replied. "Any injuries to report? Because we're not going to get an ambulance out here thanks to the weather, but I can be a field medic."

"I think Ben was doing a full body scan on Quinn when we walked over." Neil cocked an eyebrow at us. "Is she going to make it, doctor?"

It took all my strength not to make a crack about how cozy the two of them seemed.

"Not sure. Quinn, you good?" Ben asked me.

We both went quiet for a beat, because neither of us was okay after what almost happened.

"Still in once piece."

"Another run, then?" Neil asked.

Ben looked at me, hopeful, but I shook my head. I didn't trust myself enough to sit between Ben's thighs again.

"No, I'm done, you guys take our sled."

"Oh, uh," Hailey shot a look at Neil. "That's okay, you keep it. I think we go faster with the two of us on one."

I hid a smile. "Right, okay."

"Wait for us, we need to figure out dinner," Neil called over his shoulder as the two of them started walking away. "We'll be back."

We both turned to watch them trudge up the hill, silently considering what they'd interrupted.

"Probably a good thing they showed up," Ben finally said in a quiet voice. "We both have too much to lose."

"Agreed," I admitted quietly. I closed my eyes, partly because the snowflakes kept getting caught in my lashes, but mainly because looking at him sort of hurt. "And you have to maintain your journalistic integrity."

"Yup," Ben said. "Duty calls."

Neil and Hailey went tearing by us in the sled, whooping with laughter. It made me envious of their freedom.

We watched their successful run and then their slow return up to the midpoint of the hill, where we were still camped out on the snow nursing our aftershocks.

"It sure is taking them a long time to get back here," Ben said.

They looked like they weren't moving at all, two parallel, hovering shadows.

"But then again . . . be not afraid of going slowly, be afraid of standing still," he added.

"Oh, okay, coach." I said sarcastically. I glanced down the hill to watch them. "Wait a sec. Are they . . . holding hands?"

"Fuck," Ben said. "They are, and the show has a strict nonfraternization policy."

Securing my own happily ever after wasn't even a consideration, but I wasn't about to stand in the way of anyone else's, even if I didn't understand the pairing.

"Well, if you think you saw them holding hands, no you didn't," I said. I got up slowly.

"Maybe he's helping her, because it's icy?"

"Maybe," I agreed.

The mention of ice was a bitch slap of reality. We probably weren't leaving tomorrow, at least not on our original flight at eleven.

Neil and Hailey finally reached us, no longer holding hands and a safe distance apart.

"How are the rooms?" Ben asked as we started back toward the inn.

"Shockingly nice, considering how old-timey it looks from the outside," Hailey replied. "Not one haunted doll or doily to be found. We're on the second floor, and I think you two are on the third."

I hoped at opposite ends of the building.

"Any ideas for dinner?" Hailey asked. "I'm starving and it's not like we have a ton of options with the weather."

"There's a pizza place within walking distance," I answered. "It was still open when we drove by."

"Perfect," Ben answered. "The men will brave the elements to go get it."

"And I was thinking maybe we could screen a little of what we've captured so far while we eat," Neil said. "It's looking really good, if I may say so."

"I can get us set up in your room if you want," Hailey volunteered.

They exchanged a quick look. "That works. It's open on my laptop. Room two fourteen." He reached into an interior pocket in his coat and pulled out an actual key with a heavy brass keychain.

Once I'd ditched my bag-boots in the lobby and made it up to the third floor I discovered that my room was *not* on the opposite end of the building from Ben's. In fact, ours were the only two rooms on the whole floor.

I pulled off my wet jeans and slid on sweats and a hoodie. I was tired enough to fall into bed for the night, but I was also hungry and insanely curious about how the show was shaping up. I padded down the back stairs in my socks to the second floor.

Hailey welcomed me into Neil's room like it was her own.

"I think you're going to like what we've got so far," she said. "Come."

She led me over to the desk, where his laptop was set up, and grabbed a second chair for me.

"Should we wait?" I asked.

"Nope, let's go. My fingerprints are all over this edit, don't let Neil convince you it's his baby. And Ben still needs to take a crack at it. *And* the producers. They get final approval."

My stomach twisted. I'd come to trust the team, but who knew what the big guys would do to the footage?

"Ready?"

I nodded, and she pushed play.

And there was Mel, in profile and shot from a distance with me hazy in the background, spinning on the ice. It looked cinematic.

"Wow," I breathed.

"That was all me," Hailey puffed up with pride. "My vision."

"Neil let you?" I joked.

"He has his moments," she replied, keeping her eyes on the screen. "I'm not sure why the sound isn't working." She smacked the keys, becoming increasingly frustrated. "Don't worry, it's a me thing, not a footage thing. I'm not used to his laptop yet."

"I actually prefer no sound," I said.

The footage at the rink cut to a close-up of Zoey.

"Aw, she looks *adorable*." I put my elbows on the desk and leaned closer.

I watched my friend speak animatedly, probably saying nice things about me. Yeah, I definitely didn't want to hear it yet. Accepting compliments still wasn't easy for me, because I'd been taught that flattery led to ego, and ego led to failure.

An abrupt cut to me at Greta's studio. I jumped and covered my eyes. "Oof."

"What? You look incredible."

"I don't like watching myself off-ice."

Because even after all these years, I could hear the laundry list of things that weren't quite right.

The footage jumped to me in the "Movement" costume at Greta's studio, looking at myself in the mirror. There were glimpses of Greta as she bustled around me, but the focus of the shot was tight on my face and slowly moving closer.

It was like a voyeur was looking at me while I looked at myself. An intimate moment snagged without my knowledge, like the camera was a secret admirer.

"It's so close," I said quietly.

But I didn't hate it. I looked . . . beautiful.

"That was all Ben," Hailey explained. "He pushed Neil out of the way to get it."

I hadn't noticed Ben behind the camera while we were at the studio. Hell, I didn't realize that he even knew how to operate one, yet what he'd captured was perfect.

"Okay, I've seen enough."

"Are you sure?" Hailey asked. "We also started roughing the footage from today, with your parents—"

"Yikes." I shook my head. "No thanks, I'm good."

Because I *finally* believed that my story would be well told.

All thanks to the one person I swore I'd never trust again.

Chapter Twenty-Six

*T*hey'd teased me into watching a little more footage once Ben and Neil got back with the pizzas. All of it felt lovingly captured, even without the sound, which I'd forced them to leave turned off.

"Okay, that's enough for me," I said. "It looks great. Thank you."

"We're so close to the finish line," Neil said. "Just your interview, then you're rid of us until Italy."

"Speaking of that final interview," Hailey said. "It looks like we're going to need to revisit the schedule since our flight is messed up."

My stomach dropped. "It's canceled?"

She looked down to study her phone. "Delayed until six. At least for now."

Which meant I'd lose another day on the ice.

The original plan was for us to fly back, then they'd set up at the rink while I banged out a practice session, after which I'd sit down with Ben for the final solo interview. Getting home after eight meant no time for either.

"I have a feeling we'll be okay by the afternoon," Ben said. "The snow is tapering off, and if you look at the forecast it's going to be sunny after ten tomorrow."

That was Ben, ever the optimist.

"And I have an idea for the final interview," he added.

I was exhausted and ready to go comatose in my bed but I perked up at the mention of our remaining interview. "Oh?"

Neil and Hailey seemed equally curious.

"Well, now you've gotta tell us. No cliffhangers," Neil said.

"Since the flight is delayed, we're doing it here," Ben said. "Tomorrow, while we wait to leave." He turned to me. "That is, if it's okay with you."

Worry bloomed in my chest. I knew it was coming, but *tomorrow*?

"Hold on," Hailey said. "We agreed to stick to a schedule and this is a giant deviation."

"Act of God," Neil replied, pointing out the snowy window.

"But do you have anything else to wear, Quinn?" Hailey asked me, ever the ally. "And did you pack makeup and stuff?"

"I have other clothing . . ." I'd learned the hard way to always have options. "But . . ."

"No, actually it's perfect," Neil interrupted. "If we knock out the final interview tomorrow we can switch our flights and just head straight to New York instead of going back to Colorado with you."

"No pressure, though," Ben added.

With the three of them staring at me expectantly I felt plenty of pressure. It made sense. Getting the final interview over with would free all of us up. I should've jumped at the opportunity to put it behind me, but that would mean the end of whatever was happening with Ben. Thanks to our little sledding moment, our connection felt like an entirely new beast to be tamed.

"We can set up in the conference room and knock it out first thing tomorrow, which'll free you up to train until we have to leave," Ben added.

I didn't love the shift, but it made sense.

"Okay. I'm in," I finally said.

"Excellent." Ben bobbed his head. "Can we make eight happen? A quick breakfast then we get going?"

"Definitely. We'll be set and ready to go at seven forty-five," Neil answered. "Then we can pack up the second flights open up again."

"Aw," Hailey stuck out her bottom lip. "What a jump cut. I can't believe we'll be done tomorrow. This was a super fun trip."

She shot a look at Neil, and I felt like I could take a little credit for the new love match.

A wave of exhaustion washed over me out of nowhere, so intense that I wondered if there was tryptophan in mozzarella cheese. But then again, the weariness made sense given our nonstop, emotionally draining day.

"Guys, I'm out." I tried to stifle a yawn that just kept getting bigger. "Thanks for everything today."

It was still hard to believe how much we'd crammed into it. Had I really been sitting between my parents just a few hours before?

"Yeah, same. I'll walk up with you," Ben said. He turned back to the laptop and punched a few keys then high-fived Neil. "Be done for tonight, okay? Get some rest."

"Oh don't worry, I'm ready for bed," Neil agreed.

"Same," Hailey added, although she sounded more amped than exhausted.

Ben and I walked out together and headed up the narrow staircase to our rooms one floor up.

"You feel okay? About the footage?"

I glanced over my shoulder at him. "Totally. It's not what I expected."

"In a good way?"

"In the best way," I answered as I pushed through the door to our floor. "It's like a movie. I was thinking it would look more like a local news feature."

He caught up to me in the hallway. "Give us some credit. This show is one of the channel's crown jewels, they're not going to cheap out. And I've got too much on the line to deliver anything less than perfection." We paused when we got to my door. "Which you're helping to make happen." His voice dropped. "I know agreeing to do it wasn't easy for you."

It felt like the end of a date. This was the part of the evening where the obvious next step usually hovered in the air until someone bold and horny decided to make a move. It wasn't going to be me, but there was no question of what I'd do if *he* pitched it.

The air was thick with everything that was still unsaid between us.

I slapped the pocket on my hoodie looking for my room key, then my sweats. "*Damn* it. I left my key in Neil's room." I heaved a sigh and started walking back to the steps.

"Wait here, I'll go," Ben said, jogging in front of me.

There was no point trying to fight him so I slid down the wall and sat on the floor to wait. "Thank you," I called after him.

I closed my eyes, but all I could see was Ben's face watching me. A few minutes later I heard him jogging back upstairs.

"Mission accomplished?" I asked as I stood up.

Then I noticed his pained expression.

"Uhhh, not exactly," he grimaced. "I was about to knock on the door and then I heard . . . *sounds*."

I frowned at him. "They're still editing?"

"Oh, they're hard at work, just not on the show."

He widened his eyes at me and my jaw dropped.

"So they *are* . . ."

"Yup."

"And here I actually believed that they hated each other. They're great actors."

"They better be. The show's nonfraternization policy is no joke. Plus there's a noncompete. It could end really badly for them."

I hoped for their sake that they could keep their little enemies-to-lovers adventure quiet until they decided on which side of the equation they wanted to remain.

"I guess I need to go down to the front desk and get another key," I sighed.

"Uh, actually, you'd have to call the innkeeper. There's a note at the front desk that says he's only reachable by phone after eight. And with the storm . . ."

I dropped my head and sighed even harder. Not what I wanted to deal with after a marathon day.

"Just come hang out in my room. I can't imagine they'll be too long," Ben said.

I laughed despite my exhaustion. "Damn, you're not giving our buddy Neil much credit for stamina."

"I guess you're right. You might be stuck with me for a couple of hours." The way he smiled at me made me feel a little less tired.

A *lot* less tired.

Our eyes locked, like we both felt what might happen if we walked into a room with a bed.

"C'mon." He turned his back and walked down the hall, assuming I'd automatically follow behind him like a puppy.

Which was exactly what I did.

Chapter Twenty-Seven

I stood behind him as he unlocked the door and breathed in his now familiar scent. The cologne he'd put on in the morning was long gone, so what I was greedily inhaling was all Ben. He opened the door abruptly and turned around.

"After you."

Crossing the threshold into his room felt momentous. We were about to be *alone* alone without the potential for witnesses, for the first time since that night in Switzerland. The door clicking shut behind him sounded like a starter pistol.

I wasn't sure where to go once I was inside, because the desk and only chair were claimed by equipment. His room looked smaller than mine because of the sloped ceiling by the window. It seemed like the bed with the bright white bedspread filled the entire space.

"Are you hungry?" Ben asked. "Because I have apples."

"I just had two slices, which is more pizza than I've eaten in"—I tried to calculate my last forbidden dinner—"A long time. I'm good."

Normally I'd be stressing out about the deviation from my meal planning, especially with the countdown clock at full speed. Being with Ben lately had forced me to act like a normal civilian who didn't equate enjoying food with guilt.

"Sorry I don't have many seating options." He jutted his chin at the sole chair in the small room.

"I can stand."

He smiled. "Now you're the one not giving Neil enough credit."

I felt my cheeks go hot, because sex jokes landed differently in a room with a bed. I moved toward it and gingerly sat on the edge.

"I want to say make yourself comfortable but that sounds like bad seventies porn," he said as he perched on the opposite corner.

"Are you implying that there's *good* seventies porn?" I asked.

"I mean . . ." He shrugged. "That era introduced a bunch of the scenarios still in use today, so good or bad, it's got staying power."

"You're an expert in vintage porn?"

He threw his head back and cackled. "Oh, god no. But everyone knows the tropes."

"I sure don't."

"You're telling me you don't know the pizza-delivery-guy scenario," Ben asked, incredulous.

"Oh, that," I nodded sagely. "Yeah, of course."

"And the porn stache, and sax music," he added.

"Okay, maybe I know more than I realized," I laughed.

It was odd that talking about antique dirty movies finally made me feel comfortable being alone with him. It put some distance between us and the Very Big Possibility looming in front of us. Or *between* us, since we were now both stretched out on opposite sides of his bed.

But laughing about sex made it feel like whatever was simmering between us was our own trope. Two people who didn't want to admit how badly they wanted each other, alone in a hotel room with nothing to do, *ha-ha*, let the bom-chicka-wow-wow commence.

And then there was the almost-kiss just a few hours before that we were both trying to ignore.

"Hotel bedspreads are gross," Ben said. "We should take it off."

I narrowed my eyes at him. "That sounds like something someone would say in a porn."

"Oh? So you think I'm trying to seduce you by mentioning dirty linens?"

"*Are* you trying to seduce me?"

I blurted it out before I could stop myself, and my body went numb from the tidal wave of embarrassment.

"Yes," he replied. "I mean, no. But only because of—"

"The agreement," we finished in unison.

But . . . we were in the liminal space of a hotel room, during a snowstorm. A break in real life before I was back to regimented daily sameness. Maybe the rules didn't apply here? I took a deep breath as an insane idea infiltrated my good girl brain.

I sat up and leaned against the headboard. "Is it possible to amend the agreement?"

Ben tipped his head. "Depends."

It was out of character for me to even *think* it let alone say the words out loud, so I forced myself to keep going.

"Let's call it the Blizzard Clause." I prepared for mortification and pushed on. "One night. You and me. Then we never discuss it again."

Ben sat up slowly, his eyes wide from disbelief. "Quinn, hold on. We can't—"

"Why not?" I demanded.

I was so desperate for him that I didn't care that I was verging on begging him to sleep with me.

Ben looked adorably flummoxed. "Well, for all the reasons we've talked about. Focus. Distraction. Goals."

"Okay," I said, feeling like I was an attorney about to give my closing argument. I crossed my legs on the bed. "I hear you. However, we already have an agreement in place that we're doing a fine job honoring. True or false?"

"True, I guess?" Ben answered slowly.

"Exactly. Which means that if we were to introduce an amendment to it we wouldn't have a problem honoring it as well."

He frowned at me. "That's sort of a leap of logic. And there's no way I want to put anything in jeopardy, Quinn."

"Oh my god, Ben!" I smacked the bed. "Don't gatekeep sex!"

He laughed at me, which made me even more determined to prove my point.

"I'm *serious*. We agree to the Blizzard Clause, we get it out of our system, then the minute we leave Connecticut we forget it happened. Because I need you to know that this all-important 'focus' of mine that you keep mentioning? It's completely consumed by *you*."

His eyes settled on me with any levity gone. I continued with my closing appeal.

"You'd be doing me a favor," I insisted.

"By sleeping with you," he replied, incredulous.

"Yes, exactly. It would help me *recapture* my focus. One-time offer, only good for tonight," I insisted, even though I wasn't sure I agreed with that part.

I watched his profile as he grappled with what it could mean to both of us. Ben was obviously perfectly equipped to fuck and run based on his dating history, so I was sure that he was considering how guilty he'd feel if I choked in Italy due to our one glorious night.

Which, hello ego.

"I'm sure it's an exceptional penis," I assured Ben. "But it ain't magical. I'll be *fine*, I promise."

After a few seconds of silence Ben finally stood up slowly and walked around to my side of the bed.

He held his hand out to me. "I'd like to formally ratify the Blizzard Clause."

Chapter Twenty-Eight

*W*ithout a word, Ben climbed onto the bed and straddled me, his knees pressed against the outside of my thighs. My heart went slow and clumsy, like it was trying to move molasses through my veins. He held my gaze before lowering his head to brush his lips against mine, tentatively, like he was worried we were making a mistake.

Which we probably were, and neither of us cared.

The moment our lips touched I linked my hands behind his neck, so he'd understand that the Blizzard Clause was nonnegotiable.

We no longer had guardrails. Ben deepened the kiss like he'd just realized it as well, and I shivered in response.

We kissed like we'd rehearsed it, as if we'd spent the past four years nurturing what we'd started in Switzerland. I wondered if it would be strange for me to wriggle out of my sweatshirt immediately, because I was that desperate to feel his skin on mine.

Ben slid his hands under my sweatshirt and the T-shirt beneath it like he could read my mind. My body went hot, his touch a downed power line sparking along my skin.

He broke off the kiss to whisper in my ear. "Has it been obvious that not kissing you has been torture for me?"

I smiled as he pressed his lips along the side of my neck, my cheeks, my eyelids, like he needed to claim every bit of me.

"You were extremely professional," I managed as his hand traveled higher beneath my sweatshirt, smoothing along the lower side of my bra. My breath hitched as he moved his hand to palm my breast over the thin fabric.

Had I packed the sexiest black one I owned, envisioning this very scenario? Not consciously, but my subconscious clearly knew what was up.

So much of my life was spent trying to get or stay warm, but now here I was fighting to cool off, because Ben had me boiling. I pushed against him, trying to give him more access to my body, but it was no use. I arched my back and he jumped away from me, a horrified look on his face.

"I'm sorry! Did I do something wrong? Are you okay?"

Instead of answering him I sat up and pulled my sweatshirt over my head, leaving me just in my bra.

The mix of relief and awe on his face almost made me laugh out loud.

"Oh damn," he murmured. "You are . . . *perfect*."

He slid his hand behind my neck and gently drew me back to him, and then we were melting into one another again. It felt desperate and a little unhinged, and I loved it. Ben dropped his hands to my waist to shift my body and I followed his lead like I was his dance partner, moving until I was on top of him.

Like he wanted me to be in control.

I welcomed it, because I was *not* feeling tentative about what was happening. I wound up straddling him in just my bra and sweats, which still felt like too much clothing. I wordlessly reached behind me and released my bra clasp in a single motion, then slid it off.

"Oh, *fuck*, Quinn."

Ben sounded awestruck, but rather than let him admire me I lowered myself so that I was laying on top of him. Being scrutinized by the world in a barely there skating costume was a day at the office, but letting go in this kind of context was still new for me.

He slid his hands across my naked back then squeezed me, a reassurance that we were exactly where we were supposed to be. I nestled my cheek against the side of his neck as he held me close and breathed him in.

Yes, I desperately wanted to strip off all my clothes *and* his, but the embrace felt like us binding ourselves together, wordlessly conveying that beneath all the heat of the moment, we shared a tether.

In Ben's arms, I felt safe in a way I wasn't sure I'd ever experienced.

Then his lips were back on mine, and I was starving for him. All of him. I slid my hand down between our bodies to the waistband of his track pants—thank god for elastic—then his briefs, and wrapped my fingers around his hardness.

I paused at his rough exhale, still gripping him tightly.

"*Quinn.*"

He was paralyzed for a few seconds as I stroked him, until I felt his hand gliding down my stomach and beneath my sweatpants.

Then it was my turn to go breathless for a few seconds.

Ben's fingertips explored between my thighs, gently teasing me until I found myself greedily pushing against his hand, trying to tell him that there was no reason to be tentative. It was desperate, but honest. I needed him.

We moved in tandem, kissing feverishly between the moments Ben broke off to nibble and lick his way down my neck to my breasts. When his mouth found my nipple I gasped. When his tongue swept across it I heard a desperate little noise that I realized was coming from me.

I felt the sweet pressure building as Ben reached down and stroked me in smaller and smaller circles, like he was pairing his touch to my reactions. But it didn't matter what he did because every sensation left me a little dizzy and fighting to fill my lungs. I was starving for him even though he was closer than he'd ever been.

I could barely focus on what I was doing to him as Ben teased me closer to the edge, but I still gripped his cock. I wanted to make him feel as good as he was making me feel, but his fingertips made it almost impossible for me to do anything but wait for my inevitable peak and crash landing.

My lack of focused effort didn't seem to bother him at all. His quiet, strained noises made it sound like he was holding himself back from coming even though it was probably the most half-hearted hand job I'd ever given.

Then I had a flashback that made me pause. The last time we were together he'd focused on my pleasure like it was enough for him.

Not this time.

I kissed my way closer to his ear, getting more satisfied little noises from him. "You better have a condom."

He froze, his warm hand still cupped against me. "*Fuck.*"

"Yeah, that's the idea." I laughed softly and dropped my forehead to his shoulder.

"No, I'm not sure . . ." he rasped. "Fuck, fuck, fuck."

It felt impossible that Bennett Martino would travel without a case of condoms, but then again, I was starting to understand that I'd misjudged him in so many ways.

He untangled from me, trying to wrench up his track pants despite the massive hard-on. I watched him shuffle to the stack of equipment on his desk and unzip the front pocket of his backpack. I held my breath until he pulled out a worn gold foil package.

"Do they expire?" he asked as he turned it over in his hands.

"I paid attention in health class. Five-year shelf life," I said, raising an eyebrow.

"Oh, *fuck* yes," he sighed as he ripped it open.

He pulled his T-shirt over his head then slid his pants off, giving me a front-row seat to exactly why he looked so good in his skintight speed suit. The uniform didn't leave much to the imagination—I already knew about his incredible ass—but now I was treated to *all* of the body hidden beneath it. The legs, the legs, the legs . . . he was a perfectly toned specimen from top to bottom, but I couldn't stop staring at his granite thighs with the deep cut up the middle.

Then he was back on the bed, poised above me.

I raised up to kiss him as he bumped his way between my thighs, and then he pushed deep inside.

A pause to savor what we'd both been waiting for, a kiss to seal our amended agreement, and then we were moving together in rhythm. Ben didn't miss a beat as he reached over to grab a pillow and slip it beneath my hips. I'd been close to the edge before but the new angle and sweet pressure of Ben slipping in and out left me feeling feverish.

He bent down over my body to whisper in my ear. "How did I get so fucking lucky?"

I was too dizzy to reply, too close, too happy, too sweaty. And then when he reached down between my legs to make those sweet little circles again?

I shouted his name as I came.

The rush was almost too much. I clung to Ben during the aftershocks, and could feel his muscles straining as he started moving faster.

Then, a pause and shudder as he collapsed on top of me.

"Quinn . . ." he rasped against my neck between kisses. "I love doing contract renegotiations with you."

I giggled and squirmed as he hit the ticklish spot behind my ear.

Ben rolled off me, still breathing heavily. He kept his hand on my stomach, like he was trying to remind himself that I was still there as he found his way back to earth.

He rolled his head to look at me. "Sleep here."

I nodded. "But tomorrow . . ."

"I know what I agreed to," he said quickly.

We got out of bed reluctantly to clean up and found our way back to bed, and to each other. He slid under the covers in boxers and a T-shirt, while I was back in my protective hoodie and sweats.

Ben reached over to smooth my hair behind my ear, and I reflexively closed my eyes and leaned into his touch.

"You must be exhausted. Incredibly long day," he said. "C'mere."

I scooted closer to him and slotted in against his body.

"Big spoon," I murmured as I drifted off into the best sleep of my life.

Chapter Twenty-Nine

$\mathcal{T}$he library is *so* much better than the conference room," Hailey assured me as I followed her to where they'd set up for the final interview. "You're gonna love it."

Thanks to the storm it felt like we had the run of the whole inn. We knew there were other people staying as well but it seemed like everyone was opting for cozy vibes in bed instead of acting like it was a regular day. The snow had done its thing, blanketing the region in white overnight and forcing everyone to slow down, at least for a couple of hours until the plows could come through. But it was a temporary break, because the sun was already trying to cut through the gray skies.

We'd all be on our way soon enough, and it felt bittersweet, like we'd trauma-bonded through the ups and downs of our time together. Plus, I was now *very* invested in Neil and Hailey's top-secret affair. I'd liked Hailey from the jump, and Neil had grown on me, because any man open to constructive criticism couldn't be all bad.

She pushed the door to the library open and when I walked in it felt like there was a chance I'd run into a hobbit.

"Wow."

"Right?" Hailey walked backward in front of me like a TV realtor. "It's perfect."

It was, from the moss-green walls, to the floor-to-ceiling bookshelves, to the fire glowing in the hearth. The big circular window that looked out on the fields behind the inn certified it as the coziest room ever.

The two chairs with box lights shining down on them were a jarring centerpiece, but they were the reason we were in the space.

Neil walked through a door on the opposite side of the room carrying equipment. "Does this room work?"

"I never want to leave," I replied.

For a second I considered how it would feel to waste a day in the window seat, reading, daydreaming, and drinking hot chocolate.

I couldn't begin to imagine what it would be like.

"Let me get you mic'd up," Hailey said as she moved toward the setup. "You look gorgeous, by the way."

Probably because I'd had the most restorative rest of my life, nestled in Ben's arms until the sun came up. There was zero awkwardness when we woke up because we'd both slept soundly enough to miss the first alarm he'd set and had to speed through a goodbye, since we needed to get ready.

"Thank you. I have another sweater if this one doesn't read well in the room." I plucked at my pale-blue V-neck. "And is my makeup okay?" I turned so the box light was shining on my face.

Neil stopped fussing with wires to lean in next to Hailey and study me.

"Hails and I agree that you're basically the most stunning human being we've ever seen in real life," he replied, like it was a fact that he was corroborating.

"That's his way of saying that this," she waved her hand in front of my face, "is working. You look amazing."

"Thank you," I said softly.

She unwound the wires from the mic battery pack and handed it to me. "And don't worry about the interview. You've probably already picked up on it, but Ben is shockingly good at this, despite not having a background in journalism. Some people just have a knack, you know?"

Yeah, I did, because it seemed like Ben could do anything he set his mind to. If I hadn't learned to appreciate him it would've been annoying.

I paused. "Appreciate" wasn't the right word at all. No, now the way I felt about Ben was something much bigger, a feeling that I couldn't wrap my brain around to define.

"Hey, friends, good morning."

The three of us turned in unison to see Ben standing in the doorway.

"Okay, look at you," Hailey said with obvious admiration, pausing her mic'ing efforts. "I didn't think it was possible for you to level up, but somehow you managed it."

For the first time since he'd forced his way back in my life I actually allowed my heart to jig at the sight of Ben. I welcomed the butterflies swarming my belly. Our agreement was unchanged, even with the Blizzard Clause, but deep down I was nurturing tiny embers of hope that once we were on the other side of Italy, both victorious in our own ways, we'd find our way back to one another.

Ben looked . . . the only word I could come up with to describe it was *more*. More handsome, more professional, more smiley, more welcoming, more perfect than I ever thought he could be. It took real effort for me not to walk over to him and force myself into his arms.

He came over and cupped my elbow, the safest body part to touch in public. "You feeling okay? Sleep good?"

I gave him a secret smile.

"I did, actually. The beds in this place are so comfortable."

Our eyes caught, and I wondered if what we were saying without words was as obvious as it felt.

"Hey, Ben, do you want to come check out the angles?" Neil asked, pointing to the cameras. "One is pointed at Quinn's chair and two is on you."

It was another small acknowledgment that Ben wasn't just a talking head for the piece.

"Let's see what you've got," he replied as he headed over to Neil.

They had a conversation filled with words I didn't understand, and before I knew it he was mic'ed up as well and we were ready to go.

I waited for the flood of nerves to wash over me as Ben settled in the chair across from me, but all I felt was comfortable.

And shockingly happy.

I *finally* believed that my story was safe in Ben's capable hands.

"Okay, people, let's do this," Ben said. "We all have planes to catch in a few hours."

My heart sank as I realized that this time I'd be flying alone. "Is everything on time?"

"Yeah," Hailey said. "We'll be good to go by this afternoon, and you'll be back on track without us pestering you."

"Next stop, Milan," Neil added as he adjusted the lights. "Okay, I'm ready if you folks are. Can you slate, Ben?"

And we were off and running.

Ben slapped the clapperboard, took a moment to find his on-camera persona, and turned the full power of his incandescence on me.

"Quinn, tell me what you love about your sport."

The little smile, the fixed gaze, the warmth in his tone . . . every bit of it unbalanced me, but in a good way. I now knew that I could let go and not feel like I needed to be on guard.

I met his smile with my own because he'd started with a softball question. "What do I love about figure skating?"

My usual sound bite was *right* there, but I pivoted, because I wanted to give Ben my real feelings, not the same tired lines about the beauty of the sport that I'd been spitting out for years.

"I love the power of it," I replied. "People view us like these delicate little dolls, but we're hardcore athletes who are just as strong as we are graceful. We've got the endurance of a long-distance runner, and the strength of a weight lifter. Think about it—we defy gravity and fling our bodies through the air over and over, then land on a sliver of metal. On *ice*. It requires endurance and coordination unlike any other sport."

"Agreed," Ben said. "I've been skating my entire life but you've seen my sorry attempts at jumps."

Had that moment with Nate just been a few days ago? It felt like we'd been one another's shadow for way longer, in the best possible way.

"That's what I'm talking about. It's an art, but it's also a literal science. Rotational speed, friction, gravity, force of impact . . . there's a lot of math that goes into those pretty spins."

"Which you've mastered," Ben said with a nod. "You're basically Michael Jordan on ice."

I laughed at the unexpected comparison. "You think so? That's a first."

"I mean it," he insisted, shifting closer in his seat. "When you jump, you hover before landing. Gravity doesn't apply to you while you're spinning. It's like you've co-opted Jordan's hang time. I haven't seen any other skaters do it quite like you. It's beautiful."

Warmth spread in my chest. "Thank you. That might be the best compliment I've ever gotten."

"How do you make that happen? What are the mechanics of flying the way you do?" Ben asked.

"Falling a ton at first," I laughed as I admitted it. "I like to call it 'falling to learn.'"

Ben tipped his head. "What does that mean?"

"Every time I fell as I tried to master a new move, I learned something. You know, like, maybe my arms weren't pulled in tightly enough. Or maybe my takeoff was wonky. Each fall was an opportunity to dissect my mistakes, and then try it again without making them. Mel is great at zeroing in on what went wrong, and helping me figure out how to make it right."

"That's your coach, Melanie Kolakowski. Let's talk about your partnership."

"Mel," I shook my head, smiling. "She's the absolute best. We've accomplished so much since we started working together. It sounds cheesy, but I never thought a coach–athlete relationship could be like this. I, uh, wasn't always lucky enough to have the kind of support I get from Mel."

I knew exactly what I was opening myself up to by alluding to Carol. I'd never wanted to go there in prior interviews, but I felt safe with Ben. And I wanted to shine a light on what many young skaters often go through by sharing some of my story.

"What do you mean by that?" Ben probed gently, giving me the space to reverse if necessary.

I looked down at my clasped hands. "I was subjected to a fairly traditional training regime, starting at a very young age. There's a precedent for rigorous training that borders on abuse because it *works*. The podium has seen plenty of broken little girls who were taught to skate through their pain. To practice every day on an empty stomach, with just a sip of water to sustain them. It was all I knew for the longest time, so it was normalized for me. And hey, most of my friends were going through the same thing, so suck it up and skate, right? Pain fades eventually, but gold is forever."

"Ouch," Ben said softly.

"Exactly," I agreed. "And what kills me is that the oversight just isn't there, you know?" I started to say more but shut my mouth. As much as I wanted to throw a match at the governing organizations that looked the other way when athletes were hurting, now wasn't the time.

Ben picked up on my abrupt stop. "Is it safe to say that working with Coach Mel helped you rediscover your love of skating?"

Another flirtation with my past, without coming out and addressing my crash and burn.

"Oh, I never stopped loving it. Even during the tough times," I allowed. "I belong on the ice, but I definitely needed to find another way to feel at home there. Things got really bleak, as I'm sure you know. As *everyone* knows." I huffed out a hollow laugh.

His face went tight as he nodded. "But your focus is on the future. On Italy. How are you feeling about your chances?"

I wanted to jump out of my chair and kiss him on the mouth. He'd allowed me to hint at my difficulties without probing for more.

"I feel stronger than ever," I said, sitting up straighter. "I adore my programs."

"And how are you feeling about your competition? Ayumi? Beatrix?"

"Oh, they're *amazing* skaters. I love both of them. I respect their talent. But I don't focus on what everyone else is doing, you know? I'm all about bringing my best to the ice. Obsessing about other people shifts my focus."

I saw something flicker across his face. It's what we'd both been insisting since the first morning at Eagle Diner.

"Speaking of focus, there's been plenty of attention on your *skates*. Those black skates and blades. Women have skated in white skates basically forever and men in black, so why are you bucking tradition?"

"Who decided that men get to wear black and women have to wear white?" I demanded. "White skates are easier to scuff up, so why would I opt for them over black, which stay looking good basically forever? It's a silly tradition that means absolutely nothing and I'm not going to be forced to adhere to it without a good reason. I like the way black looks, and I don't think that wearing white solely because 'that's the way it's always been' is enough of a reason to do so."

"Bold stance," Ben said with an approving nod. "But I guess that's how you roll these days, right?"

"I'm glad you noticed," I laughed.

"Oh trust me, it's hard to miss."

We shared a moment that all the world would see, but somehow it felt like it was just for the two of us.

Chapter Thirty

*W*hen I picked up Ben's FaceTime call a week after Connecticut, I couldn't tell if his expression was angry or sad, but I knew for a fact that whatever had him breaking our agreed-upon low-contact scenario with just three weeks left until Italy couldn't be good. We'd mapped out a communication strategy that worked for both of us; occasional texts and nothing more until I was post-events in Italy and he'd locked down his position at *The Score*.

"Sorry for calling," he said, his eyebrows pinching closer. "Is now an okay time to talk?"

My mouth went dry. I was on the couch after a grueling day, strapped into my massage compression pants. It was supposed to be my recharge time, not processing whatever had Ben all stressed out.

"What's wrong?" My stomach twisted preemptively.

I came up with a million scenarios as I waited for him to say something.

"So, the trailers for your show are going to start airing tomorrow. I, uh . . . need to go over some stuff with you."

His face went even more pained. It didn't compute, because Ben always managed to find the sunshine in every scenario.

"You know that you and I were on the same page about the story we were telling, right?"

The joy of seeing him kept bubbling up inside me despite all the red flags from what he was saying. My body repeatedly tried to remind me that it was *Ben*, yay, you're happy! The tingly, excited feelings went to war with whatever worry was creasing his face.

"I do," I answered in a shaky voice. "Why? Did something happen?"

He nodded, his expression tightening even more. "They changed my edit. Without my knowledge or permission."

I felt my face collapse into a frown that matched his. "But I was there for like eighty percent of filming and I was totally comfortable with everything. The only part that was dicey was the solo interview you did with my parents."

"Which I managed like a conductor." Ben leaned closer to the screen and lowered his voice. "And I deleted any footage that was questionable. Let's just say that your mom won't get all of the airtime she's hoping for, because a good part of her interview disappeared. Somehow. Which is a major editorial transparency breach."

"Wait, are you serious?"

He nodded, looking grim. "I didn't get rid of anything that could change the narrative. I was just making sure that your story remained yours, the way you want to tell it."

"But isn't that like, tampering? Can you get in trouble for it?"

"If they find out, yeah, I could. There's probably something about content ownership in the contract I signed, plus there's possible reputation damage to me if it gets out. Neil, Hailey, and I agreed to keep the deletions to ourselves." He paused. "After a conversation about their own little ethical breach."

"You threatened to *expose* them?" My head started spinning at the developing soap opera.

"God no, no threats. I just pointed out how we were all sidestepping the rules in our own ways."

I much preferred him Mister Rogers–ing them to a conclusion over strong-arming them.

"So how bad is it? The edit?"

He frowned as he considered it. "I'm going to be honest; the trailer sucks. It starts with the Switzerland falling footage, and you crying. There's a cut to your mom and Carol looking very unhappy."

I could picture the moment he meant. My entire body started trembling. "Fuck."

"And then there's the ominous voice-over they used."

"Are you *serious*?"

"Yeah, it's not great. But don't worry too much, because the show itself isn't as shit as it could be given the way they positioned it in the trailer. They wanted me to do voice-over to include more 2022 backstory and I refused, so they cut it in anyway with captions."

I started spiraling, trying to sift through the competing emotions inside me. Anger at myself for believing that the show wouldn't retrigger me, fear about how it would make me look as I headed into the most critical weeks of my career, and worry about what Ben had put on the line to keep his promise to me.

"Are they upset at you?"

He gazed off-screen. "I'm not sure. Communication has been limited. But we signed a contract so I'm still going to Italy." He paused to give me a half smile. "Wahoo."

"I'm sorry," I said quietly.

He jerked backward. "For *what*? I owe you an apology for letting it get out of my hands."

"But you broke rules for me. And you're putting your future with the show on the line . . ."

"Listen, I was very clear about my angle for the story, and they agreed to it. I used my own experiences as an example of how challenging this type of coverage can be, especially so close to the games. They had no problem with how I pitched it. So it all comes down to the fact that I was honest and they weren't."

We both fell silent, staring at each other through the screen.

"Should I skip it?" I finally asked him. "Mel and I were planning to have a little watch party with Zoey."

His jaw flexed. "Hard to say because there's still *so* much good in it. I'm really fucking proud of what we made. It's a strong show. But . . ." He swallowed hard.

"Say it," I demanded.

"Quinn, what happened in Switzerland was awful, but it *is* part of your story. And while I wouldn't have presented it the way they did, it's still something that had to be acknowledged. Like it or not, you're living a comeback story."

He paused to check in with me and I managed a nod.

"If you can tolerate four minutes of bullshit out of sixty minutes of brilliance, then I think you should watch," he continued. "Because every other part of the show is beautiful and inspiring. And so is your story."

My eyes welled up. "Thank you."

His face went soft with concern for me. "Remember, the trailers are sensationalized to get people to tune in."

I sniffled and nodded.

"You okay?" Ben asked.

"I don't have a choice. I have to be," I answered. "It's the athlete's way, right?"

"The harder the battle, the sweeter the victory," Ben agreed.

There he was, coming in with the coach-y dad-isms again. Shockingly, I didn't hate it.

"I miss you," I blurted out. "I keep thinking I'm going to come out of a spin and spot you in the players' box sitting by Mel."

"Wow." He exhaled hard. "I never thought I'd hear you say that."

"You made it fun. So did Neil and Hailey. You guys work well together."

He let out a rueful snort. "Yeah, we'll see for how long."

My stomach dropped at yet another unexpected reveal. "Did word get out about them or something?"

"No, not at all. I mean because their tenure is safer than mine. They're employees."

Once again we were reminded that we were each facing future-defining battles.

"They'd be stupid not to hire you."

"I happen to agree," he chuckled. "But I guess we'll have to see."

We both fell silent again.

"Are you feeling ready?" Ben asked. "In a good headspace?"

I sat up a little straighter. Despite all the rest of the bullshit I was about to face, I'd still managed to protect my peace.

"I am. I feel phenomenal. I'm ready."

Another beat.

"I know you are," Ben replied, his face shifting back to the warmth I was now so familiar with. "And I can't wait to watch you win."

Chapter Thirty-One

It was no surprise that Mel had insisted we have a watch party at her house for my episode of *The Score*. She'd invited Sarah and Zoey over as well, and tricked out her finished basement with all the pillows, cozy blankets, and snacks we could want, like we were thirteen-year-olds at a sleepover. My guess was that she was providing as much physical comfort as possible, just in case things went sideways with the show.

Despite Ben's assurances that I'd be happy with it, the trailers had gotten under my skin. The only bright spot was that my mom had texted me to complain about the way she looked in it, probably because they showed clips of her fuming at me in Switzerland. I had to assume that someone in the edit bay was on my side, because they zoomed way in and she *did* look like her Botox needed a touch-up in the old footage.

Mel settled on the couch next to me. "I told Danny that the door is locked and I want zero interruptions until it's over. Not a peep unless someone is bleeding." She reached over to give my hand a squeeze. "It's going to be great. Stop worrying."

Zoey was nestled in on the other side of me. She held up her phone. "*Lots* of interest on social media. With all the shipping going on between you and Ben they're all going to be watching for signs of flirting. Which, duh. It was constant."

I hid a smile and gave her a little kick in the thigh. "*Stop.*"

"Sorry, but I saw it, too," Sarah said as she grabbed a blanket and plopped down next to Zoey.

"We all did," Mel said. She reached for the tray on the table in front of her and held it out. "Crudité? You guys better have some because all my boys are in an anti-veg stage right now and I can't eat all of it by myself."

"Oh, and I made kale chips." Sarah jumped off the couch and ran to her bag to grab the Tupperware container.

I snorted out a laugh. "In any other universe a watch party has alcohol and greasy food. We have *vegetables.*"

"No, hold on," Zoey said. "My mom sent her famous ginger chews, which are basically candy."

She pointed to the stack of parchment-wrapped squares on the table and I immediately grabbed one. Mrs. Chen encouraged us to eat them when we had a sour stomach, which was all but guaranteed for me as I watched the show.

"Everyone ready?" Mel asked as she reached for the remote. "Let's go."

My entire body tensed as the theme song came on and the host intro videos flashed on the screen. The announcer intoned, "with special correspondent Bennett Martino" as his handsome face came up and we all hooted in unison.

"Lookin' good, Martino!" Mel cheered.

When he smiled it felt like it was just for me, and in a way it was. What we were about to watch was his gift to me.

The program began like always, with all the hosts gathered on a blue-and-white set to give their impressions about the story to come. My heart thudded in my chest with sympathetic nervousness for Ben even though it wasn't live.

"He's so damn good," Sarah said as Ben fielded questions from the other hosts. "What a natural."

It was like he was born to be in front of a camera. He was obviously hot as hell in person, but good looks didn't always translate to the screen, which was where charisma came in.

Ben had both. If his episode—*our* episode—was as good as he claimed, his future on the show was set.

The image on the TV shifted and then there I was, alone in the middle of the ice, doing a Biellmann. Everyone squealed and clapped but of course I zeroed in on how I lost my grip on my blade and hastily came out of the spin as a way to cover up my mistake. I glanced at Mel but she seemed too enthralled to notice.

There were so many ways to begin the episode, but Ben had opted to keep the camera at a distance like a voyeur as I skated over to chat with Zamboni Frank while his voice-over described my morning ritual. Thankfully, I'd remembered to wear the pink tie-dye legwarmers that day so a certain little fan would be pleased. The footage of me laughing at Frank's jokes was adorable, then it cut to a close-up of Zoey looking gorgeous.

Another cheer. She squealed and covered her face.

"You look *stunning*," I assured her.

She peeked through her fingers. "Actually, I do," she replied with awe in her voice.

"Ben's going for the community angle," Sarah said. "It's not just about your comeback, it's about your *connection*. He's going to interview all the people around you before diving into your story, so the audience can see how loved you are. Supersmart way to reframe it."

Zoey talked about our early years together, and the show flashed photos of us as kids, which I had no idea they were going to do. She went on to talk about how she considered me a big sister and mentor, and managed to slip in some mentions about her own career.

More cheers as Sarah's interview came on, which was intercut with footage of us working together, then finally Mel. As the show rolled on we downshifted into quiet observers, so we could take everything in.

"This is amazing," Mel whispered to me. "He's telling a beautiful story."

I nodded, but I still didn't feel like I was out of the woods yet because there'd been no mention of Switzerland. Then, as soon as I thought it, the image on the screen cut to me crying.

"Fuck," Sarah said.

"It's okay, we knew it was coming," Mel replied in her reassuring mom voice. "Let's watch how it plays out."

After seeing the trailer I was expecting the worst, but what made it to the show was factual, blissfully brief, and bookended by footage that showcased the difference between then and now. A few minutes of pain, and then it moved on to clips of me kicking ass at competitions in the years since.

"You've been officially shipped," Zoe said as the show's focus shifted to the one-on-one interview with Ben. "People are already doing fan edits of you guys making fuck-me eyes at each other."

"*Zoey Chen*," Mel mom-scolded. "Watch your mouth!"

We were at the halfway point and I finally felt like I could relax, until the show shifted to a tight shot of Ben.

My heart did its own joyful Biellmann when he smiled.

It was as if I couldn't fully fill my lungs from the heat in his eyes. He looked smolder-y because he was looking at *me*. That appreciative, roving meander around my face made me want to blush, because it felt like he was letting the world in on the Blizzard Clause we'd executed the night before.

I could finally see what everyone was making a big deal about, because if I didn't know better I would've sworn that he was in love with me.

But I did know better. Ben was just being Ben.

"Damn," Sarah exhaled when the show cut to us both laughing about something. "Get a room!"

"Shh, guys, listen to how freaking insightful he is in this part! He talks about what he thinks my 'Movement' program means," I said.

"I see it as a story of self-discovery, told in three parts," Ben was saying. "The first section feels like you're waking up in your body. Like, coming to terms with your gifts. The power you have within you. The second part, after the chorus, is you enjoying that power. Harnessing it. Starting to seduce your audience with everything you're capable of."

I'd blushed when he'd said it, but he was right.

"The final act, when the music gets more intense, is *mastery*. Ownership. Triumph. It's you stepping into your full glory and loving every second of it. Your smile during that section . . ." He'd stared into space for a few seconds, like he was trying to find the right description. "It's the most difficult part of the piece because you back-loaded all those jumps, but your smile makes it look like you're taking a Sunday stroll. Like those jumps and flips are no big deal."

I'd been dumfounded by his accuracy. "*How* did you figure that out?"

Ben had looked wounded by the question. "I mean, it's obvious if you just open your eyes and watch. It's all right there on the ice."

I knew that wasn't the case for everyone. A good performance told a story, but sometimes subtext didn't register with audiences. Or judges, for that matter, since a few had called it "sexy and flirty," which was almost an insult to the depth of the message running through the performance.

But my goal on the ice was to evoke emotion in my audience, so there was no wrong answer to what my performances meant. As long as they felt *something*, I'd done my job.

The very interview that I'd been dreading had actually been the perfect epilogue to our time together. Ben had been right; waiting to do it until the end of the week had changed the shape of our relationship as well as the resulting sit-down. If we'd done it earlier I would've been guarded. Skeptical. It would've hobbled our conversation and translated as me coming across as bitchy. Instead, the interview had felt like the two of us connecting on an even deeper level, with a couple of cameras along for the ride.

I leaned back and considered how far we'd come. Four years prior Ben had promised that he'd be there for me.

Now I finally believed that it was true.

Chapter Thirty-Two

*I*f organized sports and Disney had a baby, it would be the Olympic Village.

The place was a mix of beautiful old and new architecture, cheerful volunteers, and signage so clear that there was no chance of getting lost, despite the scope of the place. The uncanny valley vibe to it all was a reminder that somehow this was *real*.

We'd made it.

I looked at the other athletes around me in their colorful Village uniform jackets. It was day one of our pre-week, and it felt like euphoria had gone airborne and we were all infected. We were enjoying a collective sigh of relief before clocking back into athlete mode.

Or maybe it was just the jet lag.

I thought I'd be the jaded second timer to my teammates Erica Saunders's and Kayla Ruffini's wide-eyed newbie status, but I was just as overwhelmed by the Olympic magic as they were. It was about to level up big time since we were heading for the Team USA Welcome Experience building, the first defining moment of our time at the Games, since it was where we'd be fitted for our opening and closing ceremonies wardrobe along with the rest of our gear.

I felt like a senior walking into high school with two freshmen beside me. Erica was just eighteen and Kayla was *sixteen*, making me crypt keeper–adjacent compared to them. But they looked up to me, and when we were together I doted on them like little sisters.

"I am so ready for the swag," Kayla said, smoothing her red hair the way she always did when she was trying to calm herself down. "Did you hear we get watches and sunglasses? And a ring?"

"Just wait. We're going to walk out of here with two suitcases full of stuff," I said.

I was well aware of just how much merch we'd get thanks to Switzerland. I hadn't wanted to look at it after what happened, so even the non-Olympic stuff like the razors and body lotion we'd all been gifted were boxed up and put away in my storage facility.

But this time would be different.

We walked into the building behind a group of guys I recognized from the curling team. I didn't know them by name yet, but we'd probably all be besties by the time we left. It was one of the many surprise joys of being there; there were plenty of opportunities to bond with athletes from around the world over shared meals in the dining hall or stretched out on adjacent tables in the recovery room.

"Ho-lee-*shit*," Erica whispered once we were inside the Welcome Experience building. "This is huge!"

The dark navy-walled hallway was punctuated by faceless mannequins every few feet, each with a spotlight on them. I'd seen videos from past welcome events and some of them looked like they took place in hastily Olympic-ified auditoriums. Switzerland had been impressive, but Milan was already raising the bar because it felt like we were walking into a high-end nightclub.

"It's all the past team gear," Kayla said with reverence as she paused in front of the first pair of mannequins. "This is from 2008." She read the accompanying description. "The first time Ralph Lauren paired with Team USA to do the opening and closing fits."

"Ours are a billion times better this year," Erica sniffed as she eyed the mannequin. "That white flat-top hat is peak grandpa cringe."

We made our way to the sign-in table, where we were handed our checklists by a smiley volunteer.

"Unreal," Erica said as she skimmed it. "They're giving us new *phones*? We're getting so much stuff!"

An attractive woman in an official white tracksuit appeared. "Hello and welcome, ladies! We're going to head for the Nike room first for your kits. Right this way, please."

We followed behind her, pausing to look at images from past Games lining the hallway.

"*Quinnnn*," Kayla sang out. She pointed to a large photo. "Your *boyfriend*!"

As expected, the gossip about me and Ben had exploded after the show. I was oblivious to how observed we'd been while we were together, because new paparazzi-style photos of the two of us kept appearing online. And yeah, most of them sold the romance narrative. Even ones sneakily taken the first morning we'd met at Eagle Diner looked incriminating. *I* could see the fury in my expression, but to the rest of the world my intensity could be misread as me wanting to swallow him whole. And how had I not noticed that Ben's feet were stretched out beneath the table and nearly touching mine? Somehow our bodies looked like we were in some stage of pre-fucking in every photo.

I joined Kayla in front of the iconic image from Ben's final Games that had wound up everywhere. It looked like an accidental Renaissance painting, with Ben skating in front of the rest of the pack, so low that he was nearly horizontal. His fingertips were grazing the ice, and his gaze was fixed in the distance. Anyone who watched the event knew exactly how strenuous the moment had been for him, but if the photo was cropped around his face it could be used in a cologne ad. Of *course* Ben's intense exertion and focus read as smolder. His expression was at odds with the four-headed Hydra of skaters behind him; one had his mouth in an O of frustration, another was flailing and about to fall, the guy directly behind him was grimacing, and the final was nothing more than a helmet peeking out from behind Ben's head.

"Not my boyfriend," I reminded her.

My heart begged to differ. Even a photo of him evoked a tingly Pavlovian response.

"Keep telling yourself that," Kayla elbowed me.

I had to, otherwise the big hopeful feelings threatened to take over. We'd been honoring our agreement to keep our distance, which wasn't easy. I'd texted him a few photos of our accommodations right after we'd arrived and gotten a thumbs-up emoji in response, a terse reminder that I needed to stay focused.

"Right this way," the tracksuit lady chirped at us.

Erica the rule follower flipped her hand at us and gave us a mom-glare as she speed-walked behind the woman.

And so our whirlwind day of gifting began. By the time we got to our final stop with Ralph Lauren it felt like we needed assistants to cart around the wheelie bags filled with merch.

Noor, the Ralph Lauren stylist assigned to me, led me to a dressing room that had all the elements of my opening and closing outfits displayed on a white table in front of a mirror with the words "Team Albright" projected onto it.

I paused as tears filled my eyes. I was embarrassed that some-

thing so simple could make me feel emotional. But it was a reminder that I was back, and Team Albright had a second chance
to come in first.

"Let's start with your opening-ceremony look," Noor said as she
pointed to the smart blazer. "Get suited up and I'll help you with
the tie."

She left the dressing room, and I snapped a quick photo of my
reflection next to my name and sent it to Mel. She'd been taking
care of my social media accounts, and the image would be a great
kickoff for my time in Milan.

The opening ceremony look was quintessentially Ralph Lauren.
The fitted navy blazer had a red, white, and blue accent ribbon
running down the top of both sleeves, the polo player logo embroi-
dered on the left chest, and a round Olympics patch on the right. It
went over a crisp white shirt, and was paired with dark-wash jeans.
The coolest part of the outfit was the red tie that made it look like
a private school uniform.

Noor came back into the dressing room and helped me with
the tie, and when I turned around to look at myself in the mirror
I teared up again.

"You look amazing," Noor said as she fussed with the lapels.
She moved in front of me and clasped my arms. "I watched your
episode on *The Score*. It was incredible. You've *got* this."

I'd been hearing the sentiment quite a bit since it aired. What a
gift Ben had given me—a chance to set the stage for my triumph
to come.

"Thank you," I smiled at her.

I could hear Kayla and Erica squealing before I walked out of
the dressing room.

"Ohmigah we look *so* good," Kayla exclaimed when she saw me.

"Selfie!" Erica held up her phone.

We clustered together while she took the photo as our three stylists watched us like proud parents.

A woman with an official-looking camera walked over to us. "Hi there, I'm with Getty Images. Can we get a couple of shots with you ladies by the logos?"

We followed her to the wall with the Olympic and Ralph Lauren logos and posed beside them. A few other people gathered to take photos as well.

The three of us leaned into the paparazzi vibes, because yeah, we'd earned this moment.

Chapter Thirty-Three

I'd only been on the ice for two minutes and I already had complaints. I skated over to where Mel was watching me and the rest of my competition practicing. She'd arrived late the night before and our reunion had been half tearful, half giddy.

It was my second Olympics, but I had to remember that Mel was a part of it for the first time. Being here was a big deal for both of us in different ways. If I medaled—no, *when* I medaled—Mel's star would rise as well. Her calendar would fill up with elite students, she'd be in the running for various coaching awards, and she could even attract her own sponsors.

So many people stood to benefit from my win. I needed to be perfect, but the current scenario under my skates wasn't helping.

"This is hockey ice," I frowned at her, tapping my toe pick against it for emphasis. "It's too hard."

The repurposed rink had been upgraded for all the Olympic figure skating and speed skating events. The ice was regulation-size but the seating area around it was bigger than most of the ones I competed in, and tricked out for the Games with new flags of every country flying from the rafters. Hockey was in a different rink entirely, so I wasn't sure why the ice was even an issue.

Mel nodded tersely, watching the other skaters. "Ingrid just told me. Pretty major oversight, but we're a week early. Hiccups happen, even here. We've already escalated it and we were told it was being addressed. Just watch the timing of your jumps for today, okay? It's not the first time we've had to compensate. Although Frank would never allow this kind of mistake."

We both went quiet as we watched Ayumi do a perfect quad flip despite the shitty ice. As always, she was flawless.

"*Fuck*," Mel said under her breath.

"Exactly," I agreed.

"She looks clean as hell."

"No surprise there," I answered. I wanted to stop staring at Ayumi, but she was just too magnetic, a mix of balletic poise and strength.

"She's a mathlete, though," Mel said with a shrug. "I swear I can see her calculating her score as she skates."

She did a flawless triple axel.

"Wish I could multitask like that."

Mel refocused on me. "You won't have to. You've been so consistent there's no need for you to shove in more technical elements at the last minute. Skate your programs exactly the way you've been during practice and you'll be fine. Better than fine."

I nodded and turned to survey the rest of my competition out on the ice. Everyone was in their own world, skating to music that only they could hear. We didn't have the leeway to skate as long as we were used to given the multi-use arena, so I needed to stop obsessing about the shitty ice, or how amazing Beatrix Syers was looking, or wondering if Petra Lurz seemed stiff or if I was just hoping that she was, and focus on myself.

Analyzing other skaters was another old habit that resurfaced now and then. Carol used to force me to study my competition's performances, which only served to make me second-guess my own abilities. Mel helped me realize that the only person I had to beat was myself. She audited what everyone else was doing to strategize the strength of my performance against the other programs, but insisted that I block them out and focus on myself.

"How do you feel? How's your body?"

I did a quick inventory. "The usual twinges plus a hint of jet lag, but overall I feel great."

Such a difference from last time. I'd spent my first Olympics pretending my injuries were ignorable. It seemed impossible to feel this good, especially given all the interruptions in the lead-up.

Although maybe those very interruptions were the reason *why* I felt so good?

"Hey, there's Ben and his crew." Mel pointed across the ice, where he was doing a rinkside interview with Yena Shí from Team China. "Have you guys connected since you got here?"

My cheeks went hot and chest constricted, because it was my first time seeing him in Milan. As much as I wanted to get together I'd held off even suggesting that we try to meet. And he'd mentioned how jammed up his schedule was trying to pack in as many interviews as possible. With five venues spread throughout the countryside, I couldn't believe that I was lucky enough to be in the same town as him, let alone the same building. He'd told me that the full *Score* team was on-site, which meant that he needed to revert to hyperprofessional mode.

"We've exchanged a couple of texts," I replied.

Which I was trying not to worry about. We'd agreed to low contact but I sort of assumed we'd at least text more frequently once we were both in Milan. It wasn't like he was ghosting me, but our communication definitely felt different than when we were stateside. Less cheery and more "just the facts." But again, he was busy too, and sticking to the plan we'd *both* agreed to.

I squinted to try to figure out who else was with him, because I didn't see Neil behind the camera, or Hailey, for that matter.

"Do you know who the blond ponytail woman is who's standing behind him?" I asked Mel.

Even at a distance she telegraphed "I'm important" energy. She was almost as tall as Ben and had perfect posture.

Mel craned her neck. "Pretty sure that's Kim Overton. I stalked her before I responded to her initial email about doing the show."

His boss. Or, his temporary boss at the moment. My stomach clenched when I thought about how different our time in Wood-spring would've been if she'd been there as well, along with the rest of the crew. I focused on the camera guy. Baseball cap, gray hair, with a middle-aged paunch.

Definitely not the sort of person who'd jump at the chance to go sledding in a blizzard.

I watched the interview process with a different eye now, since I'd been part of the editorial discussions that went into creating a show. I'd been the subject of plenty of interviews throughout my career, but my time with Ben, Neil, and Hailey had opened my eyes to just how much went into crafting a story, and how every-thing from the background music selected to the camera angles could influence the viewers' reaction to a piece.

I'd been gifted with the kindest version of my story possible. Aside from the four minutes he'd warned me about, the show had been perfect. Even the snippet with my parents. We looked like a normal family.

"Are you doing anything with him here? A follow-up interview?" Mel asked.

I nodded, still staring at what was happening on the other side of the rink and hoping that he'd feel my gaze and glance over. "Yeah, he mentioned stealing some time when I could fit it in. Nothing scheduled yet."

Ben was partially obstructed behind a post so I squinted to watch Kim instead. The perma-frown and tightly crossed arms told me everything I needed to know.

I'd gotten *super* lucky with my skeleton crew. Thank you, genetic doping.

"I understand how hard it is for you to look away from Ben, but let's get moving," Mel joked. "Are you all warmed up and ready?"

I ignored the first part. "I am. Let's go."

Mel pulled out her phone and got ready to record me.

I gave Ben and Co. once last glance as I skated to an open space, ignoring the perfect Salchows and axels taking flight around me.

The first practice of my gold medal month was starting now, and the only person I needed to worry about was *me*.

Chapter Thirty-Four

I don't think I've ever been this tired," Erica whined as I sat down beside her in the main Olympic Village dining hall.

"Same," Kayla agreed. She took a huge bite of quiche and frowned at her plate. "And those *beds* . . ."

I glanced between the two pouting teens in matching powder-blue Nike tracksuits and realized that I needed to harness my elder stateswoman energy, because they were spiraling and it was only day three.

"Remember, *everyone* is sleeping on cardboard and fishing wire, so it's still a level playing field," I replied. "And we're here a week early. Plenty of time to acclimate. You'll be fine."

Although I had to agree about the bed part, because the infamous Olympic beds made out of cardboard made it feel like we were sleeping on cereal boxes.

"How's your breakfast?" I wave my fork toward their trays.

"Amazing," Kayla sighed as she picked at her quiche.

"This frittata is so freaking good," Erica said with her mouth full. "But would we expect anything less from Italy?"

I glanced down at my selections. I'd come close to having meal-decision fatigue because the main dining hall was like a bizarro-world mall food court. It was the juxtaposition of carrying a tray to various stations with every cuisine and preparation method imaginable, from deep fried, to vegan, to kosher. I'd opted to be a little adventurous and traded my usual oatmeal for an egg and avocado breakfast sandwich on a cornetto.

"I need more coffee," Kayla complained. She craned her head to glance around the crowded space like she was looking for a waiter. "Because I have no clue how I'm going to stay awake today."

"Maybe if you put your phone away before midnight you wouldn't be so exhausted."

I was fully embracing my role as oldest team member now.

I felt someone slam into me and then collapse into a chair next to me. I turned to find women's ice hockey team captain and social media darling Campbell Pesansky panning her phone over the three of us.

"You guys, look who I found! It's members of our gorgeous figure skating team, live on Cam-cam," she said, staring at her phone instead of us. "Say hi, ladies!"

We all waved warily, shooting glances at each other.

"Is that really live?" Erica pointed at the camera and mouthed to me.

I leaned over and saw the comments streaming up Campbell's live feed. I grimaced at Erica and nodded.

We'd all gone through media training prior to arriving, and live streaming was allowed in nonrestricted areas but frowned upon. That said, the rules were different for some of the athletes with major name recognition. Obviously people knew the three of us and the rest of the figure skating team, but Campbell's fame was on a different level.

She'd mastered her social media presence during the build-up to the Games and was now exploiting it in every way possible. Her vibe was fun big sister with an emphasis on the "big" part because she was five eleven and all muscle. One of her most popular sketches was humbling guys who weren't athletes but thought that they were faster or stronger than her just by virtue of being men. Her unhinged "Cam-cam" lives were a close second because she asked rapid-fire, uncomfortable questions in a way that was so disarming that no one got insulted.

Campbell swung her camera to face me. "Okay, Miss Albright, the people want to know. Are you and Bennett Martino melting the ice or what? Hm? Because everyone is convinced you're a thing. Right, people?"

Kayla snorted in a way that sounded like agreement.

Campbell flipped her phone and slid closer to me so we were both on-screen, and I could see the comments and gifts from viewers popping up. There were nine thousand people watching her livestream.

I remembered one takeaway from the training for dealing with these types of questions; acknowledge without overexplaining, and then pivot. As much as I needed to figure out what was happening with Ben there was no way I wanted it overshadowing how the public viewed my Olympic experience. The narrative needed to be about my comeback, not who I was or wasn't sleeping with.

I manufactured a smile for Campbell and her audience. "I can understand why people would assume that given we were seen together quite a bit. But that was all for my interview on *The Score*."

I glanced at the screen and saw thumbs-down emojis falling over our faces.

"Hold up, you have angered the people," Campbell said. "Not

the answer they want." She squinted at the screen. "Or believe. FraggleFrock00 just called you a 'lying liar who lies.' Damn, that's harsh, Fraggle!"

I laughed despite my frustration about my redemption arc getting hijacked.

"C'mon, we're professionals," I joked. "Ben is just a good friend."

"I don't know," Campbell laughed. "I've never looked at *my* friends the way Ben looks at you."

I paused to read the comments scrolling beneath us and was shocked by how many people had opinions about us being together.

A *lot* of people.

I'd avoided social media postbreakdown and never got back into it, so seeing a live representation of the public's reaction to us was eye-opening. I discovered that we even had a portmanteau— Quinnett.

"I get why you'd want to put up some guardrails with that guy," she elbowed me. "He's hot as hell. I don't care that you get around, Ben baby. Call me, I love me some man-whore!"

I flinched. We both went quiet to read what the people watching were saying in the comments.

"Oh, no way," Campbell exclaimed and then looked around the crowded cafeteria. "He's *here*? That means I've got a chance! Ben, I'm comin' for ya. Quinn might not be buying what you're selling but I sure am!"

I laughed. "Good luck, I'll be crossing my fingers for the two of you."

"Okay my friends, let's shift the spotlight to your buddies," Campbell said as she pushed back from her chair and walked to where Kayla and Erica were sitting. "I've seen you guys killing viral dances, so can the three of us do "Les Party" together? Do you guys know that one?" Campbell glanced at me. "You can join us too."

"It's okay, I'll be your audience," I replied quickly.

The chance to be featured in Campbell's feed was more than enough to wake up the world's sleepiest Olympians. My phone chimed right as the three of them started dancing, and I had to hide a smile when I read the text from Ben.

> Be prepared, I'm kidnapping you this afternoon.

Chapter Thirty-Five

The whirlwind kidnapping negotiations ended up with me feeling guilty about skipping my final workout of the day, *until* we reached our destination. The promise of an authentic northern Italian meal with local wine was too good to pass up, and the town of Nizza Monferrato was absolutely stunning. I could only imagine how beautiful it would be come summer, although it was still almost too quaint to be true even in the deep winter freeze.

"Have you been here before?" I asked as I climbed out of the rental car.

We wound up at a cream-colored stone farmhouse with tan shutters and a terra-cotta tile roof. It was perched on the hillside, looking out over a dormant vineyard.

"Yup," he said as he stretched his hands over his head and rolled out his neck. "I have."

The trip from Milan wasn't long, just an hour and a half, but the narrow twisty roads and lawless drivers added some stress to the navigation.

"A bunch of times, considering it's where my dad's family is from," he added.

"Oh no way," I exclaimed. "Are there any Martinos left here?"

"There sure are," he grinned at me. "And you're about to meet them."

I froze. "Hold on. You brought me to meet your *family*?"

His expression went impish, and before he could answer I heard happy chatter heading our way.

"Ecco il mio bel ragazzo!"

A tiny, stooped, white-haired woman in a black coat ambled toward Ben, alternating between clapping and stretching out her hands to him. When she reached him she took his face in her palms and her expression turned almost wistful as she studied him.

"Sembri proprio lui!" She pulled him close and kissed him on both cheeks, then wrapped him in a hug.

I couldn't tell if he understood her or was just nodding along until a translator showed up, but I was impressed just the same.

"Zia Matilde," he laughed as she squeezed him. "Bona sira!"

"Ach, devi avere una fame da lupi! Sei pelle e ossa." She clasped his shoulders and frowned at him, then patted his stomach.

"Oh, I'm definitely not too skinny," he replied. "And we're both looking forward to your cooking."

I raised an eyebrow at him. He *did* understand.

"I've been spiegando to my, uh, fidanzata that your food is *mandato da Dio*." He pointed to me. "That's Quinn. Quinn, this is my Great-Aunt Matilde."

She turned to me and her eyes went wide. She pressed her hands to her chest. "Bella, bella, bella!"

The next thing I knew I was wrapped in a hug as well.

"Questo è l'atleta?" she asked Ben over her shoulder.

"She sure is an athlete," he answered. "Il migliori."

Zia Matilde took my hands in hers while she studied me, her dark eyes familiar. "L'é na campionessa. Dio l'ha volù!"

Ben burst out laughing. "Well, okay then. Zia Matilde says that god has willed your win, so you're all set."

I laughed with him. "Grazie."

Her eyebrows shot up. "L'é un gran bel acsent!"

"She said your accent is great," Ben explained.

A man strode out to join us and the pair looked like a matched set of salt and pepper shakers. He was just a few inches taller than Matilde, and had the same stooped posture.

"Welcome," he boomed at us. "Happy, happy!"

He walked over and hugged Ben tightly, slapping his back so hard that it probably left a mark.

"Ziu Carlo, this is my friend Quinn."

"*Fidanzata*," Matilde added.

He looked down at my hand then back at Ben.

"Fidanzata?" Carlo pressed.

Ben went white as he seemed to translate what was happening. "No, I mean *amica*! Quinn is my *friend*."

"Oh ho, very nice!" He walked over to me and wrapped me in a gentler hug. "Hungry? Yes?"

I nodded. "Always."

"Good, we eat! Come."

They started toward the house and Ben fell back to walk in with me. "Sorry I didn't tell you. I didn't want to give you a reason not to come."

"Are you kidding me? I'm *loving* this. I didn't know you spoke Italian."

"Speak," he made air quotes. "More like 'desperately tries to recall my high school Italian and the junk I picked up around the house.' I'm not conversant but I understand a lot of it. My parents both speak, and obviously with my mom's opera I heard it all the time."

I followed them inside.

"Wow." I glanced around. The front door opened directly into the dining area with a long rustic table beneath dark, exposed beams, probably unchanged since it was built. There was a fire lit, and the smell of something delicious and garlicky in the air.

Matilde went into the kitchen and came out clutching a big silver pot. "Sit!"

Carlo made a fuss as he pulled out a chair for me, then took a seat next to me. Ben sat across from me.

"Oh, Zia, did you make agnolotti del plin?" he asked.

"Sì," she nodded.

"It's my favorite. She makes her own pasta, by hand," he explained. "It's like a miniature ravioli stuffed with braised beef, sautéed spinach, and parmesan, with a butter and sage sauce." He paused. "Shit. Is that okay for you to eat, or . . ."

"Are you *kidding* me? There is no way I'm turning down handmade pasta. In Italy."

Ben rattled off something to Matilde and she started scooping pasta into bowls.

"She serves everyone. It's going to be way more than you can handle," he said under his breath.

"We'll see about that," I said as I eyeballed the feast headed my way.

"Uffa," Carlo said, jumping to his feet. "Un bicchiere di Nizza!"

"He's getting the red wine," Ben explained. "Made with grapes from this vineyard."

Carlo placed a tulip-shaped glass in front of each of us.

"Un po' for me," Ben said, holding his thumb and pointer finger an inch apart.

Carlo nodded and tipped the bottle to my glass. I laughed when he went well beyond the appropriate fill line.

"He's giving you my share," Ben said. "I'm only having a couple of sips."

I leaned across the table and lowered my voice. "Is that . . . okay for you?"

"Oh, I still drink on special occasions like this one. But it's rare. Honestly, it would be a bigger deal if I *didn't* have some. It's our family legacy."

"Alla nostra," Carlo said, raising his glass to us and kicking off a wonderful meal.

Somehow, the evening seemed to exist in a space out of time. The only thing that mattered was *this* food, *this* joyfully shouty Italian-English conversation, *this* cozy room with a roaring fire. For the first time in ages I was able to detach from my striver self and not worry about what I was eating or how it would impact me the following day. I gave myself permission to be fully in the moment, because there would never be another one like it.

We finished our meal and we all seemed to exhale in unison.

"Fare una passeggiata." Matilde swept her hand toward the door.

"Good idea," Ben answered. "I'll show Quinn the vineyard before it gets too dark." He stood up and fixed his eyes on me. "We'll stroll a bit then head back."

"Grazie for, uh . . ." I turned to Ben. "How do you say 'dinner'?"

"Cena," he answered.

"Grazie for cena," I said to his aunt and uncle.

They oohed and clapped in unison at my sad attempt at Italian. I pulled on my jacket and followed Ben into the cold twilight.

"Are you okay to stay for a little bit longer or should we head back now?" he asked.

I shook my head as I surveyed the landscape spilling out in front of me. We were in a fortress on a hill, surrounded by similar looking houses dotting hills on the horizon. The vineyard stretched down in front of us, with rows of grape vines so symmetrically planted that they looked like lines on a legal pad. The sun was just starting to dip below the horizon, leaving a highlighter trail of pink and orange along the edge of distant hills.

"No way I'm ready to go. It's beautiful here," I sighed. "This is the kind of place where you can forget everything."

"Is that what you want to do?"

"In this moment, yeah," I said quietly. "I could use a little meditation in the now instead of worrying about what comes next."

"Good," he said. "Let's walk and meditate."

The cold was bracing but not uncomfortable, like everything about the region was calibrated to be welcoming. Ben described the history of the home and land, and talked about his summer staying with his aunt and uncle back when he was thirteen, working the vineyard alongside them and his cousins. We ended up at a white stucco barn.

"Why is every inch of this place so picturesque?" I asked as we paused outside of it. "This is a utility building and I'd live in here."

"It's the way the architecture merges with the landscape," Ben mused. "There's harmony. And old-world craftsmanship."

"What's that?" I pointed up to a wall made of lattice brickwork beside an open doorway on the second floor.

"It's for air flow. We process grapes up there, and age barrels. Want to check it out?"

I nodded, and Ben led me into the barn to a floating staircase. It was dark inside so he switched on his phone flashlight.

"Careful," he said as I climbed the stairs. "It's a little creaky. Repairs happen slowly around here, if ever."

Once I got to the second floor I walked toward the light fading through the lattice. In addition to the tapestry of hills and doll-house homes dotting the landscape, I was now greeted by a field of twinkly stars waking up above us.

"Heaven," I sighed. "I love it here."

"I'm glad."

We were side by side, staring out at the horizon and pretending that the poetry of the moment wasn't having an impact on us. As if being alone in the Italian countryside with the moonlight casting a blue glow on our faces was just like any other day.

I wished I could add another amendment to our agreement.

Ben turned to me and stepped closer without a word, and my heart fluttered wildly off beat. He took my hands in his.

"Sorry," he murmured.

I willed my voice to stay steady. "For what?"

He dropped my hand and reached up to palm the back of my neck. "For this," he whispered as he pulled me to him.

Our noses bumped and we giggled self-consciously, but the moment our lips connected we melted together.

The idea that we'd maintain our boundaries despite what happened in Connecticut was laughable and we both knew it. There was no "getting it out of our systems." We were now addicts trying to navigate life with permanently altered DNA.

"This is a terrible idea," he whispered against my lips. "We can't . . ."

"But we *are*," I insisted, kissing him harder.

I squeezed my eyes shut but I was tempted to keep them open, so I could drink in the perfect moment. Stars, moonlight, Italy . . . *Ben*.

I stopped feeling the cold and instead found myself wishing I could wrench off my clothes. Ben's hands dropped to the hem of my jacket and pushed under it, searing my skin at the same time cold air grazed it.

"Do you want me—"

"Yes," I scold-panted as we kissed. "I want all of you. Why do you even have to ask? I've always wanted you."

"I guess you *don't* want me to stop, then." I could feel Ben's smile curving against my mouth.

"Never," I sighed as he dotted kisses down the side of my neck.

I'd somehow convinced myself that we wouldn't have to worry about crashing into each other this way again in the days leading up to competition, seeing as we were both here facing career-defining scenarios. *Life* defining. But the pull to be as close as humanly possible canceled out all the discipline that had defined our lives.

My body felt like it was sinking into his, and Ben adjusted to support my weight. I was letting go in every possible way, signaling to him that I was his. He deepened the kiss, sweeping his tongue over mine as his hands found their way to the bare skin of my back.

I felt weak, but at the same time my whole body was tensed, bracing for the next shock of pleasure. Ben's hands migrated from my back to cup my breasts, his thumbs grazing my nipples over the thin fabric of my bra as if we had all the time in the world. I closed my eyes, my breath coming in short bursts, like I'd just finished a marathon.

My hand moved down to the front of his jeans to find him straining there.

Ben made a deep, rumbly noise as I pushed against him and rubbed. He inhaled sharply, like my touch through thick denim was enough to leave him unmoored.

I was blinded by how intensely I needed him. I fumbled with the zipper on his pants and pushed it down, forcing my hand between the layers of fabric to grip him. He went concave as my hand circled his hardness, and then dropped his forehead to my shoulder.

"Quinn," he rasped.

We moved together, hindered by our clothing and the cold that prevented us from stripping. If we'd been in this spot during the heat of summer I had no doubt that I'd be naked beneath him, sweaty and happy. For now we had to settle for the stolen bits of skin we dared to expose.

I still felt feverish with need for him despite the barriers between us. I yanked his zipper down and started lowering myself to my knees.

Then we heard something echoing in the distance. I paused, hovering in a half squat in front of him.

"*Fuck*," Ben grumbled through gritted teeth. "The fucking bell."

I stood up slowly and listened. Sure enough, I heard the sound of a handbell bouncing off the hills.

"What does it mean?" I whispered. "Is there a problem?"

"It's how they signal the workers in the field to come in. She's trying to tell us we need to come back, probably for port and torcetti before we leave."

The bell continued calling us home.

"Will she keep on . . ."

He nodded, frowning at the timing. "Yeah. We should go. Otherwise she'll start making jokes about leaving the hay outside the barn."

I tipped my head, questioning the translation.

He snorted softly. "She told me that was how girls avoided getting pregnant back in the day. The men 'left their hay outside the barn.'"

It took a little bit to figure out what she meant.

"Oh my god," I giggled when it dawned on me. "She told you that?"

"Oh yes. Zia has no filter." Ben adjusted himself and sighed. "It's probably for the best. We're supposed to be avoiding this."

I snuggled up against him and wrapped my arms around his waist. "Then we probably shouldn't be alone together, because I can't resist touching you."

My heart fumbled at the idea of not having another chance to be this close to him.

He kissed the top of my head. "Deal. We'll make sure we have a chaperone. And I'm going to get even busier next week, once everything starts. The only time I'll get to see you is our final interview, postcompetition."

"Hold on. You're not covering the press conference we're doing tomorrow?"

He frowned at me. "They haven't mentioned a word about that. Weird."

The bell started clanging again.

"We'll figure it out," he said unconvincingly as we set off for the house.

It was fine that we'd be forced apart. Better, in fact. We'd both navigate the insane pressures ahead of us, and then once we were on the other side, we could figure out what the hell we were to each other.

Chapter Thirty-Six

The six members of the Team USA singles skaters were gathered with our coaches standing just beyond the big two-level step and repeat area for the press conference in the media center. There was Mel, along with Kayla and Erica and their coaches, as well as the three men's singles skaters, Sam, Declan, and Jae, along with their coaches. I could tell it was going to be a clusterfuck since it was the first presser with all of us gathered. The room was packed and buzzing with noise. I peeked out to see if Ben was in the crowd of reporters but couldn't find him in the sea of faces.

"Okay, are we ready to go?" a smiley woman in a blazer and headset asked us, pushing her hands through the air like she was trying to sweep us toward the stage. She'd introduced herself to us but I'd already forgotten who she was. "It's time, let's get settled in our chairs. Ladies, the three of you are on the first level, and gentlemen, you're behind them."

Normally I'd be fighting off a twist of tension in my gut at the thought of being faced with a room full of reporters, but the combination of having the team with me plus all the recent interviews I'd done with Ben had fortified me. I felt like I could handle anything they'd throw at me. *My* version of my story was out there, thanks to him.

Erica grabbed my arm and looked up at me with her eyes wide before we walked out. "It's a full house."

I smiled at her. "You've got this, don't worry."

The blazer woman moved in front of the chairs as we settled in and the room quieted. "Welcome everyone! We're so excited to have our Team USA singles figure skaters here today for the first official press conference of the Milano Cortina Olympic Games!"

The energy in the room shifted as everyone broke into applause.

"Tina Weng from *USA Today*, you're up," she said and pointed to a woman seated at the front of the crowd.

"Thank you. This question is for Declan. You've been coming really close to hitting that unicorn, the quadruple axel. How confident are you feeling about your chances here in Milan?"

The three of us in front turned around to watch him answer, because we wanted to know as well. I could see his media training bleeding through as he answered, because the old Declan would've been brash. This polished-up Olympic version was humble and hopeful.

And long-winded. I used the time to scan the crowd, hoping to find Ben among them, smiling back at me. I recognized a few of the reporters from their on-air coverage but couldn't find him. Then I spotted a familiar high blond ponytail. Kim the producer was here, which probably meant that Ben was nearby. I squinted and scanned and came up empty.

"Next question," Blazer Lady said. She pointed at a guy with gray scruff and a stack of notebooks on his lap. "Jim, go ahead."

"Thanks. Jim Kellogg from CNN. My question is for our two youngest skaters here today. Kayla, Erica, how does it feel to be in Milan?"

The softballiest question ever, and one we were all well prepared for.

Kayla leaned forward to speak into the mic in front of her. "I'll
start."

I wanted to high-five her, because she usually liked to stay quiet.
Her answer was lovely, so much so that all Erica could do was
basically repeat the same stuff about being honored and hoping to
make her country proud.

"Okay, who's next?" Blazer Lady said as hands shot into the air.
"Kim, you're up."

I swallowed hard when her eyes landed on me.

"Thanks. Kim Overton from *The Score*, and my question is for
Quinn."

Of course it was. Like I hadn't just fed their show every detail of
my life. Well, not *every* detail. I faked a smile for her.

"There must be so much pressure on you after what happened
at the last Olympics."

My stomach dropped and my palms instantly went sweaty. *This*
bullshit. I thought we were past it by now.

I nodded and got ready for my spin-filled reply, but she wasn't
done.

"It was such a shocking disappointment for Team USA, so I'm
wondering—I think we're *all* wondering—if you're worried about
a repeat performance this time around."

Deep breaths.

"I wasn't until you brought it up," I said and continued to smile
at her, but there was just enough venom in my voice to make my
feelings about the question known. A few people chuckled.

She met my smile with her own overly toothy grin that didn't reach her eyes, then shifted to a faux-concerned expression. "The world saw you broken the last time around. And then your retirement announcement was both shocking and not. So what was it that got you back out there? Do you have something to prove to your old coaching team, or is it more than that?"

Well, *damn*.

Kim Overton was playing all the old hits, from my disastrous performances to the beef with Carol and my mom. It struck me that if Ben hadn't been running point for me during our week together it probably would've included lots more of this type of questioning.

I'd assumed he was going to blow up my life, but he'd actually kept me glued together.

I straightened my back, arranged my face into my haughtiest ice queen expression, and locked on to Kim.

"My goal as an athlete is to always look forward. It's too easy to get caught up in who we *were* at the last competition, not who we're training to become in the present. And I've worked hard to be this version of me. I feel really happy skating these programs. I'm back at my second Olympics because I deserve to be here." I didn't normally brag but I wasn't going to let her get away with trying to knock me off balance to get a good sound bite. "I'm sure you've seen how hard I worked to earn my place on Team USA. If not, I can text you the YouTube clips from my performances at Worlds."

I winked at her and everyone laughed, because the clips had been impossible to avoid.

"Thank you." Kim looked down at her phone like I was boring her.

"Who else?" Blazer Lady looked around the room and pointed at a man standing along the back wall. "Yes?"

"Hi, Randall Thorpe from *The Telegraph*. We've briefly touched on age but I wanted to go a little deeper."

Easy now, Randall.

"Tara Lipinski was our youngest Team USA competitor at just fifteen. Kayla, you just turned sixteen, and we've got Quinn on the opposite end of the age spectrum competing as our oldest skater at twenty-four. Our oldest ever, I believe. Quinn, are you feeling that eight-year age gap?"

Suddenly, I understood how Ben felt when people joked about his age. Nothing worse than people hinting that you're past your prime. I knew this question would come so I already had a reply cued up.

"She's our big sister," Kayla insisted before I could say anything.

I laughed. "First of all, I want to point out that the honor of most senior competitor goes to Mariah Bell, who was twenty-five when she skated at the Olympics. And to answer your question, I actually feel amazing despite my advanced age." I said it with verbal air quotes. "I'm healthier than I've ever been, and I attribute that to the way Mel and I work together. I'm very lucky to have a coach like her. She understands that positivity lifts you up and carries onto the ice." I wanted to say more but there was no need to even hint at the troubles from my past.

He nodded at me and wrote something down.

"Lee, you're up," Blazer Lady said.

"Lee June-hyoung, *The Korea Times*, this question is for Jae. Your family emigrated from South Korea. How challenging is it facing down premier South Korean skaters like Ha-Joon and Jin?"

Ah, international rivalries with a local angle would definitely shift the vibe away from me. I took the opportunity to study the room as he answered.

Why wasn't Ben with Kim? And where the hell were Neil and Hailey? In the rush I'd forgotten to ask Ben about them. There was a good chance the three of them were in one of the other locations where skiing or snowboarding would be taking place.

But still . . . it felt odd that they wouldn't send him to cover this press event given how well the show was doing. Mel had told me that it was still showing up in the top-picks listing on the channel, even though it had been out for a while now.

Things were starting to kick into overdrive for both of us. We were preparing to do the opening ceremony Parade of Nations walk-through the following day, followed by a Team USA welcome dinner hosted by Vox Telecom in Milan.

Then?

Showtime.

Chapter Thirty-Seven

*T*he amount of fanfare at the Vox Telecom Milan building made it feel like the main drag of the Met Gala, paparazzi and all. Team USA was gathered in our red, white, and blue glory for the sponsored kickoff dinner before the Games began, which meant that the room was filled with gorgeous athletes trying hard to tamp down the urge to cut loose and party.

Some of us were doing a better job than others, seeing as the men's hockey team was strategizing to find a way to turn the Olympic Rings ice sculpture into a shot luge.

"Are we going to be forced to listen to smooth jazz the whole night?" Erica leaned close to me and shouted over the sax. "Because this is torture."

"I saw a DJ setting up by the dance floor," Kayla said. "Don't worry, you'll get a chance to shake that ass."

All I cared about was trying to spot Ben in the crowd. I hadn't seen him since Nizza Monferrato and our texting had dwindled to an acceptable but still a *little* concerning level. I kept reminding myself that this was what I wanted, what we'd agreed to, but I still had flashbacks to the way things had ended up last time.

But *nothing* was the same as last time, in all the best possible ways.

Someone tapped me on the shoulder and I turned to find a smiling woman with a press badge around her neck.

"Hi, Quinn! I'm Lucia with *The Score* and we're hoping to chat with you and the rest of your teammates. Just some quick sound bites about the event tonight."

It made sense that they were the only press on-site since CineBinge and Vox Telecom were under the same parent company. I'd heard the word "synergy" more times than I could count during the evening's opening speech.

"Yay!" Kayla said. "I look extra-cute tonight."

"Same," Erica said, doing a double shoulder hitch and pose. "I'm ready."

Lucia laughed. "Perfect. Keep that energy. We're set up right over here, follow me, please."

I immediately spotted Kim among the people gathered around the branded step and repeat, watching snowboarders answer questions. I scanned the rest of the crew and finally found Ben toward the back, arms crossed and forehead furrowed.

The crowds and noise and lights fell away while I studied him. I knew without a doubt that I was looking at Ben being benched. The interview action was all up near the step and repeat, where the snowboard team was currently trying to make a human pyramid. Kim was right at the edge of it next to correspondent Maizey Liu, along with a camera crew I didn't recognize. No Neil and Hailey.

"Excuse me for a sec," I said to Erica, and she nodded without looking at me, totally focused on snowboarder Kyle Hobbs.

I fought for control of my body as I got closer to Ben, because we were in a public space surrounded by a billion phones. The narrative about the two of us had a life of its own, but I wasn't about to add new chapters by getting cozy with him. If anyone was watching all they'd see was a friendly drive-by at a socially acceptable distance apart.

He was so locked on to the action that he didn't see me approach or notice when I paused next to him. I was almost afraid to interrupt his hardcore staring.

"Hey you," I finally said.

He jumped. "Oh, *hey*!"

His expression immediately relaxed into the Ben I'd become oh so familiar with, as if seeing me was the antidote to whatever poison his body was processing.

Ben moved a half step closer to me but maintained the buffer. "You look fucking amazing," he said quietly.

I ran my hand down the front of my cobalt velvet dress. "This old thing?"

The corner of his mouth tugged up. I knew exactly what his devilish expression meant.

"How's it going?" I jutted my chin toward the action.

His smile disappeared. "I wouldn't know. They've got me riding the pine."

My stomach clenched. So my theory was correct.

"Any clue why? Because your episode is doing great. People love it."

"*Our* episode," he corrected me. "And I'm not sure. But it's fine, don't worry about me. All good. Maybe Maizey was feeling left out or something?"

His reassurances sounded genuine but the cloud of frustration remained.

"Ben . . ." I began. I glanced around and moved closer to him. "It's me. You don't have to fake it. What's going on?"

He locked on to me, his eyes stormy. "Quinn, everything is fine, I promise. This setup is our final one for the night. I'm not hungry so I'm probably going to head out before they start serving dinner. You need to focus on the event and have fun. Drink it in. It's for you."

"Eh," I tipped my head back and forth. "It sort of feels like it's for our host, not us. *Everything* is branded." I pointed to the table of Vox Telecom water bottles behind him.

There was a fine line between celebrating the athletes and making us props in their content, and while I was honored beyond belief to be at the Games, it felt like the dinner had been born in a board-room.

"I'm leaving with you."

"Quinn, no," he insisted. "Stay."

I shook my head. "I don't want to be here. I'm overstimulated. I'll just say I need to rest, and we can hang out."

He sighed warily, because it wasn't what we'd agreed to.

"C'mon," I said, poking him in his stomach, which was un-surprisingly rock hard. "Let's play hooky. Isn't that sort of your brand?"

I could've sworn I saw tension flash across his face. "I haven't been that guy in a long time."

I'd accidentally discovered a pain point. I backtracked. "Sorry, you're right. Correspondent Ben is nothing but professional."

"Hey, Quinn? We're ready," someone called out, and the crowd in front of us turned around to stare at me.

"Please wait for me," I whispered. "Don't leave until I'm done."

He nodded and I walked up to the step and repeat to join the entire team of skaters in front of the cameras. I played along during the silly Q&A session, keeping one eye on Ben to make sure that he didn't try to sneak away.

I could sense his unhappiness despite the wall of people be-tween us. The dim lighting didn't hide the furrow between his eyebrows.

"Do you mind if I head out?" I asked Erica and Kayla as we were herded away from the cameras. "I'm just not feeling this tonight."

"Aw, are you sick?" Kayla asked, frowning at me.

I shook my head. "I'm tired, that's all. I could use a couple of hours of quiet."

With Ben.

"Okay. I'm staying here until they kick me out, so enjoy the alone time," Erica said.

"Same," Kayla echoed. "This is the last fun I'm having until it's all over."

"Enjoy. Make smart choices," I cautioned, staying true to my chaperone roots.

I caught up to Ben in the lobby that was so tricked out with red, white, and blue that it felt like a political rally.

"Ready?" I asked. "They know you're leaving?"

"They do. But you're not."

He fixed me with a glare that made me wonder if something had shifted between us. Instead of answering I walked to the coat check and handed over my ticket, staring at him with a "try me" expression. I made a show of putting my coat on and buttoning it all the way up while he watched.

"Let's go," I said, striding past him as fast as my stilettos would allow.

My hand was on the door when he caught up.

"I carpooled with them so I was planning to walk back to my hotel." He nodded toward my feet. "Those aren't walking shoes."

I pursed my lips at him. "Every jump I land puts pressure on me that's five times my body weight. On *one* leg. So I think I can handle a few blocks in Louboutins. Anyway, my toes no longer have feeling."

"Hey, at one point I wanted to shave off my pinkie toes because of the pinching, so I get it." He paused. "But are you *sure* you want to leave?"

I answered by pushing open the door and pirouetting out. I'd dressed for a "cab to curb" night, forgoing a hat and gloves to be cute. Now I was going to pay the price, but it was worth it.

Ben caught up to me and I finally saw a smile.

The quiet night felt like the perfect antidote to the energy of the party. I hadn't had much time to sightsee other than our side quest to the countryside, so I craned my neck to take in the beautiful moonlit architecture all around us. It was a place where medieval, lace-front churches coexisted with glass skyscrapers.

"What's the vibe with the crew?" I asked as we fell in step. "Is it going well?"

"Definitely," he answered a little too quickly. "The coverage has been phenomenal."

I smacked my forehead. "Oh my god, I've been meaning to ask you where Neil and Hailey are! I thought they were coming too."

"Things change all time in production," he said, staring at his feet as we walked. "Just like we experienced with your show. I haven't connected with them in a bit but I'm pretty sure they were reassigned."

"Bummer," I said. "It seemed like they were excited to come."

"It's a tough business," he answered with a shrug.

The streets turned to cobblestones as we walked through a

more crowded part of town. One of the busy restaurants had a speaker mounted outside that was playing a lovely piano song with a woman singing in Italian. I paused to listen.

"It's a waltz," I said.

I started swaying, and when it coaxed a smile from Ben I got a little more dramatic. He glanced around.

"You realize that if any of the people in these restaurants look out they'll see you."

"Let 'em," I said, amping up the performance even more. "What's the saying? Dance like no one's watching?"

I one-two-three-ed by Ben, hoping to jolly him out of whatever had parked a black cloud over his head. It felt like a role reversal, but I owed it to him. He'd spent his time with me regulating everything to help keep me sane and happy, and now it was my turn.

"Come on," I held out my hand. "Show me what you've got."

Ben looked around again. "Fine," he sighed. "But we're doing it my way."

He reached out and grabbed my hand, then pulled me to him while simultaneously walking backward toward the shadows of the buildings.

He took me into his arms and paused, I assumed to find the beat before he started twirling me about. But instead of launching into movement he pulled me tightly to his body and barely shifted his weight.

"Like this," he whispered in my ear.

He swayed, slow as molasses but somehow still in time to the music. I'd expected a big, dramatic waltz like the one he'd done with Justin, but our version was intimate. Just for the two of us clenched together and hardly moving in the dimly lit alley.

I rested my cheek on his shoulder and let him lead, the thick wool of my coat and his puffy down parka a chaperone between our bodies. The only skin-to-skin contact was our raised hands, but it was enough. I could still feel the rise and fall of his chest, and the pressure of his palm pressed against my lower back.

I closed my eyes, blocking out the cold weaving around my bare legs.

"Hey," he said in my ear.

I raised my head to find him watching me hungrily, doing that thing that rendered every human he came in contact with lulled and powerless to resist him.

I wasn't sure who kissed whom, all that mattered was that it was happening. Our dance slowed so that we could both focus on how it felt to finally kiss again. He let go of my hand to gently grasp the nape of my neck, and when I closed my eyes to savor the sensation I saw fireworks. Ben pushed against the wall and pinned me there. We kissed for I don't know how long.

It struck me how *effortless* we were together. How our body parts slotted together perfectly, like we belonged tangled up in each other's arms. Each new touch felt choreographed and surprising at the same time,

It took effort but we finally pulled apart, each breathless and pink cheeked.

"Come to my place," I whispered. "Kayla and Erica won't be home for hours. Please."

"Quinn, you know that's not a good idea. The agreem—"

I went up on my tiptoes to kiss the words from his mouth and I swore I could feel his resistance faltering.

"Abstinence," he muttered against my mouth. "Before you compete. It's important."

The way he kissed me made me doubt he believed it.

"Debunked lore," I countered and nipped his bottom lip. "There's no scientific evidence that it has an impact."

"But . . ." He kissed each eyelid then traced lower. "The cardboard bed . . ."

My head dropped back to give him more access to my neck. "I'm sure you tested them in Switzerland."

He pulled away abruptly, flustered but incredulous. "I'll have you know that I had zero sex in Switzerland."

I eyeballed him. Was it possible that he believed the abstinence hype, or was he just trying to convince me he didn't man-whore it up, considering we spent the night together?

It didn't matter now.

"Then let's go test that cardboard," I whispered.

Chapter Thirty-Eight

I was no longer feeling the cold.

Ben and I kissed our way back to the Village in every secluded patch of real estate, until we were forced to pretend to be business acquaintances just outside the main gates.

"You have your credentials, right?" I asked him as we approached the checkpoint. "Because getting in and out is intense, even for me."

He reached into his parka and pulled out the laminated badge. "Yup. And my two forms of ID, and clean hands for the finger-prints."

"Do you have an easily accessible vein for the blood draw? Because that's part of the protocol after five."

"At the ready." Ben cracked a smile as he held up his arm.

Olympic Village security was nothing to joke about, and every time I ran the gauntlet I was reminded that I had Ben to thank for the shiny new driver's license I handed over. It didn't matter how recognizable an athlete was, we all had to subject ourselves to rigorous scrutiny to get back into the Village. Not just the ID, credentials, metal detector, and bag check, but also a surprisingly thorough Q&A, with everything logged on an iPad.

It didn't matter that I had every right to be there, the stress of the inquisition still left me feeling like *maybe* I'd accidentally packed a machine gun in my evening bag and forgotten about it.

We approached the two unsmiling guards who both looked like they took their jobs very seriously. I went through the drill first, offering all my paperwork and chatting about the event we'd just left. Security felt like a different planet from the rest of the Village, where the smiles and kindness were nonstop. But I understood the seriousness of security's job given the state of the world. The uniformed pair acted like a switch had flipped once they'd confirmed that I was who I said I was, then they turned to Ben.

"Good evening, sir," the taller one said in accented English.

"Buonasera," Ben replied, hitting the accent hard. "Come sta?"

He didn't even get an eyebrow twitch in response as they looked at his paperwork.

"You're media, yes?" the taller one asked.

"Sì, sono con Vox," Ben answered.

I guessed that he'd referenced *The Score*'s parent company since their signs were all over the Village. All he got in response was a tight-lipped nod.

"I spent today at Livigno, covering freestyle skiing practice," he explained, abandoning the Italian since it didn't seem to be having an impact on the stony-faced men. "But I was here the day before, for hours."

One guard pointed out something on the iPad to the other one.

"I'm sorry, sir, your credentials don't allow you to visit the Village after five. No entry until tomorrow morning at eight."

Ben frowned at them. "Well, that's not true. I've been allowed to stay much later than that."

The taller guard nodded at him. "Capito. But it looks like something has shifted with your allowances. You're tier three now, so I cannot let you in."

He handed the stack of credentials back to Ben triumphantly, like they'd just prevented a felon from entering the safe zone. An ember of worry ignited inside me.

"No," Ben stared at the documents in his hands. "That's not correct. I'm tier one. I have been since I got here. And I'm a former Olympic athlete in addition to being a correspondent. Bennett Martino?" He tapped his chest and gave the man a hopeful look.

"I'm sorry, sir. There's nothing more we can do."

"È assurdo!" Ben exclaimed, smacking the back of his hand on the documents. "Something's broken with your check-in process, because I know for a fact that I have full-access credentials."

"Non mi riguarda," the mustachioed guard said with a shrug.

Ben started to say something then stopped himself.

I put my hand on his forearm. "It's probably just a glitch. It's okay, let's figure something else out for now."

I could see the worry creasing his face, which I totally understood. Too many signs were pointing toward a shake-up at the show. Ben was cemented in place in front of the guard box, like he couldn't believe that anyone would refuse Magic Martino.

"Come on." I gave him a gentle tug. "We can figure it out tomorrow."

"*You* can enter, signorina," the guard smiled at me. "Just not him."

Clearly. Thanks for the salt in his wound, sir.

Ben finally seemed to come back to consciousness and let me pull him away from the entrance.

"So fucking weird," he mumbled. "It doesn't make sense. I was told that our partnership with Vox and their sponsorship of the Games meant full access. And I've *had* full access since I got here."

"Just a hiccup, I'm sure of it," I said. I glanced around the street and now wished I'd worn a hat, not because of the cold but because our proximity to the Village meant that the people clustered around were starting to recognize us. Fans seemed to understand that waiting near the entrance almost guaranteed athlete drive-bys.

"Let's walk," I said, putting a few steps between us to continue the plausible deniability of us being together.

I could see a couple of people in my peripheral vision starting to speed walk toward us. I knew the always affable Ben was processing what the possible credential shift meant, so it was my turn to run front. I steered him toward an alley, then pulled him through a door with red lettering that was either to a private home or the world's smallest bar.

Thankfully, it was the second option, a windowless brick room that felt subterranean. The walls were crowded with paintings and oddities, so the décor combined with the low, sloped ceiling and dim lighting meant that we'd found the perfect hideaway spot.

"Shall we sit?" I asked him.

He was finally starting to shake out of his trance. "Sure."

We found two open chairs at the end of the bar, right near the server station. The place was crowded with people wearing shades of black and gray and not a single star-spangled banner tribute among them. No one even looked our way as we settled in.

A bartender with slicked-back black hair nodded his chin toward us.

"Hai qualcosa di analcolico?" Ben said.

"Certo," the man replied and handed Ben a small menu.

He turned to me. "Do you want a real drink? Because I'm having a mocktail."

"Mocktail for sure," I agreed. We were two days out from competition and I was doing my best to stay true to my meal planning despite the upside-downness of my life in the Village.

"What are you thinking? Sharp, or fruity . . ."

"Bartender's choice," I shrugged.

Ben rattled off our order and then started fiddling with the coaster in front of him.

"I'm fine," he said abruptly. He turned to me with his face arranged in a smile that neither one of us believed. "I'll figure out the credential bullshit tomorrow. Let's talk about something else."

I placed my elbow on the bar and leaned closer to him. "Maybe we should talk about a detour to your hotel after this?"

"Oh, sure." He barked out a laugh. "My roommate, Barry, would love it."

I hid my pout. All I could think about was getting him alone again, and we were getting derailed at every attempt.

"Are you *serious*? They're making you share rooms?"

"Yeah, a bunch of us are but Kim and the other execs aren't even in the same hotel as us. They're in some luxury hotel down the road."

"What's she like? Kim? Because her vibe is Business Barbie. And she was sort of cunty to me during the press conference."

I hadn't mentioned the tense few minutes to him.

"*What?* Seriously? What did she say?"

He sounded like a dad hearing his kid had been bullied.

"Don't worry about it. I handled it. Handled *her*. But what's she like to work with?"

His expression pinched as he considered the question with the new information. "We got along great at first. She went to bat for me despite . . . everything. Now, I'm not so sure. But she knows her shit. She has a vision for the show that can verge on dictatorial."

His tone made it sound like he had more to say but he broke off abruptly.

"Do you like her?" I asked.

"I did. We've sort of been butting heads lately."

The bartender delivered our order and I was delighted to receive a Creamsicle-colored drink with slices of orange hanging off the rim, and a black-and-white-striped straw in it. The thing was a party compared to Ben's tumbler of muddy liquid over ice.

I held up my drink. "To us."

He tapped his tumbler to my glass. "Cin cin."

I wasn't used to being the cheerer-upper for Ben, since it seemed like the man never had a bad day. It felt like every topic I wanted to get into with him was off limits, specifically what the hell was going on with the show, and more important, what we were to each other.

Ben broke the silence first. "You're ready," he said.

It was a non sequitur but he didn't have to explain what he meant.

"Yeah." I nodded. "I am. I feel really good. Confident in a way I've never experienced."

"That's the most important part," he said. "If you can keep your peace in here," he clutched both hands over his chest, "then you'll be fine. It's easy to get caught up in the weirdness of being at the Games, but all that matters is staying true to you."

"Agreed." I took a sip of the drink that tasted like dessert in a glass.

"So I'm guessing it feels different this time around?"

Here I was maintaining a boundary for him, yet he was crossing one of mine. But I'd always insisted that we couldn't talk about my past on the record. This was a case of a fellow athlete checking in on me, not an attempt to trauma harvest for public consumption.

"It really does feel different. I can't even compare the two experiences, because I was so miserable in Switzerland that my memory has holes. Like, I can't remember entire *days*."

His expression went pained as he watched me. "Trauma can do that to you."

I stopped fiddling with my fancy straw and returned his gaze.

"How much trauma are *you* dealing with right now? Because you're not you, Ben, and it's sort of freaking me out."

"Quinn," he sighed. "Let's not."

"No, *let's*. Because I'm getting some really weird vibes about what's happening with you and the show and I'm worried."

"Now's not the time," he insisted, staring at his tumbler and not me.

"Ben."

I said it so sharply that he jumped, and the couple next to us glanced over.

I lowered my voice. "Talk to me. Please. You should know first-hand that keeping everything bottled up is unhealthy. I can handle it, I swear."

He sighed again, heavier and deeper. I wanted to rub his slumped shoulders but worried that touching him might derail us.

"Fine. You want to know?" His voice was sandpaper. "I'm getting the sense that the show might not sign me, and I'm worried about what'll happen to me if they don't. I'm feeling, like, these *echoes* of how I felt four years ago." It came out in a rush, like it was hard for him to admit it out loud.

A stone formed in my chest as I watched his face go ashen.

"I feel *weak*," he whispered, finally turning to stare at me with haunted eyes. "I don't want you to see me like that, at any point, but especially now. I want to be strong for you, Quinn, and all of a sudden I'm worrying that I won't be able to. I'm terrified that I might wind up back on my couch for months if this thing doesn't pan out. Because how fucking humiliating would it be?"

He looked queasy at the thought.

"But why *wouldn't* they hire you?"

He seemed to grapple with his response. "It's complicated. All I know for sure is that it's not looking great," he finally admitted. "On paper, I have the tools to deal with a setback like this. Not getting hired. But . . . what if I can't?"

"Then *I'll* be strong for *you*," I insisted. I threaded my hand around his arm.

"No, but that's what you don't understand, Quinn. You're about to experience some pain with the transition back to being a regular human being. Trust me, it doesn't matter how strong you feel now, or what medal you bring home, the aftermath of the Olympics *will* be tough. What you experienced last time was different. This is your final Olympics, no chance for another shot at glory, and that brings a totally different kind of bullshit. That's where I'm supposed to come in to help you, because I've been there, done that, bought the therapy. But if that black dog comes back? I'm worthless."

I squeezed his bicep. "Ben, stop. You don't have to be my hero, you just have to be *here*."

He didn't answer.

The bartender came over to check on us and Ben shifted away from me. It felt deliberate.

After we finished our drinks we began the slow walk back to the Village, making small talk about the Vox party while I tried to pretend that everything was normal. But there was a new wall between us courtesy of Ben, and it was my turn to do some demolition.

It was probably the last time we were going to connect in person before I skated, and I couldn't resist pushing for a little clarification. I didn't want to have to worry about our status as I fell asleep in addition to every other challenge whizzing around my brain and keeping me awake.

It felt selfish, but I knew that we could weather whatever was to come if we faced it together.

"Are *we* okay?" I asked him quietly. "You and me?"

Saying it out loud made me feel itchy. We'd danced around defining whatever was taking root between us, but what our bodies had been saying left little doubt.

"What do you mean?"

Him not following the implication was a dagger in my heart. How could he *not* know what I was talking about?

"Nothing. All good." I pulled my coat across my chest and crossed my arms tightly.

"The only thing that matters right now is both of us doing what we came here to do. No distractions, right?"

I nodded. Not exactly what I wanted to hear, but it was what I'd agreed to.

"Focus on winning," he added. "We'll figure the rest out later."

I nodded again and hoped my heart would get the message.

Chapter Thirty-Nine

$\mathcal{M}$y former coach Carol had always insisted that competition skating order could make or break you, so it took a couple of years before I could shake the feeling that "the draw" would determine my outcome. It was a bizarre bit of theater on top of the rest of the competition stress, a secretive lottery-like drawing late at night in a dark hallway to determine who skated when. There was some validity to her claim, since the judges might score earlier skaters more conservatively before seeing the rest of the contenders. But then again, a baller was a baller whether they went first or last.

I hated that Carol was in my head, on today of all days. My first competition, the short-program skate. I'd almost exorcised her completely, but being back in the theater of the Games was enough to reawaken the demon. I tried to reframe my thoughts of her as gasoline on a brush fire, like my anger about the way she'd treated me was a performance accelerant. Add in some unwanted texting from my mom after she'd arrived in Milan and I had plenty of kindling for the inferno I was about to create out on the ice.

It turned out that the top-secret closed draw with the officials the night before had graced me with what Zamboni Frank called the catbird seat; I was the second to last skater of the evening. I would go out onto the ice knowing nearly everyone's scores, with the energy in the arena at a fever pitch.

The drawback was that I'd also been forced to listen to audience reactions as my competition skated. No surprise, Ayumi's program had left the rafters shaking. Mel had made sure that I camped out in a quiet corner of the waiting space off ice, far from the TVs broadcasting the performances. She divided her time between walking out to the rink to watch everyone else and hanging out with me as I did visualizations, stretched, and tried to stay warmed up. Her descriptions of the other performances were filled with adorably modest praise, like calling Yena's flawless jumps "decent."

As the night sped to a close we were left with unsurprising results: Ayumi was in the lead, with Yena close behind her in a surprising upset, followed by Madeline. Erica's performance had squeaked her into the free-skate portion of the Games—she landed in the twenty-second position—and poor Kayla had wound up in a disappointing twenty-eighth position, which meant that her journey was over.

So US figure skating only had two chances to podium. No pressure or anything.

Mel walked over to my little prep cave looking like a professor about to give a lecture, in a smart black blazer and black turtleneck. I studied her face as she got closer. No visible stress, just a confident smile, like the event was over and I'd already won.

"You should feel really good right now," she said as she took my hands. "That's all I'm saying."

She'd watched everyone with the exception of Beatrix Kahn, who would skate last. It was Mel's way of telling me that if I could skate a flawless performance I'd wipe the rest of the competition off the ice.

So different from last time. I'd forced myself not to think about the trauma of Switzerland, but there were moments like this one that made it impossible.

"It's time," she said, squeezing my hands. "Let's go do this."

I bowed my head, closed my eyes, and pictured myself in my final pose of the performance. Chest rising and falling from the exertion, with tears in my eyes again, but this time from gratitude.

I was ready.

I followed her out to the edge of the ice, past other skaters, staff, volunteers, and a million cameras. I took off my practice jacket and guards and placed them on the boards, then turned back to Mel for one final pep talk.

We touched foreheads, and I tried to focus on what she was saying, not the cameras pushing closer to capture the moment.

"I believe in you," she whispered. "No matter what, I'm so proud of you."

A calm unlike anything I'd experienced washed over me, like she'd just injected me with a sedative. The jangly, coiled-spring sensation I always battled prior to performances was replaced by a serenity. A *knowing*.

"Thank you for being you," I whispered back.

We locked eyes for a few additional seconds, then she let go and I skated out to the center of the ice.

I could've sworn I felt the energy in the building shift as I got into position.

There's no stillness quite like what a skater feels in the moments before the performance music begins. Members of the audience could probably hear the rustling and coughing of their fellow spectators, but to me the packed rink was tomb silent. I couldn't see anything beyond the borders of the ice. My breathing preemptively slowed to match the rhythm to come.

The first quiet notes of the song began and my focus narrowed even more. Now, I was a storyteller, not a skater.

I started off the performance graceful, like every other skater that night. I was soft, and poised, but a little reserved, skating like I was the same delicate flower of the past. People who'd never seen the performance might assume that I'd maintain the same level of doe-eyed wonder throughout the piece, but the pre-chorus tone shift and my corresponding spins signaled that I'd been holding back.

Each move was stronger than the last as the music swelled and became more cinematic. Not a single wobble, just clean, blissful skating that was so on target that I had to hold back from celebrating after every successful move. I still had a minute and a half to go, with the most challenging jumps to come.

The familiar burning in my legs signaled that I was reaching the halfway point. I could track my performance not only by the choreography I was performing, but also how my body felt as I moved through it.

I was now in a flow state so intense that it was like I was watching my own performance as it was happening. I saw myself stepping into my strength right after the chorus and embodying the sensuality of the moves. There was no truer performance for me than this one, no better depiction of how it felt to claim my power through *my* efforts, not as a by-product of someone else's tutoring.

My spectator-eye view of my performance meant that I could turn off the jump math portion of my brain. All I had to do was stick to the plan and keep skating cleanly and I'd dominate; there was no need for me to try to make up for on-ice mistakes by pushing my performance to be more challenging than it needed to be.

But I *wanted* to.

My only scheduled triple axel was in my "Bulletproof" free skate later in the week, but I'd played with adding one to "Movement" as well during practice sessions. Mel aimed for being predictably successful, and normally I agreed, but I'd also never skated quite like this before.

I felt untouchable.

I could do it. I'd never been more confident in my performance. I wanted to claim this moment once and for all as mine, and an unexpected triple A would do it.

The launch point in the song was rapidly approaching. The tension of the music narrowed to just Hozier's voice backed by a choir, and I could almost feel the collected inhalation of a thousand breaths as the sound paused for a millisecond and I launched myself into the air.

And hovered there, spinning without any concern for gravity.

I could visualize my landing before I'd even finished my final revolution, and when I actually touched down the reality of it matched what I'd seen in my mind.

Flawless.

I'd been focused inward throughout the performance, but I finally allowed myself to listen to the cheers from the crowd as I moved into the remaining components of the piece. It was the final section, where I fully stepped into my strength, and it felt right to be beaming as I finished my triple lutz and toe loop combo.

I was flying. Second half jump bonus, here I come.

The instruments quieted again after the crescendo until all that was left was Hozier's voice and the choir wailing behind him. Lush, haunting, and underscored by the slice of my skates on the ice.

And then it was over.

I froze in my final pose, bent over backward at the waist like I didn't have a spinal cord, with my arms outstretched. It was both a welcome and a threat; I'd bared my soft soul to the audience, but now every one of them knew that there was steel beneath the velvet.

When I stood up I felt like I'd just had an out-of-body experience. I couldn't remember what I'd just done, all I knew was that the entire arena was on their feet, applauding for me without any regard for the flags they clutched in their hands.

Tears flooded my eyes. I drank in the moment, alternating between covering my mouth in shock and waving to everyone in the stands. The junior skaters flooded onto the ice to collect the stuffed animals raining down from the stands.

I skated to the exit, where Mel was waiting for me, and launched myself at her, laughing and crying at the same time.

"You were *amazing*," she said as she squeezed me tightly.

The cameras crowded closer but I didn't care. This time around I wanted the world to see my face, mascara streaks and all.

When we finally pulled apart I put my guards on and practically levitated to the kiss and cry.

I felt like I was in shock as I settled onto the bench next to Mel. I was still breathing heavily, and a little sweaty, but I dialed up my smile for the camera broadcasting my every move. It always felt like the wait for scores took forever, but this time around I didn't care.

"That *triple*," Mel breathed as she leaned closer to me. "Why did you add it?"

I laughed. "Because I could."

Chapter Forty

*A*mong the many congratulatory texts that came after my triumphant performance from Zoey and the rest of my friends at the rink were a half dozen from my mom. I'd maintained a cordial distance from her prior to the competition, blaming my practice schedule, but she knew that I had a two-day gap before my free skate and wasn't letting up about us getting together.

She promised that she and my father were available to meet me for any meal I could swing. I figured it would be easiest to get it out of the way during the afterglow of my short, but with enough time padded in as I shifted my focus to my next performance.

Before I suggested a meeting time to her I crossed my fingers and reached out to Ben.

He'd been so overwhelmed for me after my short that the first three texts he'd sent were nothing more than exclamation points, heart and fire emojis, and celebratory curse words. When we finally managed to steal a few minutes to talk later that night he couldn't stop raving. Now I was hoping that he'd be willing to break our agreement in a big way to help me stay sane; I wanted him to chaperone my dinner date.

I crossed my fingers as I called him, still splayed out on my cardboard bed. I figured I earned the late start to the day after the previous night's triumph. Erica and Kayla had already left for breakfast, and I felt like it was good for me to keep my distance in the aftermath of Kayla not making the cut. She knew that her chances had been slim, but it didn't dull the pain of not moving on.

Ben's phone rang once then went to voicemail. I followed up with a text outlining why I was demanding a protocol break to our agreement with all sorts of silly faux-legalese. When he didn't reply to my legit funny message after ten minutes I got up to start my day, trying not to obsess about why he wasn't responding.

Hours later, after practice, my gym session, *and* PT, I received a reply.

> Sorry, they're shipping me off to Cortina D'Ampezzo to cover curling. Have fun.

I stared at the screen for an eternity, waiting for the follow-up text with encouragement, or an acknowledgment of how terrible the night was going to be, or an apology for not being able to go, or at the very least a muscle-arm emoji, but nothing else came through.

He understood the stakes, so his nonresponse was as loud as a tornado siren.

Ben was currently fighting his own battle.

I ignored my instincts and texted him back: I'm here if you need me.

This time his reply was immediate. Remember we're lc. Protect your peace and focus on you.

Another side step. My chest hollowed out at the thought of him struggling. What I needed to say to him wouldn't translate in a text, so I vowed to track him down somehow.

For now I needed to find alternate backup for *my* next battle. I called Mel.

MEL STRODE UP to me at the Village gates dressed for battle in her tallest heels and a black leather trench coat I'd never seen before.

"Okay, super spy," I laughed. "Look at you."

"I did a little celebratory shopping after practice today," she said and did a catwalk turn and posed. "Too much?"

"In Italy, it works. Not so sure about Woodspring. What about me? Do I look ready for intense, nitpicking scrutiny?"

I opened my coat to flash my brown sweater dress and tall boots.

"Perfection. Body is a ten, face is off the charts. Let's walk."

The vibe near the Village gates made it feel like a carnival. We threaded through the crowds and I kept my head down, hoping to stay anonymous. As much as I enjoyed interacting with fans, I needed to get in the right bitchy headspace for the family dinner to come.

"Why can't Ben make it?" Mel asked. "I can hold my own but it would be nice to have some backup."

"He's covering curling."

"This late?" She scowled. "Is this a special session or something?"

I'd tried to ignore the odd timing. "Maybe it's a sit-down interview with the team off-hours?"

The sound of our footsteps filled the silence. I could tell Mel was gearing up for *the* question.

"Are we ever going to talk about what's going on with him? Because I'm starting to feel a little out of the loop."

I felt my face going hot as she stared at me. Mel knew everything about me so it was odd that I hadn't shared the real story with her. But then again, I wasn't sure what was going on with Ben other than our rapidly shifting agreement.

"Honestly, I don't know. We have a connection—"

"Which anyone can see," she interrupted.

"Yeah, but Ben woos every human he comes in contact with," I said. "You have a connection with him. *Frank* has a connection with him. It's not hard to fall under his spell."

"True," she considered it. "But it seems different with you. When you're around, no one else matters. His focus is *completely* on you, and not just because you were his subject on the show. And it's not, like, flirty-horndog-who-wants-to-jump-you vibes. The way he watches you is bodyguard-ish. You know? Like he's scanning the perimeter with one eye while keeping the other glued to you."

"Okay, creepy visual," I replied.

She bumped against me. "You know what I mean. So what's going to happen next?"

"Not sure. We're LC until the Games are over."

But not if I had anything to do with it.

"LC?"

I chuckled. "I guess you're not on narcissist mom Reddit. It means 'low contact.' We're not reaching out to each other unless it's critical." I paused. "Or if something major happens, like, oh I don't know, coming in first in the short program."

Mel broke out in a jig on the sidewalk. "You did it, you did it," she sang.

"*We* did it," I corrected her. "Anyway, it's for the best right now. No distractions, just total focus on our goals."

It had turned into focus with a side of worry on my side of the equation, but I had a plan.

We arrived at Lucia, a small restaurant on a quiet side street that featured a menu sure to piss off my mom since the place had a strict policy of not altering their dishes to suit dietary issues. My mom didn't have any, but she enjoyed making restaurants jump through hoops to try to please her.

"Let's get this over with. Showtime," I said as I pushed the door open.

"My *baby*!"

The shriek echoed through the anteroom and drew every eye to my mom, which was the desired outcome. She jumped off the bench and ran to me with her arms outstretched.

"Hi, Mom," I said as she wrapped me in a smothering, perfumed hug. No surprise, she looked stunning in her double-breasted camel-colored coat.

My dad was right behind her, smiling his handsome-leading-man smile. Anyone watching would assume that we were a functional family.

She pulled back to study me. "I bet you barely slept last night. It's so exciting, sweetheart! You're closer than you've ever been. Now we just have to pray you don't falter in the free skate like last time." She wiped her thumb along my cheek then leaned in to whisper to me. "You missed some contour blending but I fixed it."

My dad pushed closer to hug me as well. "You were incredible last night. I'm so proud."

Somehow the p-word coming from him didn't have an impact on me. He couldn't claim an emotional investment in my journey since he'd largely been absent from it.

Mel swept past me. "Well hello, you two! Long time no see. So long that I wouldn't have recognized you without this one to ID you."

It was a vague enough comment, but I knew my mom would spend the rest of the night trying to decipher what Mel meant by it, wondering if she thought she looked older, or if her recent subtle cosmetic "upgrades" were more obvious than she realized.

"Oh!" My mom seemed confused as she glanced between us. "It's *you*. Melanie! What a coincidence."

"No," I relished dropping the first bomb of the evening. "I invited Mel! I figured since we're celebrating I should also include the person who helped make last night happen."

I roped my arm around Mel's shoulders and we grinned at my parents as a united front. Watching my mom try to maintain a happy expression as she recalibrated our dinner date was priceless.

"How *sweet*," my mom fake-gushed. "I guess you're acknowledging all your mentors, since you wouldn't be here without your parents."

I felt Mel stiffen in response.

"And we're going to turn that spotlight right back on our star, right?" Mel said. "I'm not taking *any* credit for what she's done. I'm just along for the ride at this point."

"Exactly," my mom laughed awkwardly. She glanced back toward the host. "Shall we get sorted out now? They wouldn't give us the table until the full party was here, and I was starting to get worried since you were late."

"It's four minutes after seven," I said through gritted teeth.

"But we were here early, and you know what I always say: Early is on time, and on time is late."

"Aw," Mel said. "That must be super helpful for all those little ones you teach. Start those life lessons young!"

My dad chuckled and followed behind my mom as she stomped to the host stand.

Thanks to my mom's tendency to "run cold because she's so tiny," we had to switch tables three times due to phantom drafts. I could see the waitstaff rolling their eyes at us. When we finally found one that met her approval she sharpened her claws and got to work.

"*So* much pasta and cream sauce on this menu! Mel, I'm assuming you picked this spot since you obviously don't have any dietary restrictions." My mom glanced at her over her readers.

Mel laughed good-naturedly. "You're right, Tricia, I *don't*. It's so freeing to just enjoy food. I had to do some retraining with her but now this one does too." She nodded her head toward me.

"Funny you mention it, I did notice how . . . healthy she looked last night." My mom reached over to poke me in the side. "But you wear it well, sweetheart! Such a cutie."

My throat tightened reflexively. The old grooves were still there despite all the work I'd done to pull myself out of them. I started to answer but Mel beat me to it.

"Isn't it crazy that eating real food can change *everything*?" Mel said with amped-up awe. "Quinn started eating bread again and bam, all of a sudden she's winning! I think there's a correlation. Maybe carbs are the secret to success?"

She reached for the bread basket, grabbed a breadstick, then held it out to me. "Cheers. Here's to gold."

I took one as well and touched it to hers, laughing. "Cheers."

My mom watched in horror as I took a bite so huge that it reduced the thing by half.

Maybe dinner was a good idea after all?

Chapter Forty-One

Campbell Pesansky had become Ben's number one stalker.

True to her creative social media'ing, she'd turned her silly obsession with him into an ongoing meme she called "Ben Watch," where she crowd-sourced his location on a map of the Village and surrounding sports complexes. Anyone who spotted him was welcome to report where he was to her so she could update the map with his cartoon avatar.

According to the map, he had indeed been in Cortina D'Ampezzo the previous night, which was a relief. I'd been watching her page all day, hoping for updates that put him back in the Village. As always, my schedule was packed, but I'd find a way to reach him with Campbell's help.

I'd set up a massage for after my on-ice practice, but when I checked the Ben Watch map I saw that he was on the far side of the Village doing "people on the street" interviews.

My sore muscles could wait.

I'd opted to wear the most basic Team USA jacket in my collection—basic blue with minimal embellishments—and over-size sunglasses so I could disappear, and hid my hair under a knit hat. I refreshed the map and saw that someone had posted a comment with a photo of him five minutes prior. I broke into a speed-walk, since a true jog would attract attention. Athletes ran, civilians strolled.

I came up on a crowd just outside the gates and sure enough, when I jumped up on a nearby retaining wall I spotted Ben chatting with a camera operator. It was like he was a zoo animal, with people milling around and watching his every move.

I searched for Business Barbie and was both happy and bummed that she wasn't nearby. It meant that she was focused on someone more important.

Ben was officially b-team now, although you wouldn't know it from looking at him. He posed for selfies with his arm around fans, wearing a big smile even though he probably wanted to disappear. My heart splintered for him.

I glanced around looking for a spot where we could have some privacy, because my next move had to have the precision of a military operation: Go into the throng, extract Ben, then take him to a quiet location for a loving beatdown.

The fates were on my side when I spotted Team USA snowboarder Luke Milberg strolling by, a man who knew how to attract attention. He was walking alone and had his signature pink mohawk hidden under a hat, probably going incognito himself. We'd met in the training room and had a long conversation about the benefits of arnica gel, and I'd wound up giving him one of my special tubs of the stuff from Germany since he was nursing a bruise that extended from his knee to his butt cheek.

He owed me.

I explained to him that I needed to cash in on my favor, and he was more than happy to walk into the middle of the crowd around

Ben and remove his hat like it was a striptease. Once he had everyone laughing and focused on him I swooped in and grabbed Ben's hand.

He turned, smiling his performance smile until he realized that it was me. He glanced around.

"What are you doing here?"

"C'mon," I insisted, dragging him when he refused to move.

"But I'm working."

"So am I. Give me four minutes."

He must've just walked out of the gates because the guards waved both of us through without an interrogation. I pulled Ben into the Welcome Experience building with him and startled the young volunteer standing in the lobby with a clipboard.

"Hi folks, I'm so sorry but this area is closed right now—" She paused when she saw Ben, then looked at me. I begrudgingly pulled off my hat and sunglasses, exposing Quinnett like the two of us together equaled an all-access pass.

"Ohmygosh! Hi, you guys! Can I get you anything? Is there a problem with your merch, Quinn?"

"No, everything is wonderful, thank you so much," I answered. "We just need to find a quiet spot to talk about, uh, ratings from *The Score*. Is that okay with you?"

"Totally! Follow me, I'll show you where to go."

The young woman seemed thrilled to be tangentially involved in our mission. She pushed a door open and gestured into the room. "This was our welcome suite for sponsors. No one is here now so please feel free to make yourselves comfortable."

I glanced around and realized that the organizations that bankrolled the Games got the kid-glove treatment as well. The room was a calming navy and filled with plush velvet couches and chairs that looked 100 percent more comfortable than a cardboard bed.

"I'll be right out here. Holler if you need me!"

She gave us a little wave then disappeared.

We were finally alone.

"What are you doing, Quinn?" Ben sighed.

Stage-Ben disappeared and was replaced by a version of him I hadn't encountered. Pale, with bruised-looking half-moons beneath his eyes.

"I'm saving you from you," I answered, moving closer to him. I grasped him on both arms.

He froze as he processed what I was saying. I watched his shoulders slump.

"It's literally the day before the biggest competition of your life," he complained and tried to pull away, but I tightened my grip. "Whatever you want to say to me can wait."

"It absolutely cannot." I shook my head. "Now listen to me."

He frowned even harder.

"I. Am. Here. No matter what color dog winds up sleeping on your chest, I need you to know that I will be right beside you trying to evict it. You decide to bed rot for a week or two? I'll be sprouting mold one pillow over. You stop showering and brushing your teeth? I'll plug my nose. You refuse to answer your phone? I'll become your social secretary. But the one thing I *won't* do is leave. Got it? I will be there for all the dark shit that you think is going to drag you under, because guess what?"

"What?" Ben asked warily.

"I'm your motherfucking life preserver."

I watched his face transform as I spoke, from anger, to disbelief, to gratitude that nearly made his eyes brim, which made mine actually spill over.

"Okay?" I sniffled. "You are not weak, Bennett Martino. You are *everything*."

"But . . ."

I wordlessly shook my head.

There was nothing more he could say and he knew it. Ben was now well acquainted with my single-minded focus, and now that I had a mission he probably correctly assumed that my loving steamroll was unstoppable.

A knot untwisted in my chest when he finally broke from being Mr. Tough Guy and pulled me into a tight hug. He exhaled when our bodies connected. I pushed my cheek against his chest and breathed him in.

We *both* needed this moment.

"You don't have to face it alone," I murmured.

"Don't worry, I'll snap out of it," he said into my hair.

"If you do, great. If you can't, I'll help you find a way to make it happen. You mean too much to me, Ben. We're getting through whatever comes next together."

"But you might be dealing with—"

I squeezed him like it was a punishment.

"Nope. Whatever comes next is *we*."

Chapter Forty-Two

I was crying on the ice again.

And not in a cute way. In a runny nose, hiccupping, laugh-crying, this-is-going-to-be-the-photo-they-run way.

But I didn't care because holy *fuck*, I'd just skated my heart out.

From the minute the song began, I'd felt nothing but pure joy. People had questioned my music choice since "Bulletproof" obviously wasn't a typical sweeping orchestral piece to which I could perform lots of balletic moves like the rest of the skaters. And Mel, Sarah, and I had had a few tense conversations about the possibility of more traditional judges having a grudge against my performance before it had even really started, but it was a risk I was willing to take. I'd spent the better part of my career bowing to what other people wanted to see from me, and since this was my final shot at gold, I was going to do it *my* way.

It turned out to be the best decision of my skating career.

The performance took everything I'd endured in my early career and transformed it into an absolutely kick-ass, take-no-prisoners performance. I hoped the cameras had zoomed in on me during the line in the song about burning bridges shore to shore, because I always visualized my mom and Carol as I skated it.

And I never stopped smiling the entire time. Every flip and jump I'd executed had been textbook. It didn't even matter to me if my fellow competitors skated better than I had, because *my* performance had felt perfect for me. And the audience reactions throughout it had lifted me up, because every move I nailed was met with roars. By the end, the crowd was on their feet.

I wasn't about to hurry off the ice to the kiss and cry. I needed to drink in what I'd practically killed myself to earn. All the pain I'd endured, mental and physical, had brought me to *this* moment.

I was having trouble catching my breath, not only from the intensity of what I'd just done, but also because I could feel the waves of love rolling down on me from the stands, practically drowning me. The applause and foot stomping sounded as sweet as Beethoven.

It felt like I stood there for an hour, just swiveling slowly and taking it in. This was my second and final Olympics so I wasn't about to speed to the end.

The sweepers skated out to grab the rainbow of stuffed animals being tossed out onto the ice and I took it as my cue to go.

As always, Mel was waiting at the edge of the rink beaming at me.

"I'm *so* proud of you," she told me as she swept me into a hug.

I could feel her crying as well, because even though we didn't have scores yet, we both knew that based on my "Bulletproof" performance, there was a spot on the podium for me.

Exactly where, we were about to find out.

I got hugs from my teammates and then we headed for the kiss and cry. I smiled for the camera and waved with both hands while upbeat music echoed around the stadium. My entire body was buzzing with the zingiest, most overwhelming endorphins I'd ever experienced.

I was so deer in the headlights that Mel had to bump her shoulder against mine to get me out of my trance. "You were perfect," she beamed at me. "Flawless."

"Seriously?" I asked, even though I knew she was right.

"*Stunning.*"

It felt like we'd just sat down and all of a sudden . . . my scores.

For a split second, numbers stopped making sense to me. It was all hieroglyphics. But the corresponding roar from the crowd and the way Mel grabbed my arm jerked me back to reality.

Eighteen years of devotion were finally paying off.

I'd won gold.

It was silly of me to scan the crowd thinking I'd see anyone I knew as I waited to step up on the podium they moved out onto the ice. I was smiling so hard my eyes were almost squeezed shut, but still I searched for that one achingly familiar face. I knew that if we locked eyes even from a distance, we'd still be able to have a conversation.

I told you, he'd say.

Yes, you did, I'd answer.

I scanned the camera crews ringing the rink but couldn't find Ben among them. There was no way he'd miss it since there was nothing else scheduled at the same time.

And of course there was no way he'd miss it since it was, well, *me*.

The music shifted as the officials walked out on the navy carpet they'd placed on the ice.

I glanced at Ayumi, then Yena. I had plenty of challenges throughout my career, but I'd never made an enemy of my fellow skaters. I knew Ayumi wasn't thrilled to be coming in second to me, but she smiled graciously and bobbed her head when I caught her eye. Yena seemed overwhelmed that she'd actually made it to the podium.

The announcer introduced Yena, they played her national anthem, and then she bent over to accept her bronze. The process repeated with Ayumi, and then time stopped.

When I'd visualized this moment I'd somehow forgotten to include how it might *feel* for me. I'd had a hard enough time even allowing the picture to sharpen into focus, so including sense details like how deafening the crowd would be hadn't even occurred to me. Now it felt like everything was heightened to extremes.

The lights were brighter, the audience was louder, the cold was chillier.

And me? I felt *transcendent*. There were almost no words to describe it. Joyful, proud, grateful, lucky . . . it was a mix of every good feeling I'd ever experienced amplified to the extreme. I felt like my face was cracking open from smiling so hard, but I couldn't stop it.

Until the national anthem began.

I wasn't expecting the tears again, but hearing the song and seeing the flags unfurling in the crowd was a reminder that I hadn't just skated for me, I'd done it for everyone back home as well. Frank, Zoey and the Chens, and all the little kids who crowded the ice every weekend and dreamed that someday they'd find themselves on top of a podium.

And yes, even my parents.

I swallowed hard as the officiant walked toward me with the medal on a tray. I moved forward, accepted his congratulations, and bent down and closed my eyes as he slipped the ribbon over my head.

When I stood up, the medal bumped heavily against my chest. I reflexively grabbed it, and the three of us held up our medals in unison to the cheers of the audience.

My dream was achieved, and no matter what happened next, no one could take the feeling I experienced in this moment away from me.

Chapter Forty-Three

$\mathcal{I}$ opened the door of my temporary home to find Ben on his knees bowing down to me.

"Stop," I laughed. "Get in here."

We'd managed to steal exactly two minutes the night before during my whirlwind postceremony press tour. I felt like I did a thousand interviews, followed by the Team USA party until early in the morning, then my first day as an Olympic gold medalist kicked off with even more commitments and a million different kinds of media. I'd had to beg off from a dinner event because I knew that I was getting close to burnout. I needed rest.

And I needed *Ben*.

He walked through the door and crashed into me without pausing, wrapping me in his arms in the world's tightest hug.

As always, I had to fight through layers of his down jacket to grip his actual body.

"Fuck yeah." His voice was muffled against my neck. "Fuck yeah, Quinn Albright. You fucking did it."

Another laugh bubbled out of me. It wasn't the most eloquent congratulations I'd gotten but it was probably the most heartfelt.

I pulled back to look up at him and was rewarded with a kiss that made me forget everything else.

The moment I won it was as if a switch had flipped in Ben. *I* knew there were still clouds in his heart, but his happiness for me seemed to cancel out everything else.

"How do you feel?"

I'd been asked the question so many times and I still couldn't find the right descriptor. I defaulted to the ones people expected, like "proud" and "thankful," fully aware that there was another sensation lurking in the shadows that I couldn't understand, or even admit.

"Of all the people in the world asking me that, *you* would know," I answered.

He started to pull away but I squeezed him tighter to keep him nestled close. He relaxed against me and rested his chin on top of my head.

"Oh, I'm *very* aware of what you're going through. It's almost undefinable, yet you have to come up with these pithy, quotable sound bites."

We finally pulled apart and he unzipped his jacket and dropped it on a chair. "Did Kayla and Erica leave?"

I nodded. "This morning. Feels weird being here alone."

"Get used to it," Ben said softly as he surveyed the place.

"What do you mean?" I asked as I followed behind him.

He shook his head. "Nothing."

Ben explored the bland but serviceable apartment that had been my home base for the past few weeks. It felt like the spirit of the place had left along with my roommates, although not the mess, since Kayla was incapable of picking up after herself and had left anything that she didn't pack or throw out strewn around the place.

"So what now? Are we thinking a big, fancy dinner? Or a night of nonstop clubbing? Whatever you want," Ben said. "Because you're dressed to impress."

"*Please.*" I gestured down my sweatsuited body. "I'm not leaving this apartment until tomorrow. All I want to do is sit."

"Then let's sit," he said agreeably. "Are you hungry, though? Can I bring you food?"

I paused when I noticed the time, since it had ceased to exist for me for much of the day. "No, they fed me dinner earlier. I think it was dinner. Linner, maybe?"

We both dropped onto the uncomfortable couch and I let out a long exhale. I was exhausted in a way I didn't know was possible, but still contemplating tackling Ben and ripping off all his clothes.

"Weird, right?" Ben asked.

The non sequitur made complete sense to me, because everything I was going through and feeling was weird as hell.

"Beyond. I don't know what to do with myself. Like, I don't have to get up tomorrow morning and train at the crack of dawn. The next few weeks are filled with press, not practice." I stared into space. "Who even am I now?"

"You're a freaking Olympic gold medalist," he cheered and punched the air.

I covered my mouth and giggled like a little girl.

"So where is it?" Ben asked, craning his neck to glance around the messy apartment.

I stopped laughing. "Don't judge me . . ."

"Oh shit."

I leaned closer to him. "It's in the bottom of my suitcase," I whispered. "Looking at it freaks me out."

I never would've admitted this to anyone else, even Mel.

His eyes scanned my face as he nodded. "Yup. I get it. The paradox of victory."

"It's all too much to process," I said, my heart heavy and airborne in a way I couldn't understand.

Ben reached over to palm my cheek. "But you're happy?"

I closed my eyes and leaned into his touch. "I am now."

He stroked my cheek with his thumb until it became a kind of touch meditation, lulling me into a Zen state. But one thought kept crowding out my peace.

I opened my eyes and stared at Ben's beautiful, open face, registering how he looked before I asked the question. "How are *you*?"

He dropped his hand.

"Happy."

I squinted as I studied him, waiting for the telltale furrow and tension around his mouth. *Any* hint that suggested he was hiding something from me.

Either his poker face was exceptional, or he was being honest.

"For you, and us," he continued, his eyes softening even more. "Because the agreement has expired."

I took a deep breath. I'd been so focused on the lead-up that I'd barely had a chance to consider the now.

"We're free agents?" I mused.

"Not exactly," he replied, reaching over to take my hand and thread his fingers through mine. "I'm not going anywhere, but *you're* going into an insane post-Games period, so in the short term there's not going to be much room for me in your life."

I started to respond but he held up his hand to quiet me.

"Quinn, I've been there. I know how all this rolls out. You're on a rocket ship for the next couple of months." He waited until I looked him in the eyes before he continued. "All I can do is wait until you come back down to Earth."

It was vague and undefined, but for now it was exactly what I needed to hear.

"You'll wait for me?"

A smile tugged at the corner of his mouth. "I have been. For the past four years."

My nervous heart finally relaxed into a regular rhythm, until I slid my leg over his and straddled him. Just the notion of what was about to happen was enough to make me want to start grinding against him.

"Colorado to Brooklyn is awfully far," I said as I leaned down to kiss him.

"We'll figure it out," he replied as his hands snaked up my back. "I promise."

We regarded one another like we'd finally gotten the right prescription lenses, like we could now see clearly things that had been hazy. I placed my hands against his chest and could feel his heart thumping like he'd just finished a long run.

He gave me a series of tiny kisses, pausing between each one to pull back and stare into my eyes. "You know, when I was watching you last night I wanted to scream 'She's *mine*' to everyone around me."

I felt a blush creep onto my cheeks. I dipped my head and pushed it against his sternum. He stroked my back

"But I guess I should confirm that. Are you?" Ben asked after a few minutes of silence from me. "Mine?"

My entire body turned effervescent at the question.

"I am. Always have been, agreement or not."

It was the green light he seemed to be waiting for. Ben scooted to the edge of the couch and then stood up effortlessly, clutching me against his chest.

"Room," he demanded.

"There," I pointed.

Chapter Forty-Four

*B*en wordlessly stomped down the hall, kicked open the door, and walked directly to the cardboard bed we were about to christen. The room was dark and half packed up, with the only light coming from the streetlamps through a small rectangular window.

"Is it okay if we break this thing?" Ben asked as he lowered me down onto the worst bed I'd ever slept on.

Although sleep was the last thing on my mind.

"Exactly how much force are you planning to use, sir?" I teased.

He straightened and looked down at me through narrowed eyes. "As much as it takes."

Ben couldn't maintain the tough-guy act and broke into a laugh.

"Get over here," I giggled as I grabbed his hand and pulled him down on top of me.

The running joke around the Village was how strong the things were, with social media posts featuring athletes doing all sorts of jumps and suggestive contortions on top of their beds to prove the readiness. I was about to find out for myself.

"Ah yes, just as shitty as I remember," Ben said as we tried to get comfortable on the equivalent of a refrigerator box.

He raised up on his elbow to stare down at me.

"What?" I whispered, feeling studied and adored at the same time.

"I've just been thinking about this since Connecticut."

"Then stop waiting and do something," I teased.

Instead of moving he remained there, hovering above me and taking me in, one centimeter at a time. He finally reached down to tug at the zipper of my hoodie, raising one eyebrow as if asking for permission.

I nodded, holding my breath.

Ben drew the zipper down slowly, pausing when it cleared my breasts. I hadn't worn a bra or underwear, hoping for this very happy ending.

I shivered and sucked in a breath as he gazed at me.

He swept his palm across my chest, partly to move the fabric away and partly to tease me with the faintest drag across my nipples. I squeezed my eyes shut and arched against his hand, desperate for more contact.

Ben sat halfway up and wrenched his thermal over his head. He tossed it on the ground by the bed, then lowered himself on top of me again.

I sighed when his naked chest came down on top of mine and I felt the faintest tickle of his coarse hair. Our eyes met and we smiled at each other in unison.

"I'm really happy," I whispered.

"You don't even know," he replied, his dark eyes glinting hungrily.

He leaned down to kiss me and our tongues connected immediately, fast-tracking us to what was to come. Ben's kisses managed to find hidden spots on my body that I had no clue were sensitive, and I was surprised by the noises that came out of me when he took my earlobe into his mouth for a suck and nibble. But then he moved on to twisting my hair around his hand and tugging ever so slightly to give him access to more of my neck to kiss, which sent a roll of pleasure through me.

I wiggled beneath him to get all the way out of my hoodie. After being encased in down and wool and more down every time we tried to connect, I was eager to give him as much access to my body as possible.

He seemed to understand and hooked his thumbs under the elastic of my sweats. I raised my hips up and he inched them down, planting kisses as each new patch of skin was exposed.

"Commando," he murmured appreciatively and kissed each hip bone.

I couldn't answer because he continued moving his mouth down my body, sparking every nerve to life. I rolled my hips up to meet his lips, hoping for the second time in just a few minutes that I didn't seem desperate for him.

But I was, because Ben was making my skin shiver with each kiss. He pulled my sweats all the way off, then paused to take my foot in his hand and plant a kiss on top of it.

"These poor little feet," he whispered as he switched to kiss the other one. "They worked so hard."

He crawled back to me, easing my legs wider then dipping between them so quickly that I let out a little squeak of shock. Within seconds it became a sigh of pleasure as Ben's tongue pressed into me, making me melt against him.

He was deliberate, like he was pacing his pressure on the way I moved and moaned with each flick of his tongue. His little circles narrowed around my clit and the tension continued to build until I felt like I was about to pass out. I moved away.

"Are you okay?" he asked, his voice thick with concern.

I was already on my knees in front of him on the bed, working the button on his jeans. "I'm a one-and-done kind of girl and I want *you*."

He went concave as he watched me struggle with his zipper with shaky hands. "One and done, huh? Oh, *that's* going to change."

I finally managed to get his zipper down and he slid off the bed to pull down his jeans, but not before grabbing something from his back pocket. Then he hooked one hand beneath my knee and the other behind my shoulder to gently guide me to the edge of the bed. He stepped closer before I could fully take him in, but I got a glimpse of a body that I'd been dreaming about since our night at the inn.

I closed my hand around his hard length and he let his head drop back. He groaned as I started sliding my hand along him.

But then it was his turn to move away. I heard the telltale crinkle of a wrapper.

"I don't trust this thing," he nodded toward the bed.

"Do your worst," I teased.

He moved me to the very edge of the bed and bumped between my legs. By some engineering marvel the bed was the perfect height, and within seconds Ben had pushed deep inside of me.

Every part of my body tensed for a moment as we adjusted. Ben paused to savor the connection between us, then started rocking against me. He rolled his hips slowly and let out a low groan as I locked my legs around his waist and pulled him closer to me, driving him deeper.

I felt like I couldn't get close enough to him after maintaining our polite boundaries for so long. But now he was truly mine, which gave me the freedom to claim him. I dug my nails into his back and bit his shoulder, an exclamation point that suggested I'd eat him whole if he let me.

He leaned close to me, never breaking his rhythm. "You're so fucking amazing," he rasped in my ear.

He kissed me hard on the mouth before I could reply, then reached down between our bodies. His fingertips found their way back to my heat and the sweetness I was feeling quadrupled.

It was like the ground beneath us was shifting, and then the pressure within me released, rolling through wave after wave of pleasure. I cried out as I came, arching closer to him, and within seconds he tensed, shuddered, and called out my name.

He fell toward me and we both collapsed onto the bed in a pile. We breathed each other in, panting and a little sweaty.

"Cardboard bed for the win," he said weakly against my neck, putting a fist in the air.

Chapter Forty-Five

I woke up in Ben's arms, but we didn't have much of a choice than to sleep coiled around each other given how small the bed was. Shockingly, the humble cardboard bed had risen to the challenge of three rounds of lovemaking and co-sleeping.

"*Food*," Ben said with his eyes still shut. "Dying of hunger. You destroyed me last night."

I stretched as an excuse to squeeze him tighter. "You're in luck. Someone sent me a fruit basket, and someone else sent me a dozen cupcakes. Does that work?"

"Oh, hell yes, but first?"

Ben wrapped his arms around my back and barrel-rolled me so that I was on top of him.

"Good morning," he whispered.

"Hi," I whispered back. I raised my hand to palm the stubble that had sprouted on his cheeks overnight.

"How's life postagreement?" he asked.

"I'm into it." I rolled my hips against his suggestively. "*Very* into it."

"Oh trust me, I'd stay trapped in this cardboard torture box with you all day, but how many appointments and meetings do you have lined up?"

I dropped my head to his chest. "A billion. Starting at ten."

"Then let's get moving, it's already eight."

"Are you sure?" I kissed his neck and slid my hand under the blanket and wrapped my fingers around him. "Because I think you want to stay for a few minutes more."

He groaned. I was right.

Thirty minutes later we were back in bed with a fruit basket and a box of fancy cupcakes between us.

"Best breakfast ever," he said with his mouth full of salted caramel cupcake.

"It's quite literally the breakfast of champions," I laughed. "*Two* gold medal winners."

"Look at us," he mused.

"How much longer are you staying?" I asked him, eating a cupcake with zero guilt. "Downhill finishes up tomorrow, right?"

His face hardened for an instant, a microexpression of discomfort that was there then gone. "I'm still working on my departure plans."

"When will you know for sure?"

"Soon," he said noncommittally as he grabbed another cupcake.

My chest hollowed out. He knew something he wasn't saying.

"What's going on?" I asked. "And don't give me any agreement crap, I deserve the whole story now."

"Quinn, let's talk about this later. You need to get moving."

I felt a shift in the air and I refused to ignore it.

I reached over and put my hand on his leg. "Please tell me."

The physical contact was enough to make him pause. He sighed. "I wanted to wait. This isn't the time."

Worry bubbled up inside of me. "Ben . . ."

His shoulders drooped as he looked down at the pile of cupcake wrappers in front of him. "They're not hiring me."

The news sent me into free fall. Any happiness I'd been feeling vanished at the thought of what Ben had probably been going through while he was cheering me on.

"*Why?*" I practically shrieked. "How does that even make sense?"

He drew a breath and stared off into the distance like he was trying to get his story straight before speaking the words.

"Honestly? They're sort of assholes. I didn't want to tell you before you competed, but they fired Neil and Hailey. Someone found out about them and the powers that be freaked out about their zero-tolerance policy, and how fraternization opens them up to lawsuits. Absolute bullshit."

My mouth dropped open. "Fired?"

He nodded.

"But what does that have to do with you?"

Ben looked like it was hard for him to get the words out, and the longer the silence stretched on the more seasick I felt.

"It doesn't, it's just another example of them being shitty. As for my issues, Kim and I didn't see eye to eye on your story." He couldn't look at me as he spoke, focusing instead on turning a cupcake wrapper into origami. "She wanted to do an old-school interview. Ask uncomfortable questions, get you a little unbalanced, and *boom*, your pain is nothing more than content for the world to consume. I kept pushing my vision for the piece and she eventually agreed, but I think she assumed she could wear me down, or edit my footage to craft the story she wanted to see." He half grinned. "Little did they know I made sure that couldn't happen. They weren't happy with my angle, so they obviously edited the show to be closer to what they wanted to see. It could've been so much worse for you, though. Consider me your bulletproof glass."

I felt the blood draining from my body as I tried to piece together the subtext of what he was saying.

"But . . . why did they bring you to Italy if they didn't like the show?" I asked.

"Contract." He shrugged. "They had to. And Kim pushed for me to 'fill in some plot holes' while we were here. I think she assumed that her presence could bully me into getting the full backstory from you, but I wouldn't agree to it. That's why I wasn't in your press conference. She didn't trust me to ask the right questions."

The generosity of what he'd done left me hollowed out. Tackling my story while knowing every gory detail, but refusing to cash in on it. Standing up to his boss. If he'd been a little more cutthroat he would've gotten the story *and* the job.

But not me.

"Oh my god." My eyes brimmed. "It's my fault you didn't get it."

"No, absolutely not." He pushed the cupcake remains aside and slid closer to me and pulled me into his arms. I almost felt too guilty to hug him back. "It was my choice. I agreed with your boundaries. Hell, I wish I'd been more rigid with mine back in the day. I wasn't willing to sacrifice your peace for my ratings. No way."

The pressure in my chest felt like a stone crushing me. The fact that he could mask his pain to share my joy was terrifying, because how could I help him if I didn't know he was hurting?

I scooted away so that I could study Ben. I'd seen the bleak version, and shockingly the man sitting across from me wasn't him.

"Are you okay?" I asked, my stomach weighted with worry.

He cleared his throat and fiddled with the blanket. "No and yes. I spiraled when they told me. Punched a wall, that sort of bullshit.

But then I took some time to think about the reality of working for them long term. Do I really want to produce pieces that aren't truly my own? And profit from another athlete's pain, knowing what I know? I got so caught up in my drive to win this shiny new prize that I never stopped to question what I was chasing."

"Ben, I'm sorry. I feel like it's my fault—"

Ben grabbed my wrist and dragged me back into his arms. "*Stop.*"

I nestled against him, making myself as small as possible so I could fit on his lap. We breathed in synch while I came to terms with everything he'd done for me.

"Is the dog back?" I asked tentatively.

I felt him shake his head above me. "Not yet."

But we both knew that darkness could seep in from nowhere, especially without something concrete to focus on.

"What are you going to do now?"

He sighed so hard that it ruffled my hair. "Well, I guess we both have some stuff to figure out, huh? But you know what's amazing about that?"

I shook my head silently.

"We'll be doing it together."

I tried to take a deep breath but it stuttered in my lungs, and the tears I'd been trying to suppress broke free, crying for him, for me, and the indecipherable feelings that kept washing over me when all I should've been feeling was joy.

"Quinn, I've got you," Ben whispered as he wrapped me in his arms yet again. I rested my cheek on his chest and hoped my nose wasn't draining onto his shirt. "You're going to be okay. I promise."

He rubbed my back until I downshifted to shuddery sighs. All the confusing sad-about-my-life-but-overjoyed-with-Ben feelings congealed into a single thought that I could no longer ignore.

"I love you."

The three words came out in a rush, like I wasn't sure I wanted to say it even though I felt so much love for him that it was practically boiling over inside of me.

His hand froze on my back, and I immediately regretted opening my mouth.

Ben pulled away from me in slow motion, and I tried to come up with a way to play it off, because it was too early to say it out loud even though I'd been feeling it for longer than I wanted to admit, to myself or him.

"*Damn* it," he said softly, his dark eyes glinting at me.

I jumped off the bed, too mortified to say anything else, but he grabbed my wrist before I could get away.

"Sorry. I made it weird," I muttered, trying to blink back a fresh tickle of tears that were about humiliation this time around.

"No, you *won*," he said with awe in his voice, still gripping my arm. "You beat me. I've been sitting here trying to come up with a way to tell you how much I love you without making it sound like I'm some sort of prize that's going to help you through this weirdness. I didn't want it to seem like I thought that me loving you is enough to get you past all these shitty feelings you have every right to be feeling. I mean, it helps a *little*, but you still have to sort through the origins of the way you feel in order to really—"

I bent over, grabbed his face between my hands and kissed him, hard.

I could feel him smiling at me through the kiss, confirming that the three words he hadn't actually said to me would've come if I'd just given him a few more seconds to pontificate. But at this point he didn't have to say them, because Bennett Martino had been trying to show me that he loved me since our reunion in the diner.

When we finally pulled apart Ben reached out to cup my cheek.

"Yeah, I fucking love you, too," he said, sounding a little dumbfounded. "From the first moment we met, and for the rest of them that we'll share."

Chapter Forty-Six

The Greater Woodspring Skating Arena looked like a high school gym at prom time. There were twinkly lights strung up on the plexiglass surrounding the rink, and crepe paper and balloons hanging in the common areas. The lights were dimmer than usual, like the rink was putting on a showcase, but the ice was crowded with skaters of all ages and abilities, inching and gliding along to overloud pop music.

The big handmade sign in the lobby said, "Farewell Quinn!" and was covered in so many signatures that the lettering was almost obscured.

Zoey skated to the edge of the ice, where I was watching everyone. "You having fun?"

"Is it possible to have fun and be sad at the same time?" I mused. "Because I miss you guys already."

"Yeah, same. I hate this for me, but I love it for you," she agreed.

We both went silent as we scanned the crowd.

"Nate's been hogging your boyfriend the whole night." She pointed at the two of them in the far corner of the rink. "Poor Ben."

Speedskating and free skate were dicey rinkmates but they were making it work. Nate had committed to the change in sport months ago, and the chance to pick Ben's brain had Nate shadowing him since we'd arrived.

"Please, he loves it. He claims that he could never be a coach but he's *really* good at it."

"That means he's got a backup plan if his next gig doesn't work out."

"Check out Justin and Sarah." I jutted my chin toward the center of the ice. "The man can do *everything*."

It looked like my former dance instructor was getting a private lesson from my former choreographer. Somehow, even though he'd only been on skates a handful of times, Justin was managing a decent two-foot spin.

But that was the power of a good coach and a committed student.

"How's your new program coming along?" I asked Zoey. "I feel like I've missed so much."

She pursed her lips and glared at me. "That's because you *have*."

I reached over and put my hand on top of hers. "Sorry. I'm with you in spirit. I hope you know that."

"I do, I was totally kidding. The new program is going great, actually. My parents are having a hard time with the music, but they'll get over it. No more classical!"

I smiled. I liked to think that my win was influencing other skaters to branch out and skate to what *they* loved, not what tradition demanded of them. I was also noticing way more black skates and blades than ever. Even Sarah was sporting them now.

"Are your parents still here?" I asked, craning my neck to look over my shoulder to the common area. "I need to say bye to them."

"Oh trust me, they won't leave without giving you a squeeze," she said. "Are you going to . . ." she trailed off and pointed at the ice.

I shook my head. "I didn't even bring my skates tonight. I just want to soak everything in and say my goodbyes, you know? If I skate it'll turn into the Quinn show."

I realized after I said it that I was echoing what Ben had told me in this very rink. I understood the sentiment now. I wanted to participate in the celebration in a different way. I still loved being Figure Skater Quinn—I'd spent a few hours on the ice by myself this morning, skating an emotional goodbye to the place that had helped me win gold—but tonight I was a just a Woodspring resident saying farewell to my beloved community.

"So, tomorrow?" Zoey asked.

I nodded and swallowed the lump in my throat. "Bright and early. The truck is packed."

She stomped her skate petulantly. "I can't believe this is real, Quinn. I miss you already."

"Don't," I cautioned. "Not yet, at least. Let's have fun until we have no choice but to say goodbye. And you know you're welcome to visit any time. We have an extra bedroom."

"If I ever get a break in my schedule I will. Count on it."

We turned to watch everyone out on the ice.

"Look at Mel and Josh," Zoey said. She leaned closer to me. "Does she realize that her firstborn is *not* a skater?"

I laughed. "She does. She claims he got his lack of coordination from Danny. I think she's happy she didn't give birth to a prodigy. Although little Caleb might surprise us."

I watched Mel chasing Josh around the ice. It was skating in its purest form, just a family enjoying the freedom of zipping around the rink, or in Josh's case, falling but not caring.

We still hadn't said goodbye. In fact, it almost felt like Mel was avoiding me.

I spotted Frank hovering just inside the Zam doors, watching the action with a big grin on his face.

"I need to go say bye to Mr. Zamboni. I'll be back," I said to Zoey.

The dim lighting around the edge of the ice allowed me to head over without being spotted. I'd spent the better part of the night answering and reanswering the same questions, which all included some variation about what I was going to do next (parents), if Ben and I were going to get married (young girls), if I brought my gold medal with me (young boys), how much money I made at the Games (tween boys), and if I knew that companies were now knocking off my costumes and selling them online (tween girls).

Frank didn't hear me approaching so I studied him as I got closer. I hated that the "play through the pain" mentality of his hockey years had taken a toll on his body that he was paying for now.

"Hey, you," I said as I got closer, so I didn't startle him.

"Sweetheart!" Frank's face lit up. "Get over here and give an old man a hug."

I stepped into his embrace and was hit by a million sense memories from the scent of pipe lingering in his clothing. When we moved apart he was beaming at me, but his eyes looked watery.

"I'm going to miss you, lady," he said as he wagged a finger at me.

"Same," I said. I couldn't offer much more, because I was dangerously close to crying as well. "Thanks for giving me perfect ice every day."

"Oh, go on," he pshawed at me. "Just doin' my job!"

We caught up a little bit before I finally gave him one last hug, and I tried not to think about the fact that there was a chance it was the final hug I'd ever have with my favorite senior citizen.

I walked away wondering why the hell I was being so maudlin. I was moving to New York, not the moon.

"Quinn!"

I had to fight back tears yet again as I turned to find Mel staring at me.

"Hi."

The worst goodbye. The one I'd been dreading.

We walked toward each other slowly.

"Now you listen to me." She was already scolding me, something she never did about my performances but always did when I mentioned my perceived shortcomings. "We are *not* going to cry, got it? What's happening is a good thing. It's growth. And it's not like we won't see each other. I'm going to be in your underwear more than ever as you get everything off the ground. And once you're up and running, well, we both know what happens then. You're going to regret asking me to be a part of it."

"Never," I replied, biting the inside of my cheek to keep from crying, because I'd spent the past four years in this rink listening to her instructions, and it had worked out pretty damn amazing for me. "You're a pivotal part of what's to come."

"Good," she bobbed her head once.

"Thank you," I began, my chin quivering. "You are—"

"*Stop.*" She threw her hand in the air in front of me. "I suck at goodbyes, and anyway, this is a farewell. I'll see you soon enough."

I opened my arms to her, frowning and sniffling. When we finally connected, the floodgates opened.

"I told you not to cry," she scolded through her own tears.

"Guess it's a good thing you're not coaching me anymore. I suck at listening now."

We laugh-cried and finally broke apart.

This woman had stepped up and opened my eyes to my true potential. She'd seen through my damage because somehow she could sense that there was more to me. Mel believed I was a winner before anyone else did, even me. She'd shown me that victory could be nurtured with the delicate touch of a bonsai keeper instead of the brute force of a lumberjack.

I owed her so much.

"I love you, Mel," I said.

"I know," she replied with a wink.

"Hold on, did you just quote Han Solo to me?" I asked.

"I have to keep it light," she shot back. "Otherwise I'll be in a corner rocking and drooling, and my kids will wonder what you did to their mommy."

We laughed and embraced one more time, then Danny walked over with a screaming Caleb and we both were relieved to have a distraction.

The night wore on. I hugged a few million people and cried with a bunch more, until it was time to head out.

Ben took my hand when he saw me lingering in front of the trophy case that was filled with dusty medals and trophies and photos with curled edges.

"You okay?"

"No." I shook my head. "*This* was my home. It's really hard leaving."

"I know," he said and squeezed my hand. "I get it. But you know what you're about to do could potentially help a little girl just like . . ." He scanned the photos. "Just like that one."

He pushed his finger on the glass on top of a photo of ten-year-old me. I remembered smiling for the picture because I'd won a junior title but feeling worried because I'd come in second.

Only I could see that worry, just behind my tight smile.

My chest swirled with conflicting emotions, so many that I wasn't sure what I was feeling.

"If you need more time I can wait," Ben said. "We're not in a rush. And you can sleep in the truck if you're tired tomorrow morning."

Gratitude consumed me as I watched him study me, because I knew what he was doing. It was a skill we'd both mastered, the gut-check scan that went deeper than the surface-level stuff we showed the world.

Ben knew how to see me, and I could see him.

I looked away from the ancient memories in the case to the new banner they'd hung up at the beginning of the night. It was a photo of me from the awards ceremony, holding up my gold medal and beaming, with the words "Home of Olympic Gold Medal Winner Quinn Albright" below.

Yeah, I'd won. More than I ever dreamed was possible.

Epilogue

One Year Later

"Feels like old times," Neil crowed as he worked on the camera setup.

Hailey was a few feet behind him with her arms crossed, staring at a monitor. "Um, I think we need a little more negative space to the right of Quinn. Can you come check the blocking, Ben?"

He was already in position in a chair across for me, looking at pages of notes. "I trust you guys. You know what you're doing, fight it out like the old married couple you are."

"Engaged," she corrected, holding up her left hand. "And we don't fight, we disagree loudly."

I laughed. Nothing had changed but everything had.

We'd set up the master interview in the front room of our Brooklyn brownstone, but we'd already shot plenty of footage for the show. They'd captured me giving a speech in front of a five-hundred-person audience, and we'd shot some walk-and-talk footage on the street, as well as a brief segment on the ice, because you simply cannot have two Olympic skating athletes and not film them performing their sport.

Or at least that's what Ben had insisted. It was his show, so we did things his way.

And now that he'd landed a program on CineBinge's primary competitor StreamPlay, it meant that he had a budget to hire more people, which was why Hailey could boss Neil around while two other employees worried about the lights and sound.

"Okay, so just to give you a heads-up, I'm going to go into how you got the idea for the youth foundation, some of the pushback you've gotten from the skating committees, how you vet the mental health professionals you work with, and who's involved in your mentor program."

"And the camp?" I asked.

He nodded. "Of course. You think I'm going to miss the chance to mention *my* role in *your* foundation? Come on. I guarantee I'm going to be everyone's favorite counselor."

Stereotypical Ben still reared his head every so often.

The idea for the foundation had come to me in a dream shortly before I'd left Colorado. The endorsement deals that paid bank but did nothing for my soul kick-started the formation of the group, and thanks to a team of like-minded former skaters and coaches who wanted to be a part of it, the whole thing had taken off super quickly. We were united under one goal: giving young athletes the tools to navigate their sport without losing themselves to it, or to the coaches still clinging to outdated methods, who valued winning over health.

We were already starting to make an impact.

The first episode of Ben's show had set the tone for everything he wanted to do with the series. In stark black and white, he'd faced down the camera and talked about his struggles with depression for the first time, and then cut to athlete after athlete who'd dealt with their own versions of Gold Medal Syndrome in the hope that their openness about their struggles could help others. It was a vulnerable and powerful episode that was destined to win some sort of award.

But of course, winning was no longer the sole goal.

The Comeback had been on the air for three months, but it was the first time he was interviewing me since our time before the Games. He was different now. Still observant and insightful, but clearly the bossman who was worried about so much beyond what happened on-screen.

I'd done plenty of interviews since ours for *The Score*. No one came close to how Ben had made me feel when I was his subject.

Okay, maybe the whole secretly being in love with each other stuff played a part in my feelings, but it was more than that.

I watched Ben study the papers clutched in his hand and felt my heart flooding with love for him. Of all the gifts he'd given me, the one I treasured above everything was the understanding that he would always, *always* look out for me. He'd proved it in so many ways, and after a lifetime of feeling like it was me against the world, Ben had shown me that I wasn't alone.

But it was a two-way street. He knew that he had a fighter in his corner who could see through the mask he wore when he was hurting. If his black dog ever returned it would have to get through his guard dog first.

"What?" Ben asked when he looked up from his papers, his lips twitching into a smile. "You're staring."

"Just thinking," I smiled back.

"Nervous?" He pointed at the cameras and equipment around us.

"Please." I laughed in his face. Being interviewed by him felt like going home and he knew it.

He stood up, cupped my chin, and gave me a quick kiss.

"Good, because we've got this, Albright."

We.

It was such a little word, but it signified so much.

We.

A promise that he'd always be my teammate.

We.

A reminder that our *new* agreement, the one that actually counted, meant forever.

Acknowledgments

I grew up ice skating on a frozen Michigan lake, and I considered myself a decent skater *until* I took a formal lesson during the research phase of this book. Even though I could make my way around the rink forward and backward, and even do some spins, I discovered that my technique was basically garbage. Each week my talented and patient teacher, Niki Anderson, explained the nuances of the sport, and I quickly went from cocky know-it-all to overwhelmed newbie. If I wanted to improve, I had to throw out all my self-taught workarounds and learn how to skate the right way.

Reader, I was humbled.

Taking lessons was the perfect jumping-off point to begin writing this book, because they helped me rediscover my love of skating *and* they gave me the chance to ping Niki with a billion background questions as we worked through my foundation skills. She was a perfect resource for both, so major thanks to Coach Niki.

Word about my book traveled around the rink, and coach and champion ice dancer Shay Sterlace also stepped up to help field my endless questions. During my lessons I was able to keep one eye on Shay as she worked with her students, and even that undercover spying gave me plenty of insights into the coach-student relationship. Shay was yet another amazing resource, and we spent time on the ice and the phone getting into the minutiae of everything from music selection to costumes.

When I met author and speaker Ashleigh Renard at a book event years ago, I didn't know that she had an undercover backstory as a former synchronized skating instructor. True to her coaching roots, Ashleigh spent plenty of time helping me understand the mindset required to be a champion, as well as some of the lesser-known realities and gossip of the skating ecosystem. "Generous" doesn't begin to cover Ashleigh's willingness to help me bring the story to life!

Figure skating was only half of the equation in this book, which meant that I needed to dive into the world of speed skating as I built the story of Quinn and Bennett. I lucked out when I discovered that the East Penn Speed Skating Club was only an hour away, and got doubly lucky because I reached out *two days* before their final practice of the season! Bill and Penelope Romanelli welcomed me to that session, and they fielded my many questions as I kicked off my own speed run into learning about the sport.

That research was augmented by insights from an Olympic speed skater who gave me an insider's view of the drive to be a champion, as well as the pitfalls that can occur post-Games. The Olympic Village came alive for me thanks to his descriptions of his time there.

The vastness of social media made my author life and my dog background converge in a wonderful way as I worked on this book; pet entrepreneur Joanna Russell, the creator of the Hide&Scent pet enrichment game, reached out when she saw my speed skating posts to let me know that she was a former competitive speed skater. We wound up having a fantastic conversation about her time in the trenches, from the day-to-day requirements to the social side of the sport. Our conversation gave me a new appreciation for what these athletes put themselves through to win.

Of course, this book is also the product of the phenomenal Avon team, including my cheerleader of an editor, Tessa Woodward; associate editor, Madelyn Blaney; and marketing associate, Deanna Bailey. It's a dream team rounded out by my author-whispering agent, Kevan Lyon, who works hard to keep me sane in an unpredictable business.

Finally, and as always, massive thanks to my family, friends, and readers for your endless support. Gigantic and endless appreciation for all of you!

About the Author

Victoria Schade is a celebrated author of contemporary romance novels and a dog trainer who seamlessly combines her love for animals with her passion for storytelling. When not working on books with tons of sparks and heart, Victoria enjoys dancing, baking, reading, and perfecting her dink shot. She shares her 1850s always-in-need-of-renovations home with Millie the senior Smooth Brussels Griffon, Boris the Chihuahua/pug mix, the occasional foster pup, and her incredibly tolerant husband.